The Mountain Mother Cipher

The Arkana Mysteries, Volume 2

N. S. Wikarski

Northgate Press

THE MOUNTAIN MOTHER CIPHER

Third Revised Edition 2017.

ISBN: 9781468127591

Written by N. S. Wikarski.

Also by N. S. Wikarski

Gilded Age Chicago Mysteries
The Fall of White City
Shrouded in Thought
The Black Widow's Prey

The Arkana Mysteries
The Granite Key
The Mountain Mother Cipher
The Dragon's Wing Enigma
Riddle of the Diamond Dove
Into the Jaws of the Lion
Secrets of the Serpent's Heart
The Sage Stone Prophecy
Lucifer's Triangle

The Trove Chronicles
The Crone's Legacy

Watch for more at https://www.nswikarski.org.

Table of Contents

Chapter 1—In the Beginning

Caucasus Mountains – East of the Black Sea Coast – 5600 BCE

THEY HAD BEEN FLEEING for weeks now. At first, running just to keep a few paces ahead of the flood water. The water that no longer ran fresh but tasted of salt. It had swallowed their dwellings, their crops, and even their livestock and children. Many had perished. Some had been quick enough to escape. There was nowhere left to go but into the mountains, so they stopped running and began to climb.

It was summer when they left the shore. They had now reached the heights where summer never came. Some had wrapped their feet in rags to keep away the frostbite for a little while longer. Others had already died along the trail. That was when they still had meager food supplies. When they were not yet tempted to feed off the dead to keep themselves alive.

Now they were reduced to a band of twenty. Some old, some young. She was the oldest. The only clan mother who had not drowned in the flood or died on the trail. Not yet anyway. They had stopped to rest on the top of a snowy pass while the shaman cast for signs.

The clan mother looked around at the pinched and frozen faces surrounding her. Their troubled expressions prompted her for guidance.

"Let us see what the signs will tell us." She shuffled over to a woman who was crouching above a pile of flat stones with markings incised on them. The woman wore an amulet bound to her forehead. A polished piece of copper inscribed with a five-pointed star.

"We should go down that way." The shaman pointed toward a decline that led off to the right.

"And I say we should go up instead!" challenged a burly young man. He pointed toward a gap between two mountain peaks to their left. The clan mother didn't know his name or who his mother was. He had attached himself to their band during the flight. He possessed a bad temper, and the chill in his eyes whispered to her that he had been born without a soul.

"The signs say we should go down," the shaman murmured, still intent on her casting.

"And I am sick of listening to you and your signs!" The stranger advanced and stood menacingly above the shaman.

She looked up at him in surprise. "Do you think the Mother of All would lead us into harm's way?"

He spat behind him. "I think she has already led us into harm's way. Where was she when the waters rose? What good have your prayers done so far?"

"We're still alive, aren't we?" The shaman rose indignantly.

"And you would give her credit for that?" The stranger's tone was incredulous. "For starvation?"

The shaman's voice became hard. "She will not fail us."

"She has already abandoned us!" he shouted back. "She is not to be trusted. She has turned her back on us, and now we should turn our backs on her."

The clan mother stood apart, considering the situation in silence.

"We go this way." The shaman pointed emphatically to the sloping trail on the right.

"Enough talk!" Without warning, the stranger's obsidian knife slashed across the shaman's throat.

She gave a single choking gasp before falling backwards, her blood staining the white snow.

A few of the older men drew their knives, but the clan mother stopped them. "No, let him go," she said sternly.

The stranger backed away from the group, his knife still drawn. He held up the star talisman he had snatched from the shaman's forehead as she fell. "Look how well the Mother of All protected her priestess. Do you think she will do any better for you or you or you?" He pointed in turn to each of the shocked faces that confronted him. "Anybody else who wants to live can come with me!"

They looked at one other dumbly. Exhaustion and starvation had rendered them slow-witted. After a few moments, a handful of the younger folk straggled toward where the challenger stood. His eyes glittered as he stared at the clan mother. "Hah! You see who they choose to follow now. I will lead them to a new world with new gods who won't betray us."

The clan mother watched him and his little band disappear in the gap between the peaks. She and her tribe had no place in the world of which he spoke. Nor would she have wanted one. She glanced down at the shaman lying at her feet, blood still gushing across the snow.

IT WOULD BE MANY THOUSAND years before men would spin the memory of what had happened on that desolate mountain and weave it into their myths. It could be reduced to two words. Original Sin.

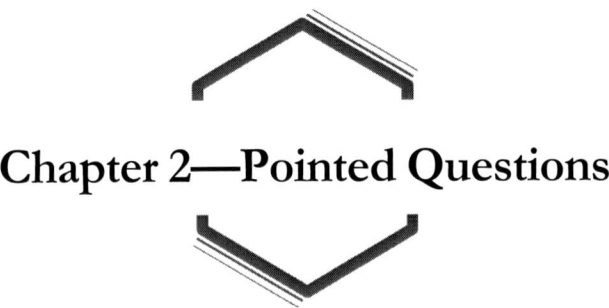

Chapter 2—Pointed Questions

STEFAN KASPRZYK KNELT on the edge of a man-made crater in the earth and stared at a small object in his hand. He couldn't understand what it was doing here. There were times, he thought irritably when he wondered what he, himself, was doing here. Stefan was supervising the excavation of a Kurgan burial mound in Kazakhstan, a country that had the distinction of being one of the most godforsaken places on earth. It was situated right in the middle of the Eurasian steppes. His team might as well be digging on the bright side of the moon. The landscape was barren and treeless as far as the eye could see. A monotonous series of low hills that dipped and rolled off into infinity. No shelter from the cold or the heat. It was summer, and the temperature was nearly one hundred degrees. He pulled his hat brim lower to shield his eyes from the sun. The excavation into the hillside had liberated a quantity of sand which the unremitting wind was blowing directly into his face.

He dusted himself off and walked over to examine the portion of the grave that had been unearthed so far. The skeleton it contained was a chieftain of some sort. His remains showed signs of trauma. A gaping hole in the skull suggested he hadn't died peacefully in his sleep. An occupational hazard, Stefan thought grimly, for those who lived by the sword.

He shifted his attention to another part of the grave. Prominent Kurgan chieftains never died alone. Their burial rites demanded the death of others. A female body posed in a crouched position to his left suggested this was his wife. Quite possibly a bride captured from a neighboring tribe who didn't care for her role in the funeral ceremonies. Her leg bones had been broken to keep her from running away, and her throat had been cut prior to interment.

Her function was to serve her lord in the afterlife. Slavery in this life meant slavery in the next.

Stefan removed his hat to wipe the sweat from his forehead. He fanned his face with the brim for a moment before kneeling down to continue his inspection of the grave goods. They were, for the most part, exactly what he expected to see. Items emphasizing the martial nature of the male buried here. Wooden bows and flint-headed arrows. Bone knives and spears. A stone mace. The skull of a slaughtered horse—probably the chieftain's favorite. The artifacts spoke of a life steeped in blood. A voracious need to subdue everything within reach.

Stefan shook his head. He would much rather be working on one of the Arkana's other digs where the artifacts were less grim. But, he reminded himself, as the Kurgan trove keeper, his work was vital to their understanding of this anomaly in human behavior. How and why it all went wrong. The jumping off point when peaceful nomads became overlord invaders. His work might someday answer those questions. At the moment, he had more questions than answers. He looked down again at the object in his hands. It baffled him. An obsidian knife with an antler handle. What on earth was it doing here? Obsidian was volcanic glass, and the nearest volcano was a thousand miles away.

Even if the object had been obtained by trade or conquest, obsidian weaponry had become obsolete in the millennium prior to the burial of this chieftain. If that weren't odd enough, its sheath presented another mystery. A hammered gold scabbard ornamented with lions. The decorative style of the sheath was consistent with the dead chieftain's culture, but the knife was not. The combination was as anomalous as someone storing a medieval French dagger inside a gun holster from the American West.

He jammed his hat back on his head in exasperation. What was this knife doing here? His speculation led nowhere. He simply couldn't answer that question. He paused as a thought struck him, and a slow grin spread across his face. Perhaps he didn't know the answer himself, but he had just thought of the one person in the world who might be able to help him.

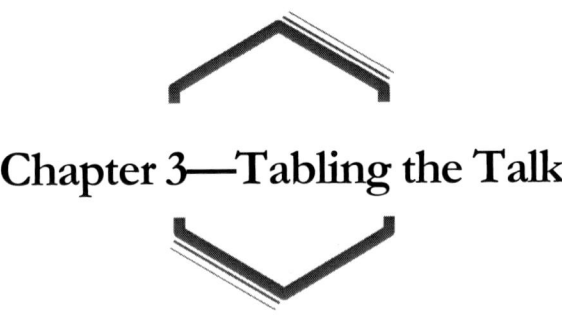

Chapter 3—Tabling the Talk

CASSIE FORSYTHE WAS running late for lunch. As always, finding parking in the trendy but highly congested Gold Coast neighborhood took longer than she expected. She rushed through the revolving door of the restaurant only to be escorted back outside by the hostess who seated her at a bistro table overlooking the sidewalk.

She hadn't wanted to be late, but it appeared she was early. Relaxing a bit, she tried to smooth her hair. It was dark brown, straight, and had a tendency to hang over half of her face like a curtain. Pulling a compact mirror out of her purse, she scrutinized her appearance. To a casual observer, she would have seemed like any other college student. A petite frame clad in jeans and cotton T-shirt. Nondescript features, or at least Cassie thought so, but people always commented on her eyes. They were an unusual opaque grey. She rubbed away a smudge of mascara that had fallen on her nose. Slipping the compact back inside her purse, she surveyed the passersby. It was the typical upscale Chicago crowd of lawyers, stockbrokers, and high maintenance spouses but she couldn't see Rhonda anywhere.

Cassie was nervous about this interview. She mentally repeated the word—interview. It really wasn't that. She had agreed to meet her sister's former business partner for lunch. That was all. A simple meal with a friend.

"More like the third degree," Cassie muttered under her breath. Given the strange events which had unfolded after her sister's death two months earlier, there were too many things she couldn't tell Rhonda. She would have to waltz around the truth like a debutante at a cotillion, and she'd never been a good dancer to begin with.

"Hi, sweetie, how are you?"

Cassie jumped at the soft pressure of a hand on her shoulder. Rhonda had walked up behind her while she'd been busy with her internal monologue.

"Hey Rhonda," she replied shakily, rising to hug the plump older woman. She didn't know why but every time she saw that concerned maternal look in Rhonda's eyes, it made her want to cry. It would have been such a relief to pour out all her cares to a sympathetic ear, but she couldn't allow herself to do that. Instead, she blinked back a few tears and resettled herself in her chair.

A brisk waiter arrived to fill their water glasses. They sat patiently while he regaled them with the day's specials. Once he had retreated back inside, they took a long look at one another.

"So?" Rhonda began tentatively.

"So?" Cassie echoed warily.

"So, how are you?" her friend added. "I haven't seen you since that one time you stopped by the shop, and it's been nearly two months. What have you been doing with yourself?"

There it was. Out in the open. How could she answer that very innocent and entirely awkward question? Cassie's mind flashed back to the night her sister died. How she had wakened from a nightmare that showed her every detail of the crime as it was being committed.

"What have I been doing?" She repeated the question to buy time. "Oh, I found a few things to keep me busy." Busy didn't begin to describe it. Cassie had discovered her sister was part of a secret organization called the Arkana and that its mission was to collect ancient artifacts that revealed human history to be radically different than the version being taught in schools.

"Care to elaborate?" Rhonda urged.

Cassie shrugged. "Nothing earth-shattering." That's a lie, she thought to herself. Her sister Sybil had stumbled across an artifact which a fundamentalist cult known as the Blessed Nephilim killed her to get. If that wasn't enough, Cassie discovered she, herself, could touch a relic and instantly receive visions about the object's past. Her sister had possessed the same gift, and Cassie had been persuaded to step into Sybil's role as the Arkana's seer—their "pythia."

"If I didn't know better, I'd say you were trying to avoid giving me a straight answer," the older woman teased.

Cassie smiled nervously. "That would be silly," she demurred. "What have I got to hide?" What have I got to hide, she asked herself. Absolutely everything! For starters, there was the trip to Crete. Together with two other agents, she'd been sent to retrieve a vital artifact, and they were all nearly killed by a Nephilim and his henchman. Now she and her team were on the brink of finding another relic somewhere in Turkey which the Nephilim coveted too. It was quite a lot for your average co-ed to juggle between classes.

Rhonda was giving her a quizzical look.

Cassie rolled her eyes, trying to breeze through the interrogation. "OK, mom. If you need the details, I got to know some of Sybil's friends in the antique trade, that's all."

"Really? I'm glad," Rhonda commented encouragingly.

The waiter returned to take their order. Cassie's digestive system was churning so violently that all she wanted was a bowl of soup and iced tea.

"I know Sybil was active in the antiquities market, but she was always very close-mouthed about who she worked with." Rhonda stirred cream into her coffee. "Are they nice people?"

Cassie mentally reviewed the staff that ran the Arkana. Faye: a mild-mannered granny by day, the head of an international secret organization by night. Griffin: the mentally hyperactive *wunderkind* who managed the global catalog. Maddie: the frizzy-haired chain-smoking Amazon who controlled worldwide operations. And Erik: the annoyingly handsome smart ass who arranged security for the team when they were in the field.

The pythia paused and stirred a packet of sugar into her tea before replying. "Yes, they're very nice," she answered noncommittally.

Rhonda reached into her purse, drew out an envelope and handed it to Cassie.

"What's this?"

"Your share of last month's profits from the store."

"Oh, right." Cassie had forgotten that since her sister's death she was now Rhonda's business partner in the antique shop she co-owned with Sybil.

"Last time we spoke, you mentioned that you wanted me to buy back your interest in the store." Rhonda hesitated. "Do you still want that?"

Relieved to be away from touchy topics, the pythia answered decisively. "Actually, I don't. I mean, if you don't mind, that is. Sybil wasn't an active partner anyway. She just put up the front money, didn't she?"

Rhonda nodded. "Yes. I ran the store, and we divided the profits."

Cassie shrugged. "Why mess up a good thing, right?"

The older woman seemed relieved. "Honestly, I'd prefer it that way. It would take years for me to buy you out."

The pythia sipped her iced tea, her stomach calming down a bit. "No worries, then. We'll just keep it like it is." She opened the envelope to take a peek at the size of the check. Her eyebrows shot up in surprise. "Wow. You must have had a good month!"

Rhonda smiled. "Not especially. That's about average."

Cassie couldn't see a downside to collecting a tidy sum every month for doing nothing, especially now that she had become so deeply involved with the Arkana that the idea of a job was out of the question.

"I expect you'll be going back to school in the fall," Rhonda hinted gently.

Cassie knew that the older woman was worried about her lack of academic interest. "I'll be going back at some point," she hedged. Given her intense involvement with the relic hunt, college wasn't an option for the foreseeable future.

"Then what will you do in the meantime?" Her friend sounded mystified.

"I... uh...well, those people I told you about. Sybil's friends in the trade. They asked me to help them with something." It was the closest she dared come to the truth.

"Asked you?" Rhonda frowned in puzzlement. "Why on earth would they ask you for help?"

Cassie took a large gulp of tea. "Um... uh... because of some antique that Sybil had at her apartment. I knew a few facts about it, so I was able to give them the history. They want me to help them sort out some other things of hers."

"How well do you know these people, Cassie?"

The pythia avoided eye contact. "They're OK, Rhonda. Like I said, they're really nice."

Her companion reached across the table and squeezed the pythia's hand. "I'm not going to pry but, whatever you do, please be careful. The antiquities market can sometimes attract a bad element."

Cassie smiled weakly. "I will be careful. I promise." The pythia flashed on the memory of Leroy Hunt pointing a gun at her head. A bad element. Rhonda had no idea how right she was.

Chapter 4—Heavenly Mansions

ABRAHAM METCALF TURNED *in a circle to survey the landscape around him. He stood in the center of what appeared to be a dark valley ringed by hills. For some strange reason, he was holding a trowel. A bucket of mortar and a pile of bricks lay at his feet. He picked up a brick and attempted to fit it into a wall that stood knee high. He worked frantically to slap mortar between the layers and stack brick after brick, but his wall sagged and buckled. He could barely see what he was doing. It was a moonless night, and the stars afforded him scant light to work by. He paused to rest, breathless from his efforts, when he saw something bright approaching in the sky. It was a glowing orb which grew brighter as it drifted near him. It came to a stop and hung suspended above his ill-made wall.*

He shielded his eyes from the glare.

Unexpectedly, the orb began to speak. "Abraham, I bring you tidings from our father."

Metcalf fell to his knees. He cast his eyes downward, afraid to gaze directly at the light. "What are you?" he asked in wonder.

"A messenger."

Abraham glanced furtively at the glowing orb. It seemed to be metamorphosing into a young man with flowing golden hair. He was dressed in a long white robe and wings sprouted from his shoulders. On his feet were golden sandals.

The angel spoke. "The Lord of Hosts bids me tell you that your house needs a firm foundation, or it will crumble."

The old man gaped open-mouthed at the seraph.

"Observe," the messenger instructed.

Metcalf fixed his gaze upward to see an image of his son Daniel forming in the night sky. Daniel held the granite key in his hands. The key that would lead him to the location of the Bones of the Mother and give Abraham all he needed to remake the Fallen world in God's image. The angel floated behind Daniel and lifted a halo above the young man's head. Then the scene dissolved into blackness.

METCALF TWITCHED AWAKE and heaved himself upright in bed. He clicked on a reading lamp and glanced at the alarm clock. Two-thirty AM. He had awakened for a reason. This dream was a portent. As the diviner of the Blessed Nephilim, Abraham's dreams were never ordinary. They were the voice of God whispering in his ear. On this night, the Lord had shouted rather than whispered, but Abraham felt frightened at his own incomprehension. What did his vision mean? He dreaded the thought of failing his Master. Rubbing his hands across his face, he tried to clear his mind.

Metcalf cast a brief glance at the woman slumbering peacefully beside him. She was one of his older wives. Was she his tenth? He couldn't remember her rank. No matter. His mind drifted as he gazed detachedly at the woman's face. He noticed the grooves forming around her mouth, the crow's feet at the corners of her eyes. She was nearing the change of life. Soon her body would be impervious to his efforts to build the kingdom through her. The thought that female nature could thwart his will so easily annoyed him.

Abraham fidgeted and pulled the covers around his shoulders. He felt chilled and, for the first time in his seventy-odd years, he felt old. This was no time to fret about his age, he reminded himself sternly. There was great work yet to be done. He was on the brink of laying the entire world at the feet of his Master. The means would shortly be at his disposal. Daniel was instrumental to the fulfillment of his plan.

Then a troublesome thought struck him. What if he were called from the fray early? What if he were asked to follow the example of his divine brother Jesus in an act of blood sacrifice? Who would carry on the fight after he was gone? Who would finish the job of remaking the world? He snapped to attention.

"Your house needs a firm foundation, or it will crumble."

There was the connection. Daniel was meant to be that foundation. Abraham paused to consider the idea. It had been generations since a diviner had designated a scion during his own lifetime. When Abraham's father had died, he was forced to contend with his brothers for the mantle of diviner. It had cost several years of struggle and confusion in the church hierarchy for him to emerge victorious. Given the plans he was about to set in motion, Metcalf couldn't afford a lapse in strong leadership. It was distasteful to contemplate his own mortality, but there was no help for it. He must name Daniel as the scion before the entire congregation so there would be no question of who would succeed him as diviner.

Another alarming thought followed fast on the heels of the first. Daniel had three wives, each of whom had produced only one child—disappointingly female in each case. This would never do. The diviner's dynasty could not be built on such a feeble foundation. Daniel must father sons. Abraham stroked his beard contemplatively. Perhaps to do so, he only needed the right stimulus. The old man smiled and switched off the lamp. He lay down and pulled the quilt up to his chin. He believed he knew exactly what God wanted him to do.

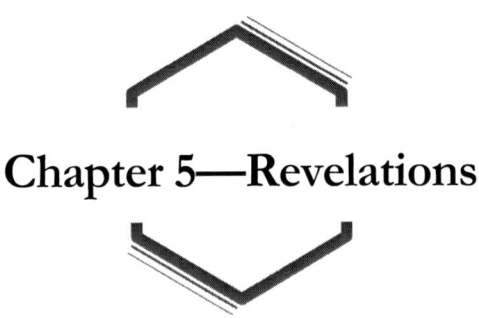

Chapter 5—Revelations

THE BELL HAD BEEN RINGING for at least ten minutes. Everyone in the compound had heard it. They were all hurrying to the Worship Hall. A nondescript twentyish blond woman named Annabeth scurried along too. She didn't want to be late. The rule was strict. Every adult member of the Blessed Nephilim who could be spared must answer the summons immediately.

It had to be something very important for the diviner to call them together in the middle of the week. She could hear voices around her speculating, but nobody seemed to know what this was about. Annabeth tried to catch her breath and smooth her hair when she entered the hall. Nearly everyone but she had already found a place.

The men in their black suits and white shirts sat together in the forward rows. Behind them sat rows of women clad all alike in grey dresses and white aprons, their hair chastely braided and coiled around their heads. Annabeth dove for the first open seat toward the back of the room. She stammered an apology as she stepped on someone's toe before sinking into a chair. She didn't like to stand out. Nobody wanted to be singled out for the diviner's attention.

The whispers in the room all died when he entered. Father Abraham was a daunting figure. With his mane of white hair and carefully trimmed beard, he looked like a patriarch straight from the pages of the Bible. He strode to the pulpit and rested his hands on the stand. Leaning forward, he began to speak. "My children, I called you together today to give you news of great joy."

Whispers of speculation rippled around the hall.

"Before I do, let me remind you who you are."

Annabeth didn't know what the diviner meant. She looked at the women around her. They were all staring forward blankly.

"More than two hundred years ago Jedediah Proctor was granted a vision. A vision of God's plan for the Blessed Nephilim. If we kept ourselves blameless in his sight and waited patiently for the Day of Judgment, then we would be restored to the ranks of the angels from whence we sprang."

Annabeth could see some of the men in the front rows nodding in agreement.

"My children, you know you are God's chosen ones. Set apart. Pure. The only bright light in a vast sea of darkness."

"We are the chosen ones," they echoed approvingly.

"Two hundred years ago God's will for us was revealed." The diviner paused to stare out at the congregation, holding his eyes locked on theirs. "But two centuries, my brethren, is a very long time."

A hush fell over the crowd.

The diviner stepped in front of the podium and began to pace. "For two hundred years we have suffered the scorn of the Fallen in our efforts to keep ourselves sinless."

"That's right!" A few of the men muttered.

"Two hundred years we have watched as the world became ever more corrupt, yet we kept the faith."

"Yes, we did," other voices affirmed.

"You know how we have been mocked by the ungodly. Made to appear foolish in the eyes of men for what they call our outlandish beliefs. Where is the savior of the Nephilim? They laugh at us and claim he is nowhere to be found!"

"Speak, diviner!" another male voice shouted.

"It must have seemed to many of you that the Lord has forgotten his promise to us. I know how you have prayed that God would give us a sign that he still remembers our plight."

Annabeth stirred uneasily in her seat. She couldn't see where all this talk was leading.

"I am here to tell you, my children, that the Lord has answered your prayers!"

The congregation sat forward, their curiosity piqued. Annabeth had to crane her neck to see the diviner.

"Do not believe the whispers of the outside world, my children! They spread lies. I bear witness that the Lord has not forsaken us!" Father Abraham punched the air with his fist for emphasis. "Indeed, he has not! I have received a sign from above that the Lord is with us still."

"A sign. A sign!" Dozens of voices chanted.

The diviner nodded and paused until the chanting died down. "Yes, my children. A sign! A sign as sure as the signs which God gave to the prophets of old. As sure as the signs He showed to our founder, Jedediah Proctor all those long years ago."

The murmurs rose again.

He raised his hand for silence. "Last night, the Lord granted me a revelation. He sent an angel to me in a dream."

Annabeth's attention was caught by the woman seated next to her who was rocking forward and back in her chair with eyes shut, a secret prayer on her lips.

"The angel showed me clearly that the Lord has prepared a glorious future for the Blessed Nephilim. His works are mighty, and he is mindful of his children. Let us praise his name!"

"Praise his name! Praise his name," they echoed, filled with the spirit of the Lord.

Annabeth watched several women fall to their knees, whispering prayers of gratitude.

"The Blessed Nephilim shall be raised high in glory above the heads of the Fallen. This mighty day will come long before the Final Judgment, my children. I have God's word that the Nephilim are meant to lead the world through the darkness of the next millennium. In preparation for that glorious time of our ascendency, the Lord has selected my successor to carry our pure faith forward unto the next generation. Today I name him. My son Daniel is God's own choice as scion of the Blessed Nephilim." Father Abraham pointed to the back of the room. "Let all here present bear witness that he will ascend to the title of diviner once I have gone to glory."

In a state of shock, Annabeth swung around in her chair to regard a rumpled man in his early thirties who had been slouching against the rear wall. Her husband Daniel was to be the scion! People stood up to get a better look at where the diviner was pointing.

Daniel's pale face flushed in embarrassment at the scrutiny of the entire congregation.

The diviner forged ahead. "The Lord has commanded me to give Daniel a new bride that he might ensure a firm foundation for our faith."

Annabeth's shock was rapidly turning to horror. A new wife! She cast a glance toward her husband to see how he was taking the news. Daniel's flushed countenance had drained of color.

She looked back toward the pulpit to see the diviner's eyes scanning the room for a different face. "Rise, Hannah Curtis. You are to be elevated to the rank of consecrated bride. You will be my son's next wife."

A pretty blond girl of about fourteen gasped and covered her mouth. She rose uncertainly at his command, looking around in dismay at the faces gawking in her direction.

"Wives. Go and greet your sister wife," Father Abraham commanded.

Annabeth felt as if she were sleepwalking. She rose on cue with Daniel's other two wives and scurried over to the bewildered girl. Each one kissed her on the cheek and led her to the back of the room where her husband-to-be stood.

"My children, I give you leave to offer your congratulations."

The rest of the congregation rose and filed toward Daniel and his newly betrothed.

Annabeth stood with her sister-wives behind the new girl. Her mind was racing. She saw all her hopes evaporating. No more than a month ago, the diviner had berated her for her lack of offspring. He had called her a disobedient wife. Not worthy of the name of consecrated bride. In terror of being cast out of the kingdom, she had pleaded with Daniel for more children. Male children. Her husband had promised her they would try to have more. He even went so far as to suggest she lie to the diviner about the state of their relations if she were questioned too closely. She had agreed, but her husband had never come to her since that day. What chance did she have now? The newest wife was always the favorite, and this pretty little girl was fourteen. Annabeth was twenty and already an old story. She bit her lip in frustration. She needed the diviner to know it wasn't her fault. She had tried to be a good wife. Perhaps there was still a way. She would wait and watch. Perhaps God would give her the proof she needed.

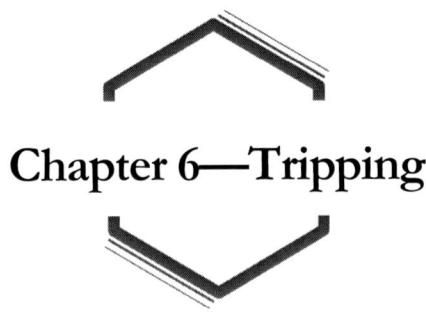

Chapter 6—Tripping

THREE DAYS AFTER HER lunch with Rhonda, Cassie Forsythe received an urgent phone call. It was Griffin. "Faye called an emergency meeting. We need you at the vault right away."

Without hesitation, she jumped into her car and left the city behind. She drove through fields of ripening corn far beyond the last stretch of urban sprawl. Out here, progress had managed to slow its inevitable march. Farmhouses looked much as they had a hundred years earlier.

She maneuvered her car down the dirt road that led to an old schoolhouse set off by itself in a clearing in the woods. Cassie smiled to think how innocent the structure looked from the outside. The secrets it protected from an unsuspecting world. This was the Arkana's Central Catalog, often simply called the vault. The unassuming nerve center of the entire global operation.

She parked and trotted up the now-familiar stairs to the front door and let herself into the deserted schoolroom. A room that had been abuzz with life only a month ago when she had witnessed her first assembly of the Concordance. Their decision to pursue the mysterious relics known as the Bones of the Mother had changed her life.

She crossed the room, her footfalls echoing, and entered the vestibule at the back. Swiping her keycard, she waited for the hidden elevator. The fact that she now had a keycard of her own was a sign of trust. Why shouldn't they trust her? She had risked her life helping them track down the first clue they needed to find the relics.

The elevator door opened. Swiping her card again, she descended to the vault below. Every time she entered this space, she was struck by the ingenuity of the design. Everything was meant to remind the occupants of the natural world above. An underground ceiling that mimicked sunlight and moonlight. A ventilation system that created gentle breezes from different directions. Waterfalls trickling at the corners of the room and, oh yes, the animals.

A Springer Spaniel came racing toward her when she exited the elevator. She bent down to rub his ears as he bounced up trying to lick her face. "Hey, buddy. How are you doing today?" Having greeted her, the dog trotted back to a desk halfway down the row where his guardian was filing some paperwork.

Cats slept on desks or curled in chairs. Birds squawked from cages. The occasional iguana crawled across the top of a computer monitor. It was the most exotic office space Cassie had ever seen—one where flora and fauna were welcome. Without asking for directions, she made her way to a door marked "Scrivener's Office." She knocked briefly and then let herself in.

"Griffin, how's it going?" she asked.

A lanky young man with curly brown hair swung around from the book case where he'd been examining the spines of several volumes. "Oh hullo, Cassie." He spoke with a precise British accent. "Did you happen to see Faye on your way in?"

He was referring to their elderly leader.

"No, isn't she here yet?"

He shrugged. "Not yet. Would you mind awfully going back topside and collecting Maddie? We'll be meeting in Faye's office on the second floor."

"Faye has an office in the vault?" Cassie registered surprise. She was accustomed to the memory guardian conducting her business from the comfort of her suburban farmhouse.

Griffin glanced up briefly from the volume he was perusing. "Yes, it's the closed door at the far end of the second floor. She rarely uses it."

Cassie nodded. "OK, then. See you upstairs in a bit."

FIFTEEN MINUTES LATER the key members of the Arkana were assembled in Faye's office waiting for Griffin.

THE MOUNTAIN MOTHER CIPHER

The space was cozy, as Cassie imagined it would be if it belonged to Faye. A lacquered chinoiserie desk sat in the front window which overlooked the lawn. There were antique bookcases lining the walls, and one corner of the room was reserved for guests. A leather sofa and loveseats were arranged in a horseshoe around a coffee table set with a silver tea service. Cassie wasn't sure who had bustled up to brew tea, but Faye was already playing hostess and handing out cups of the steaming beverage.

Maddie refused the refreshment. She sat with her arms folded, clearly in a grumpy mood. "You'd think Griffin could be on time."

"What's the matter? Did we pry you out of the chimney too soon?" teased Erik.

He was referring to the bell tower that Maddie had commandeered as a smoking lounge.

"How'd you guess?" Maddie asked, chewing on the end of an unlit cigarette in an effort to calm herself down.

"Let's just wait a few more minutes for him before I begin," Faye said. She sat perched demurely on the edge of the couch, sipping her tea. The quintessential grandmother in her flowered dress and cardigan, a little pillbox hat balanced on her head.

Cassie was secretly amused by Faye's appearance. Like the schoolhouse itself, she was far less bland than she seemed to be.

At that moment, Griffin came skidding through the door, a pile of papers under his arm, and breathlessly took a seat next to Erik. "Very sorry I'm late," he offered apologetically.

"You ought to be," muttered Maddie.

"I'm sure you're all wondering what this is about." Faye handed Griffin a cup of tea. She looked mildly distressed as she gazed from one quizzical face to another. "I'm afraid we must speed up our timeframe a bit."

Her listeners still appeared confused, so she elaborated. "Ever since you returned from Crete, I've taken the precaution of keeping close tabs on our adversaries."

Eric raised his eyebrows in surprise. "I don't see how you managed that. I couldn't sneeze within twenty feet of the Nephilim compound without somebody seeing me."

"Quite right." The memory guardian nodded. "Fortunately, there is a weak link in their chain mail. Mr. Hunt is not of the brotherhood."

Griffin sat forward intently. "Of course. He doesn't live with them. Not difficult to set someone to keep watch of his whereabouts."

"Or to monitor his communications." Faye smiled sweetly.

Cassie laughed to herself. Harmless little granny. Yeah, right.

The old woman's smile faded. "Unfortunately, I just received some disturbing news this morning. The Nephilim are mobilizing once more. We intercepted a message between Mr. Hunt and Abraham Metcalf. Apparently, Mr. Hunt has been instructed to prepare for another trip to Crete."

"When?" they all cried at once.

"I gather the departure could be any time now."

"How's that possible?" Maddie barked. "I thought you all were convinced they weren't going to move on the relic for months." She turned to stare at Erik. "Didn't you tell me they couldn't find their way out of a paper bag without help?"

Erik shrugged. "Guess it was a paper bag with a map printed inside."

"Oh, but this is terrible." Griffin ran his fingers through his hair—an unconscious gesture whenever he was perturbed about something.

Faye noted the reaction to her announcement. "I see you all understand our dilemma. I'm afraid you'll have to leave for Turkey much sooner than anticipated."

"But how can we?" Cassie asked. "Last time I checked, Griffin still couldn't make heads or tails of that clue we discovered in Crete. The one that's supposed to lead us to the first relic. How does it go again?"

"You will find the first of five you seek, when the soul of the lady rises with the sun, at the home of the Mountain Mother, where flows the River Skamandros." Erik rattled off the lines in a sing-song voice. "That little ditty has been running through my head for weeks now, and it still doesn't make any sense."

"Well, we do know a few things," countered Faye. "We know that the artifact is somewhere on Mount Ida and since the Nephilim are missing the critical fourth line of the riddle, they will be searching Mount Ida in Crete rather than Mount Ida in Turkey."

Griffin appeared panic-stricken. "Yes, but I remain utterly baffled by the second line. 'When the soul of the lady rises with the sun.' What does that mean? I've searched every reference book I can think of. There is simply no context in which the ancient Minoans used the expression 'soul of the lady.'"

"Despite your hesitation, we must act and soon," Faye said softly. "I'm open to all suggestions."

Griffin glanced at her sheepishly. "Under the circumstances, our only hope is for Cassie to touch things."

Erik swiveled in his seat to stare at the scrivener as if he'd lost his mind. "That's your idea of a plan? You expect us to go stumbling up and down a mountain while the kid trips over rocks and gets a vision?"

"I'm not a kid," Cassie corrected him, trying to sound dignified. Although Erik had become far less hostile to her presence as a member of the Arkana since Crete, he could still be thoughtlessly insulting. For someone who was only in his mid-twenties, he considered himself the wise old man of the team.

"Sorry, toots!" He gave her a half-smile, knowing that this new name would irritate her even more.

"My name isn't toots, either," she retorted in an injured tone. "I'm the pythia. Try to remember that! If it wasn't for me tripping over rocks in Crete, we wouldn't have any intel at all about where the first relic is hidden."

"That's true," Erik said more seriously, "but the area we were searching around Karfi was a fraction of the size of Kaz Daglari."

"Kaz what?"

"Daglari. It means Goose Mountain in Turkish. That's the modern name for Mount Ida which, by the way, isn't a single mountain. It's actually a mountain range. That's a whole lot of tripping for one pair of size eight sneakers to handle."

"Six and a half," Cassie protested. "I don't have floppy clown feet!"

"My dears," Faye chuckled. "Calm yourselves. Have some cookies. They're homemade." She held out a plate of sugar cookies. The two combatants helped themselves and began crunching loudly.

Faye gave her full attention to Griffin. "I do believe Erik's point is well-taken. We will need to focus the search in a specific direction if Cassie's talents are to be used effectively."

"There are a few ways we could narrow the field," Griffin answered. "I expect we're looking for an ancient ruin. That would be the most likely place the Minoans might have hidden the relic."

"Good luck with that idea," Erik snorted. "You should know better than anybody that Mount Ida is riddled with ruins. They're scattered all over the countryside."

"I beg your pardon. Will you be contributing anything to this discussion other than disparaging remarks?" Griffin drew himself up. "I wasn't proposing we go there without a plan."

Maddie sighed and shifted her position causing the couch to squeak under her ample weight.

"Then what are you proposing?" Erik challenged.

"We should start with the Anatolian trove keeper, obviously. Find out if he can recall any sites that bear unidentified marks that might match our translation key."

"Anatolian?" Cassie asked. She still wasn't up to speed on all the Arkana terminology.

"Anatolia is the name for the Asian part of Turkey," Griffin explained. "It was once known as Asia Minor. I think the trove keeper has been dividing his time between the excavations at Catal Huyuk and Hacilar."

"OK, slow down." Cassie held up her hands in protest. "What does that mean?"

"Here, I'll show you." Griffin selected a page from among the stack he'd brought with him. Spreading it out on the coffee table, he revealed a map of Turkey.

"This is Mount Ida." He pointed to a mountain range on the west coast of the country. "It's very close to the ancient city of Troy. So close, in fact, that Homer mentions it in the *Iliad*. He describes the gods standing on Mount Ida and watching the conflict in the valley below from its slopes." He moved his finger in a line due east of the mountains and about halfway across the country. "This is the ancient city of Catal Huyuk. It has provided invaluable information about matristic civilization in this part of the world. The same is true on a smaller scale at Hacilar." He pointed to a spot to the southwest of Catal Huyuk.

"So why would the Anatolian trove keeper know anything at all about Mount Ida if he's hundreds of miles away?" Cassie challenged.

"Because he's responsible for every find that's catalogued in the Anatolian trove all across the country. He's also very old and has a long memory."

"I suppose that makes sense," Cassie conceded. "But I'm still not sure I understand what all the rush is about. So what if the Nephilim are on their way to Crete way sooner than we expected? I mean it isn't as if they're going to magically figure out they're looking for the relic in the wrong country, jump on a plane, and beat us to Turkey."

The scrivener shook his head. "I don't credit the Nephilim with an overabundance of brains, but it would behoove us to be on our guard."

"Behoove?" Erik echoed incredulously "Did you actually just say behoove?"

Ignoring the security coordinator, Griffin continued. "I'm merely pointing out that we can't afford the luxury of complacency. We must still move with the utmost speed especially because of that one devilish word in the riddle."

His listeners looked at him blankly.

He clarified the point. "When the soul of the lady rises with the sun. 'When' is the word that's most worrisome."

"Nice alliteration," Erik joked.

Griffin sprang out of his seat unexpectedly and began to pace "Don't you understand? We're looking for an object that isn't merely hidden in space. It's also hidden in time. Some event that happens at sunrise must occur in order for us to find the relic we seek. For all I know, we're running out of time with respect to that event if we haven't already."

"I see," Faye murmured speculatively.

"All I can glean with any certainty from that line of the riddle is the direction we must be looking toward. East." Griffin sat back down and glanced helplessly at Faye.

"You've just demonstrated that we know a good deal more than nothing," she consoled. "Perhaps once you're searching the landscape, the meaning of the line will become clear." Turning to Maddie, she asked, "Do you think you can coordinate the trip for them on such short notice?"

The operations director frowned. "Not overnight I can't but give me a couple of days to pull the arrangements together." She glanced briefly at the security coordinator. "Erik's going to need a few days to get their papers in order."

He nodded in agreement. "The Turkish government likes to keep an eye on visitors. We're going to be poking around places we may not be welcome or authorized to visit." Erik looked earnestly at Cassie. "Crete was a walk in the park compared to what's coming next. I hope you're ready for it."

With all the bravado she could muster, Cassie replied, "Only one way to find out."

Chapter 7—A Bedtime Story

HANNAH CURTIS SAT CROSS-legged in the middle of a strange bed. Everything was strange. Her entire life, in fact, had taken a strange turn. She came from Missouri and was raised in a house surrounded by brothers and sisters and a mother who was always ready with a hug or a smile of encouragement. Her father had been a distant figure. He was the leader of the Missouri Nephilim and therefore a man of importance. When he came to visit, the children were expected to put on clean clothes and brush their hair thoroughly. They would line up in a row, and he would ask them if they were good children. Once they replied that they were, they would be dismissed. That was all.

She hadn't been unhappy although it never occurred to her to ask herself what that word meant. Not that she knew what happiness was either. She just went along and did what she was told and stayed out of trouble. It was safer to avoid being noticed. That way everything proceeded more or less as it was supposed to do. As God willed it to do.

But now, she could tell the difference between happiness and unhappiness, and she didn't much care for it. Unhappiness was an aching emptiness in the pit of her stomach. Unhappiness was being told she could never see her mother again. It was being separated from her brothers and sisters. Being moved a long distance from the only home she had ever known.

Her father had angered the diviner somehow. It was so serious a matter that all his wives and children had been reassigned to other men. Hannah's mother had been her father's favorite. She had pleaded to be allowed to stay with him. In order to teach her a particularly harsh lesson, the diviner separated Hannah's mother not only from her husband but also from her own children. They were distributed among the other compounds. Hannah

31

had been taken to Illinois. She knew which state it was from the geography map in the schoolroom. She didn't know anybody here. Her foster mother had a dozen children of her own to look after. She seemed tense most of the time, and Hannah was afraid to ask her anything.

The girl reached into the pocket of her nightgown and drew out a small wooden doll. Her mother had pressed it into her hand when she was being taken away. "Remember me," was all she had time to say. The doll had been one of Hannah's earliest toys. It had sat neglected in the locker at the foot of her bed for some years after she decided that she was too old to play with dolls. She slipped it back into her pocket. It didn't matter if she was supposed to be too old for toys. She always kept it with her now. It was all she had left.

In this strange new place, all the women spoke in whispers. They stopped speaking altogether if she happened to walk by. She pretended not to notice. All of them, men and women alike, seemed terrified of the diviner. She was scared of him too. He was old, and he scowled most of the time, and he talked directly to God. She wondered if that meant God liked him. God didn't seem to care much for the rest of his creation, as far as she could tell. He was always punishing people who disobeyed him. Killing them in floods or banishing them from gardens. He even made his son Jesus die to make up for all the things that displeased him about human beings. She wasn't sure she wanted to talk to God even if he wanted to talk to her. He would probably just yell at her.

She picked absentmindedly at the quilt on the bed. The fabric felt odd to her touch. As if this was a dream and she was touching a dream quilt instead of the real thing. It all felt like a very odd dream. Two days ago, the diviner had called everyone together to announce her marriage to his son Daniel. They all came crowding up to congratulate her. They all told her what a good thing it was for her. In spite of her father's transgressions, the diviner was allowing her to marry one of his own sons, and the scion at that. They all told her how happy she must be. There was that word again. Happy? She didn't think that she felt happy. Numb, maybe. Shocked definitely, but not happy.

The wedding had taken place just this afternoon. Again, she was singled out in front of the whole congregation. She changed her grey smock for the garb of a married woman—a shapeless grey shift and apron. Instead of wearing her hair in a long braid down her back, the braid was coiled around

THE MOUNTAIN MOTHER CIPHER

her head. All those things meant she wasn't a child anymore. How did that work exactly? Changing her clothes didn't change how she felt. She still missed her mother and her sisters and brothers. She didn't feel very grown up, but everybody told her she would learn to be.

She got off the bed and walked over to the dresser. Picking up a hair brush, she combed out the braid and brushed her hair. She looked at her reflection and couldn't see any difference between her married self and the way her face had always looked.

Her mind drifted off to her husband. It felt so odd to say that word. He slouched. His suit seemed two sizes too big for him, and his voice quavered when he said, "I do." She guessed he must be about thirty. Twice her age though she supposed that wasn't too bad. Many girls were married off to men much older than that.

She knew what was expected of her on her wedding night. Women were meant to breed heirs to the kingdom. That's how they were allowed to enter heaven. Only if they became wives and mothers, consecrated brides, would they be worthy. She knew that was her duty, but she didn't know why. It was God's plan and not for her to question. Who was she, after all, to ask about such things? It had all been set down many generations ago by wise men.

She had braced herself when her husband had entered the room, but he didn't appear as she expected. She was dressed in a cotton nightgown, but he was still wearing his black suit.

He cleared his throat and asked, "How are you?"

"I'm fine," she replied uncertainly, balancing on one bare foot. "How are you?"

He paced around the room, pretending to examine the window shade. "Oh, I'm well. Thank you for asking." He spun around and asked, "Do you like the room? It's yours now."

Taken aback, she answered, "It's alright, I guess."

"Good," he seemed relieved. "That's good." Approaching her awkwardly, he kissed her on the forehead and patted her shoulder. "Well, good night then."

She opened her mouth to speak, but no words emerged. She was too taken aback.

With a brief nod in her direction, he left.

She stopped brushing her hair and simply stared into the mirror, puzzling over everything. God told her it was her duty to increase his kingdom. The people around her told her she was lucky to be married to the son of the diviner. They said she should be happy. Everybody had an idea about what she was supposed to do and how she was supposed to feel about it. Everybody except her, that was. Most of the time her insides felt like an overpacked suitcase. Stuffed with all the things other people told her she should want. She wondered what she wanted for herself. The question took her completely by surprise. In all her life she had never asked herself that. It seemed like a selfish thing to want to know. Still, she wondered.

Turning away from the mirror, she walked back toward the bed. She switched off the light and crawled under the strange quilt in the strange bed still thinking about the strange man who was now her husband. What did he want from her? What did she want for herself? Maybe tomorrow she'd ask herself that question again. Maybe tomorrow she'd know the answer.

Chapter 8—Run from Your Wife

BRIGHT AND EARLY ON the morning after his nuptials, Daniel knocked warily on his father's office door.

"Enter!" a magisterial voice commanded from inside.

The visitor took a deep breath before entering the lion's den, anticipating how awkward this conversation might be if he didn't handle it just right.

His father glanced up from his paperwork. When he saw who his caller was, he actually smiled. That was a rare occurrence. Daniel wasn't sure if he didn't prefer the characteristic scowl after all. The smile reminded him too much of a grinning skull.

"Hello, Father."

"Good day, my boy. Have a seat." The smile remained. "I trust you slept well last night?"

The question hung in the air like an axe poised to fall. Daniel remembered his awkward encounter with Hannah and his hasty retreat from the very idea of consummating the marriage. He looked down at the carpet. "I, uh, that is, well... um. Yes, I did." He allowed his father to draw the obvious though incorrect conclusion.

"I am glad to hear it! Please sit down," he urged.

The younger man sank into the low visitor's chair in front of the massive desk. It automatically forced him to look upward to carry on a conversation. His father always liked to keep the high ground.

Folding his hands across his papers, the old man asked, "What is it you want to discuss?"

"I'm ready to leave for Crete now." The words came tumbling out too abruptly.

"What?" The smile finally left his father's face. That at least was a relief.

"Yes, there have been some new developments." He wasn't actually lying. He did believe he might know where to find the relic his father had become obsessed with recovering. The first of five. As for the need for an immediate departure, that was motivated by more personal concerns. He didn't require another wife making awkward sexual demands upon him. He already had three wives toward whom he felt no inclination. Daniel had performed the necessary, though distasteful, duty of providing each one with a child and had hoped the matter would end there. But that was before his father singled him out for this relic hunt.

Daniel's entire life up until that time had been spent in pleasant anonymity. One of twenty sons of the diviner and a middle son at that. Unexceptional but for his unfortunate ability to translate ancient languages. That ability had caused him to give Abraham what he wanted—or at least the hope of obtaining what he wanted. As a consequence, Daniel had been elevated to the rank of his father's favorite, even named as his successor—a role which his brothers envied and which he would gladly have exchanged for obscurity once more. Being the favorite meant his father had taken too keen an interest in his son's business. Daniel had succeeded in fathering only three children, all of them disappointingly female. This was unacceptable behavior for the son of a diviner. How ironic that his father would choose to show his favor by giving Daniel a gift for which he had no earthly use— another wife. Better to leave the country and let the dust settle for a while. Perhaps if he could bring back the first relic, his father's attention might be diverted. He paused as a more appalling thought struck him. Perhaps if he succeeded, his father would show his appreciation by giving him a fifth wife! He brushed the thought aside. He would cope with that calamity when, and if, it ever materialized.

Focusing back on the present moment, he continued his explanation. "I believe I've isolated the location of the relic to a specific cave on Mount Ida."

His father nodded approvingly. "That is excellent news, my son. Excellent! I had already begun arranging your next trip, but I didn't anticipate you would be ready to leave immediately."

"Since I know you have a pressing need for these artifacts, I thought I should go as quickly as possible."

The old man seemed puzzled. A rare occurrence. "But surely you want to spend at least a little more time with your new bride, don't you?"

Daniel didn't want to arouse suspicion. He skirted the question. "You misunderstand me, sir. While I mean to make immediate preparation, it could take a few days to assemble everything I need for the expedition."

"Oh yes, quite right."

Abraham's concerns seemed alleviated. He once more incorrectly assumed his son would spend some of that time in conjugal visits. Daniel was content not to contradict him.

The old man stood up and walked to the window, his hands clasped behind his back. "I'll get in contact with Mr. Hunt again and alert him to these new developments."

Daniel swallowed hard at the sound of the name. Leroy Hunt. A mercenary his father had employed in the early stages of the project. A man who seemed to delight in violence. In his nightmares, Daniel still saw Hunt herding three innocent people into a cave, ready to shoot them at point blank range. He would have done so without remorse if an unexpected rockslide hadn't buried them alive first. He shuddered at the memory.

"Father, must we involve Mr. Hunt again?" Daniel deliberately kept a detached tone. He didn't want to sound recalcitrant.

His father turned from the window to regard him with surprise. "Do you have an objection to his participation in this great work?"

Grasping at straws, Daniel said, "But he isn't one of us. He isn't a Nephilim."

Taking his son's protest seriously, Abraham sighed. "Yes, I know Daniel. It's unfortunate that for the type of work required, we have no one in the brotherhood who has the necessary skills."

The necessary skills to commit murder? Daniel remained silent and let his father continue.

"I intend to correct that deficiency very soon."

The young man wasn't quite sure what his father meant by that cryptic statement, and Abraham didn't elaborate.

"Mr. Hunt has shown himself to be an invaluable ally even if he is a worldly man and one of the Fallen. He is the strong right arm of the Lord."

"As you wish, Father," Daniel murmured. If Leroy Hunt was the price he had to pay for a temporary respite from domestic tension, then so be it. He rose to go, but the old man stopped him at the door.

Abraham placed his hand on his son's shoulder in an awkward gesture of affection. Patting him on the back, he added, "I'm very glad you have entered so wholeheartedly into doing God's work."

Daniel nodded but said nothing as he closed the door behind him. Apparently, theft and murder were now a part of God's work. It had been a long time since his heart felt whole. He doubted it ever would be again.

Chapter 9—A Room with a View of the Past

CASSIE WOKE FROM A deep, dreamless sleep to hear an insistent tapping on her hotel room door. She shook her head to clear away the cobwebs. What time was it? What day was it? The flight from Chicago to Istanbul had taken almost eleven hours. The minute she got to her hotel room, she'd thrown her duffle bag on the floor and passed out on the bed. She never slept well on airplanes. Twenty winks had apparently turned into sixty.

She stood on tiptoe to check the peep hole in the door. A globular face was staring back at her.

"Oh jeez!" She jumped back, startled. Then she fumbled with the lock.

"Hey, toots."

"My name's not..." she trailed off. "Oh, never mind. Come on in."

Erik sauntered past her, hands dug deeply into his jeans pockets. Looking around at the suite assigned to Cassie, he said, "Guess now we know who Maddie's favorite is."

"What? You guys don't have rooms this nice?"

He shrugged. "I can't speak for Griffin, but mine's a broom closet." He scratched his head. "I think she's still ticked at me."

"Why?" Cassie scurried to the foyer mirror to comb her bed head back into shape.

"We have what you might call a complicated relationship."

Cassie paused to look in the mirror toward Erik's reflection. "You mean she doesn't like you either?" Her tone was teasing.

"Love—hate. Depends on the day." His eyes swept the sitting room again. "Right now, I'd say accent is on the hate. There was an alleged incident where a hotel room in Venice might have gotten set on fire while I was retrieving an artifact. The Arkana was stuck with the bill. In case you didn't know, Maddie hates writing big checks."

"Alleged?"

"That's the way I remember it." Erik folded his arms across his chest, refusing to offer any further information.

Cassie's brain still felt fuzzy. She went to the sink in the luxurious marble bathroom and began splashing cold water on her face. "How long have you been here?" she burbled through the water.

Leaning against the door, Erik replied, "Since yesterday. I had to get a few things squared away on another project. As long as I was here, I decided to kill two birds. Thought I'd give you a couple of hours to get some sleep before swinging by."

Cassie reached for a towel. "What time is it anyway?" She patted her face dry and moved back into the sitting area.

He checked his watch. "Around five PM local time."

"Feels more like four AM to me after being out all night." She rubbed her head. "I think I need an aspirin." She dove into her duffle bag in search of the tiny green bottle. "When's Griffin supposed to arrive?"

"Last I heard, he caught the flight after yours. Should be here any time now."

As if on cue, someone knocked tentatively on the door.

Erik went to answer while Cassie downed two aspirin and a glass of water.

"Hello all," Griffin chirped brightly. Apparently, he was one of those lucky people who could sleep on airplanes. He looked around Cassie's suite. "I must say Maddie outdid herself in arranging our accommodations this time. Absolutely first rate."

"You too, huh?" Erik asked glumly.

To Griffin's puzzled look, Cassie replied, "He's bent out of shape because he got assigned a broom closet."

"Ah, I see," the scrivener nodded sagely. "She still must be upset about the Boetian vase incident."

"Guess so," Erik replied sourly. "I wonder how long it's gonna take her to forget about it."

"I fear she's rather like an elephant in that regard," Griffin commented.

"Guys, check this out," Cassie called out eagerly. "There's a balcony." She threw open the double glass doors and rushed outside to a picture postcard scene. Her room overlooked the oldest section of the city with its mosques and minarets. Beyond them lay the blue ribbon of water that was the Bosporus Straits.

"What a view!" she exclaimed. "I was in a fog during the taxi ride from the airport. When I got here, I dropped off to sleep right away, so I didn't get to see the city. It's amazing!"

The two men came out to join her at the railing.

"Yes, Istanbul does have some interesting features," Griffin observed. "Over there is Hagia Sophia, the church of Holy Wisdom. Its huge dome is an architectural wonder. At the time it was built in the 6th century, the structure was the largest cathedral in the world and remained so for a thousand years. It was converted to a mosque at which point the minarets surrounding it were added. Now it's a museum."

Cassie studied the four slender towers that surrounded the building. "That's something I'm not used to seeing. I've seen cathedrals before, but not with little towers around them. In fact, they're all over town."

Griffin assumed full lecture mode. "Five times a day, the muezzin, a man appointed to lead prayers, will climb the stairs of those minarets and call the Muslim faithful to praise Allah."

Cassie squinted in the late afternoon sun. "The tops look so sharp from here; it's almost as if they're trying to poke a hole in the sky."

Directing her attention elsewhere, Griffin pointed. "Over there is the Blue Mosque, built by a sultan named Ahmet who wished to outdo the splendor of the Hagia Sophia."

"It doesn't look blue to me," Cassie noted.

"That's because you have to be inside to see the blue tiles that it's named for," Erik offered. "That green space around the mosques is where the Hippodrome used to be. It was like the Coliseum in Rome. Chariot races and lots of blood sport for the masses. Not to mention a few riots and massacres."

"People had an odd idea of fun back then." The pythia shook her head.

Erik continued. "On the other side of the Hagia Sofia is the Topkapi Palace. Sultan central. Now it's a museum, too. The harem is always a big tourist draw."

"Hmmm." Cassie scowled in disapproval. "I'd rather not know about what went on in there."

"Actually, it's quite a fascinating place," Griffin chimed in, "and not for the reasons you would imagine. The harem was a microcosm of Ottoman society with its own bureaucracy and political power struggles. The sultan's mother, the Valide Sultan, had a great deal of influence over her son's decisions in governing the empire. Sultan Padishah Ahmet is even quoted to have said that the world lies at the foot of the mother."

Erik snorted sarcastically. "Harem life was pretty good for the sultan's mother but not so good for his brothers."

"Why not?" Cassie turned from the railing to look at him. "Being related to the head honcho couldn't be all that bad."

The two men glanced significantly at one another.

"You tell her," Griffin instructed Erik.

"Sure." Erik grinned. "Back in the bad old days, there was cutthroat competition to be the next guy in charge, and I mean that literally. Multiple wives meant lots and lots of half-brothers all itching to take the crown, or turban anyway. Succession by murder."

"That's awful." Cassie gasped. "You mean they'd kill their own relatives to become sultan?"

"Well, what do you expect? Overlord culture rules applied. The world had become a dog eat dog kind of place. After Sultan Mahomet III murdered all his brothers and most of their mothers, he came up with a kinder, gentler way to deal with the problem of his own sons."

"If you can call it kind," Griffin muttered.

Cassie shot him a puzzled look but said nothing.

Erik leaned his elbows on the railing and continued. "Instead of killing all the guys who might be future competition for the throne, the reigning sultan decided to shut them up in a part of the harem called The Cage."

Cassie blanched. "Was it an actual cage?"

"No, it was more like house arrest, but they were always watched by guards and weren't allowed outside. Of course, they were provided with female company to pass away the time."

"Sorry, but I don't find that idea any less disturbing," the pythia grumbled. "The women couldn't have been any more happy to be shut up for a lifetime than the men were."

"Yeah but they got to go outside sometimes," Erik corrected. "Shopping trips to the bazaar."

"Swell," Cassie retorted.

Griffin concluded the story. "In the long run, the practice of caging rivals for the throne wasn't a success. By the time a prince was allowed to assume power, he was usually incompetent to rule if not outright insane from having spent all his life in confinement. Although one poor sod endured fifty-six years in the cage, others chose a quicker release by committing suicide."

"I can believe that," Cassie agreed. "It's all so creepy."

"It was a violent time, and the men in charge could only retain their power by using violent means." Griffin sighed. "Even by the standards of overlord culture, this city has had a frightfully bloody past."

Cassie turned from the railing and flopped down in one of the balcony chairs. Her companions followed suit.

"What made it so frightfully bloody?" she asked.

"This spot was a battleground for nearly all the overlord kingdoms during the past two thousand years," Griffin explained. "The Bosporus is the only waterway that connects the Black Sea to the Mediterranean. Istanbul itself straddles two continents. Anyone intent on building an empire in this part of the world would eventually have to pass right through it. First, it was conquered by the Greeks, then the Persians, then the Romans, then the Crusaders and finally the Ottomans in the 15th century who held it until the country became a republic in the 1920s. As the conquerors changed, so did the name. Initially, it was Byzantium, then Constantinople, and finally Istanbul."

"OK, I'm sorry I asked." Cassie rubbed her head distractedly. "Too much information. I already had a headache before you guys got here, and I think my brain just reached its capacity for processing new data."

"When did you eat last?" Griffin asked solicitously.

"Not since I left Chicago," she replied glumly. "I have a thing about airline food."

"Maybe a meal would help," the scrivener suggested. "I confess I'm a bit peckish myself."

"We might as well order room service and eat out here," Erik said. He walked back into the room and returned with a menu. "At least if we charge it to Cassie's room I won't get an earful from Maddie about my expense account."

"Surely, she's allowed you a per diem for meals?" Griffin asked.

Erik gave a short bark of a laugh. "Like you said, man, elephants."

Chapter 10—Flooded with Information

HALF AN HOUR LATER their room service order arrived, and the Arkana team hungrily dove in. Cassie's headache evaporated once she started eating.

Griffin looked at Erik's plate disparagingly. "Thousands of miles from home and all you can think to order is something as prosaic as a hamburger?"

"It's a cheeseburger," the security coordinator replied defensively taking a large bite. "I like cheeseburgers."

Cassie and Griffin had opted to try a sample of Turkish dishes called meze.

"What's that you're eating?" Cassie scrutinized an interesting item on Griffin's fork.

"Its name is *patlican salatasi* in Turkish. I believe it's cold aubergine salad."

"What's that in English?"

"Oh, sorry. You Yanks would call it eggplant."

Cassie smiled. "I can't pronounce any of the names, but these dishes sure are good."

"Just don't drink the tap water," Erik cautioned.

"He's right about that," Griffin concurred. "Bottled water only."

Cassie sat back in her chair taking a break between courses. She watched the aquatic taxis and commercial ships making their way up the thin blue ribbon of water separating two continents. "It's hard to believe a place as pretty as this has seen so much death."

Erik looked up briefly from his burger. "You mean all the battles? That's nothing."

She fixed him with a stare. "What do you mean?"

"Some places just seem to attract disaster. And this one had a dark history long before the first Greek decided to settle here."

Cassie turned her attention to Griffin. "What's he talking about?"

Griffin hurriedly swallowed a mouthful of food. "He's referring to the flood."

"The flood," the pythia repeated skeptically.

"Yup, the flood," Erik echoed, shifting his focus to his french fries.

Cassie gave a huge sigh. "OK, I've eaten. My head's clearing up. Tell me the rest."

"In the beginning..." Erik intoned pompously.

"You've no doubt heard of the flood in the Bible?" Griffin dabbed his mouth with a napkin.

"You mean Noah and two by two and the ark?"

"The very same."

"Of course, I have. So what?"

"There's a very good possibility that a flood of epic proportions really happened and that it happened not very far from where we're sitting."

"Get out!" Cassie blurted, intrigued.

"Other cultures have recorded the story of a similar catastrophe. The most well-known is the Babylonian epic of Gilgamesh. But there is also a Sumerian deluge myth and the Akkadian epic of Atrahasis. Of course, by the time these stories were written down, the event itself was several thousand years old."

"Then what did happen here?" Cassie sat forward, looking at Erik inquisitively.

"Let him tell it, I'm still eating," the security coordinator growled.

"Very well." Griffin cleared his throat. "You may think of global warming as a modern occurrence, but it's quite old. The catastrophe of the Black Sea flood was the result of global warming on a scale that is nearly incomprehensible. You see until quite recently a large part of the northern hemisphere was covered in ice."

"You mean as in glaciers?" Cassie offered helpfully.

"Precisely. Around 10000 BCE, the last ice age was coming to an end, and those glaciers began to melt. The process took thousands of years.

46

During that period, the Black Sea was a body of fresh water called the New Euxine Lake."

Cassie looked out at the Bosporus in surprise. "But how's that possible? Doesn't this channel connect the Black Sea with the ocean somehow?"

Griffin smiled knowingly. "That's quite correct, but at the time of which I'm speaking, there was no strait here. Just a rocky shelf separating the Sea of Marmara to the south of us from the Euxine Lake to our north. There was a tiny rivulet called the Bosporus that let fresh water out into the sea." He paused, looking out at a boatload of sightseers bobbing on the strait.

"Sumeria is often credited with being the cradle of civilization, but it's far more likely that the signal honor belongs to the coastline of the Euxine. Humans had left their gatherer-hunter ways behind and become settled agriculturists all along its shores. They set up villages that traded with one another for hundreds of miles around. We assume they were peaceful matristic communities though we can't be sure. The Arkana is in the process of collecting evidence to that effect. The pleasant life along the Euxine may, in fact, be a memory fragment that eventually found its way into the Bible as the Garden of Eden—a land which was supposedly fed by four rivers. It can't be proven, of course, that the writers of Genesis were referring to the Black Sea basin, but it is fed by four major rivers: the Dnieper, Dniester, Danube, and Don. An interesting coincidence, don't you think?"

"Get to the good part," Cassie urged. "How did the lake become a sea?"

Erik leaned back in his chair, propped his feet on the balcony railing and closed his eyes.

Griffin forged ahead. "As I mentioned, the glaciers had gradually been receding and dumping an enormous quantity of melted ice into the world's oceans. It was only a matter of time before the sea level rose higher than the fragile little outcropping of rock which separated the Sea of Marmara from the Euxine Lake. The salt water first began as a trickle through the tiny outlet of the Bosporus. The trickle grew into a stream, then the stream grew into a river, and the river finally grew into a cataract that became unstoppable."

Cassie jostled Erik's arm to waken him. "Are you listening to this?"

He yawned and resettled himself "I've heard it before. Wake me up when he's done."

47

The scrivener rolled his eyes and resumed. "Try to imagine a waterfall cascading with two hundred times the force of Niagara Falls and a velocity of over fifty miles an hour. The sound of the water crashing across the breach in the sill would have echoed one hundred and twenty miles away. The lake's water level would have risen so rapidly that the shoreline may have expanded by as much as a mile a day, drowning everything in its path. One can only imagine the catastrophic impact this would have had on the people who lived along the shores of the lake."

"I'll say," Cassie exclaimed in shock. "They wouldn't have known what hit them."

"Those living closest to the Bosporus would probably have drowned, of course, but those farther away may have had time to pack some meager belongings, collect their kin and livestock and flee."

"Where did they all go?"

"It depends on which side of the lake they inhabited. The ones to the north and west were luckiest. They fled up the river valleys into the heart of Europe. Since those river valleys were incredibly fertile, the people who emigrated there were able to continue living as peaceful agriculturists. Others were not so fortunate."

"That sounds pretty ominous."

"Indeed it was. To the east and south, the Black Sea is rimmed with mountains. Anyone lucky enough to scale them would find their problems just beginning. Those who skirted the Caucasus Mountains and fled to the northeast would have ended up in the Eurasian steppes. A very inhospitable landscape for farming."

"What did they do if they couldn't farm?"

"They became nomads and grazed what little livestock remained. Scarcity became a way of life. There was never enough food to go around, so eventually, they raided nearby groups and stole their livestock. Their neighbors retaliated, and raiding became a way of life for everyone on the steppes. A harsh landscape produces harsh people."

"Overlord cultures," Cassie exclaimed, finally comprehending. "Now I understand what Faye was talking about."

"Oh, there's much more to the story of what turned them into aggressive, sky god worshippers but I think the Anatolian trove keeper may have more insight to offer on that topic than I do."

"When do we get to meet him?" Cassie asked eagerly.

Griffin took a sip of his Turkish coffee. "If all goes as planned, tomorrow afternoon. We have to travel to the dig site first, of course, but he did say he would have time to speak with us when we arrived."

Cassie gazed out over the darkening water and noticed with a start that the sun had already set. She hadn't realized how long they'd been talking. "I think we need to get some actual sleep before we pick up and go anyplace else." She rose and turned to regard Erik who was snoring slightly. Pursing her lips, she said, "Guess we should wake him up and tell him to go to bed."

She was about to nudge Erik when Griffin stopped her. Poising his foot to deliver a well-aimed kick to the legs of Erik's chair, he said, "Please allow me to do the honors."

Chapter 11—Flight of Angels

LEROY HUNT LOOKED AT his wristwatch and let out a bored sigh. This flight was taking forever. He didn't much care for flying to begin with. Airplanes always seemed like coffins with wings. "If God had wanted us to fly," his momma always said, "He'd have made us rich enough to afford a plane ticket." He chuckled at the memory. If momma could see him now. She'd been praying over his soul right up to the day she died. Bet she'd be proud to know that he was rubbing elbows with churchy folk these days. Hell, the Nephilim claimed they were part angel. You couldn't get any churchier than that. According to crazy old Abraham, Leroy was actually doing the Lord's work. That was neither here nor there as far as he was concerned. He got paid real well and sometimes got to shoot folks, which he always enjoyed. Leroy believed that unless you were aiming at a live target, you were just wasting good ammo.

He cast a glance at the man in the window seat who was literally rubbing elbows with him. He sighed again. The only part of this job he didn't relish was babysitting the old man's weasel of a son. Daniel was about as hangdog and gutless a piece of humanity as Leroy had ever seen. Hunt bitterly recalled the time when Daniel had interfered with his hired duty to kill those three thieves who wanted to get to the relics before the Nephilim did. Messing with God's plan for the merchandise, as it were. Leroy never mentioned the incident to the boy's daddy, but he never forgot it. Didn't like the kid and didn't trust him either.

Hunt reached up and pressed the call button for the stewardess. When she arrived, he asked, "Darlin', think you could scare up another one of them tiny bottles of whiskey?"

He looked ruefully at the three dead soldiers already lined up on his tray table. Even booze couldn't seem to move this boat any faster.

The stewardess poured him another drink. He downed it in two gulps and then turned his attention to the sad sack next to him. Daniel was staring at his computer like he was praying over the dead.

"I see you got yourself a new toy," Hunt observed.

Daniel jumped and stopped mumbling to himself. "Sorry?"

"Your shiny new computer, son," Leroy hinted.

"Oh, yes that." Daniel collected his wits. "Father gave me permission to have one because I told him we could recover the artifacts much quicker if I had my own access to information on the internet."

Hunt registered surprise. "You mean none of you all got computers of your own?"

Daniel shook his head. "Only Father and the heads of the other compounds are permitted to have them. Father believes the internet is a corrupting influence."

Leroy chuckled. "He ain't wrong about that. You stumbled across any free porn sites yet?"

The young man peered at him earnestly. "I don't know what that word means. Is porn an abbreviation for something?"

His companion let out a guffaw and slapped his knee. "Hooee! I tell you what, boy. You're greener than acorns in June! Porn is short for bare-naked ladies gettin' up to all sorts of mischief and lettin' us fellers watch."

Daniel blushed to the roots of his hair follicles. "I... I... I've never heard of such a thing."

Still grinning, Leroy replied. "No, I don't expect you would've. Your daddy likes to run a tight ship. Still and all, can't say that you'd need to watch porn much since you got all them wives. What's the body count up to now?"

"Four," Daniel said in a tight voice. "I have four wives."

"Must keep you busy most nights," Leroy opined.

"I'd rather talk about something else."

His companion nodded affably. "OK, no harm in askin'." He tilted his head in the direction of the computer. "Then if it ain't porn, what are you starin' at on that screen?"

The young man transferred his gaze back to the monitor. "I'm trying to find as much information as I can about the Idaean Cave."

"The Idea cave?" Leroy repeated, bemused.

"I-D-A-E-A-N." Daniel spelled out the word. "It's a cave on Mount Ida where we are most likely to find the first relic."

Leroy studied the image on Daniel's computer. "It looks like a big hole in the side of a hill, son. What makes it so special?"

"The cave was sacred to the heathens of the island. The Minoans built a shrine there several thousand years ago which was then taken over by the Greeks. In the original myth, the Minoan goddess gave birth in that cave to the annual god of fertility. Actually, there are two caves on the island associated with the myth, but our clue points to the one located on Mount Ida. When the Greeks conquered Crete, they changed the myth to say that their chief god Zeus was born in the cave."

"Oh, I heard of him. Big fella with a white beard. Liked to wrap hisself up in a bed sheet and run around smitin' folks with lightnin' bolts. Ain't that the guy?"

Daniel cast a dubious look toward the man seated beside him. "Why, yes, Mr. Hunt. Zeus was associated with lightening in many of the myths. As for the bed sheet, it's called a toga."

"Don't care what it's called," Leroy retorted. "It ain't manly attire."

Ignoring the comment, Daniel retrieved a map on his computer. "We're flying to Heraklion. Over here, you see?" He pointed to a dot on the northeast coast of the island.

"Yup, I gotcha."

"Brother Nikos will hire a car and meet us at the airport."

"Oh, so it's Brother Nick again, is it?" Leroy flashed briefly on the little rat-faced convert who sucked up to Daniel because he was the son of the diviner. He'd be over the moon knowing the kid had been promoted to something called a scion.

"Yes, he will drive us to Mount Ida which is over here." He pointed to another dot on the map, southwest of Heraklion.

"So, the two of you plan on crawlin' over rock piles again like you done last time?" Leroy asked bleakly.

"Fortunately, the area we will have to cover is very small. It's a single cave, Mr. Hunt."

"Still, if it's all the same to you, I'll wait for the pair of you at the nearest tavern."

"As you wish."

Leroy pulled his cowboy hat over his eyes and pretended to doze off. He didn't want to shoot the breeze with the kid any more. This was shaping up to be even more dismal than the first trip. But then again, he consoled himself, somebody might turn up who needed shooting. That thought was a comfort.

Leroy had a couple of other comforting thoughts to keep him warm. No matter what Daniel said and no matter what his daddy said, Hunt was sure there was money in those relics. He wanted to stick close and see what shook out. Maybe if the kid turned up something valuable enough, Leroy might help the little punk to have an accident and go into business for himself.

Hunt wasn't the only one forming a new game plan. The cowboy's mind drifted back to the last conversation he had with Daniel's old man. Abraham had asked him for the name of somebody who had experience with weapons training, but Metcalf wouldn't tell him why. Leroy had put him in touch with an army buddy. Maybe it was worth hanging around just to find out what the old coot had up his sleeve. Hunt was sure he could turn it to his advantage somehow. His momma always told him, "Leroy, you're too smart for your own good." He didn't think so. Not too smart. Just smart enough to make it pay.

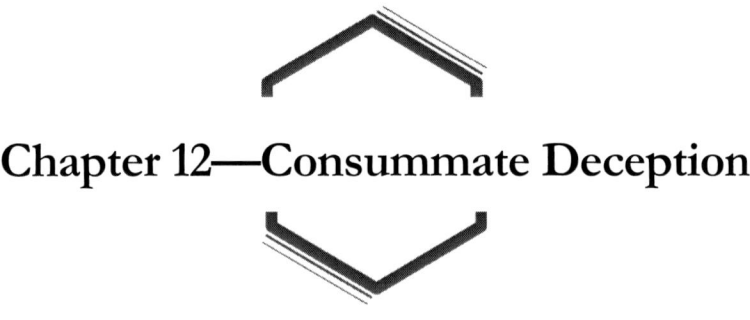

Chapter 12—Consummate Deception

ANNABETH SKIDDED TO a stop in front of the heavy oak door. She took a moment to smooth her hair and straighten her apron. She waited several seconds for her breathing to slow down. It didn't want to cooperate. Her heart was still hammering a mile a minute even though she mentally willed herself to be calm. She jammed her left hand into her apron pocket, fighting the urge to bite off a hang nail. In all her life, she never thought she would do something this bold. Request a personal interview with the diviner. She'd almost hoped he would refuse to see her. But then, she supposed, since she was one of the wives of the new scion that gave her some special status. She braced herself and knocked on the door.

A deep growl from the other side of the partition told her to enter. The sound almost made her squeak in fright, but she did as she was told.

The diviner was standing in front of a Bible lectern on the far side of the room. He didn't turn around. "Sit down, Annabeth," he instructed.

She looked around nervously for a chair. She had never been inside his prayer closet before. Directly to her right she saw a small table and two chairs. She dove into the nearest seat and folded her hands in her lap to wait.

Father Abraham resumed reading his Bible.

Annabeth glanced up at the portrait of the last diviner which hung above the table. She averted her gaze just as quickly. The face seemed to be staring directly back at her in an attitude of stern disapproval.

"What do you wish to speak to me about?"

She jerked to attention. The diviner was walking across the room toward where she sat.

He took the chair opposite and waited for her reply.

She cast her eyes down at the floor in confusion. "I'm sorry to bother you, Father. I... I... know how busy you must be."

"Yes," he said coldly. "My time is valuable. I don't want it wasted on trifles."

She gathered the courage to look at him. Her hands were no longer folded in her lap. They were clenched together in a tight little ball. She wanted to fly out of the room, but she had to hold her ground and speak. Her own salvation was at stake. "I have come to tell you some news." She hesitated. There was no good way to say this.

"Yes?" His tone was impatient.

"I... uh... I think there may be something wrong with the scion's new union."

"What?' he bellowed, rising and standing above her. "What on earth are you jibbering about, woman?"

She tried to blink back the tears, but she had been on edge for so long that it all came flooding out and she began to sob. Hiding her face in her hands, she bent over the table and cried.

The spectacle took Father Abraham by surprise. He seemed perplexed and sat back down. "There, there," he said stiffly. "There's no need for tears, Annabeth. Now, what is the problem?"

She blew her nose, sniffled and tried to regain control. "I... I... had to make sure you knew that it wasn't my fault, Father. I'm not a bad wife."

"A bad wife?" he echoed. "Who said you were a bad wife?"

"Y... you did." She began to wail all over again.

The diviner drew himself up. He seemed offended. "I said no such thing."

Annabeth struggled to breathe. Her sobs left her gasping for air. "Y... yes. Y... you told me that I was disobedient and that's why my husband didn't seek out my company. But it isn't only me!" She dug her fists into her eyes to clear them. "I don't deserve to be cast out of the kingdom, Father. I don't want to be left behind on Judgment Day."

The diviner kept his tone level to avoid upsetting her further. He chose his words carefully. "You just said it isn't only you. Explain what you mean by that."

Annabeth blinked back the last of her tears and let out a huge sigh. She blew her nose again and regarded the diviner gravely. "I don't believe the problem is with us, Father. I talked to my sister-wives, and Daniel has showed no husbandly affection to any of us for years now. And then yesterday I asked my newest sister-wife Hannah about her wedding night, and it seems…" she trailed off, unsure of how to phrase a subject so delicate.

The diviner appeared stunned. He sat perfectly still for several seconds, staring off into space. Finally, he asked, "Are you trying to tell me that my son did not consummate his union with Hannah?"

Annabeth nodded solemnly. "That is what she told me, Father. She seemed very confused by it too."

"Woman, you know it is a grave sin to lie about such things."

Annabeth nearly stopped breathing altogether. "Oh, Father, no! I would never lie about this or anything."

Father Abraham stared at her in silence. His face wore exactly the same expression as the man in the portrait. "If you aren't lying then it is plain you are being deluded by the Father of Lies. The devil has tricked you into believing you are not to blame."

Annabeth faltered in her conviction. The thought had never occurred to her before. "He has?" she asked limply.

The diviner rose and paced around the room, his hands clasped behind his back. "There is no other possible explanation. He has hoodwinked not only you but your sister-wives as well."

She gaped at him in shock.

He continued. "You are being seduced by the sin of pride. Satan has whispered in your ear that there is no fault in you, so it must be your husband who is to blame. Women are foolish and easily led astray. If your husband is avoiding all of you, perhaps he has detected some flaw that you are too prideful to admit. His judgment is to be trusted not merely because he is my son but because he is the scion. He will one day speak directly to God as I do now. God himself chose Daniel to succeed me." He wheeled around and glared at her. "Do you think He would have chosen a man who was fallible and lacking in discernment to lead the Nephilim?"

"N… no, Father." She couldn't bear to meet his eyes. She stared at the floor. "That isn't possible."

"I advise you to examine your heart most carefully, Annabeth. The foe of mankind has made an abode for himself there."

Annabeth felt a thrill of horror running through her. Satan in her own heart? How could she trust the evidence of her senses? Was any of it real? The devil could be whispering lies to her even now. She sat transfixed until she felt a firm hand grasp her by the elbow and propel her toward the door. The diviner was speaking again. She heard his voice echoing from a great distance.

"...the matter of your sister-wives. I will question each one separately."

She could feel him shaking her by the shoulders. "Annabeth! Pay attention."

"Y... yes, Father."

"You will not speak to anyone about this matter ever again. Do you understand me?"

She nodded mutely as the door slammed in her face. She felt sick with dread. A demon had taken possession of her body. Someone else was peering out from behind her eyes. Hell wasn't simply some faraway place where the Fallen would go on the Day of Judgment. Hell was as close as the beating of her own heart.

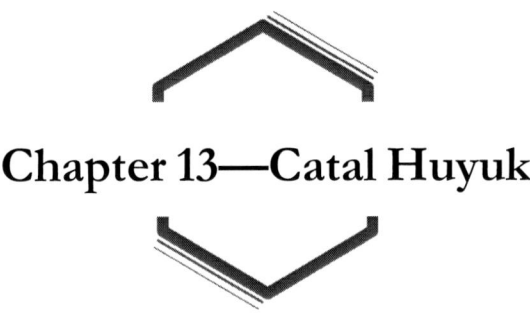

Chapter 13—Catal Huyuk

CATAL HUYUK. CASSIE thought the very name sounded mysterious and exotic. They were on their way to an honest-to-goddess archaeological dig site, but she couldn't help feeling slightly disgruntled. Nothing was turning out the way she'd expected. It had all started going sideways that morning. She imagined they would make the cross-country journey from Istanbul by train in something that looked like the Orient Express. Instead, they took a commercial flight to Konya—a large town in central Turkey that had traffic signals and chain hotels. When their plane landed, she imagined they would be met by a vaguely sinister contact wearing a fez with a tassel. His name would be Ali Ben something. Instead, they got a balding American guy named Fred who picked them up at the airport in a minivan. Fred's only distinguishing characteristic was that he was so utterly ordinary that he had no distinguishing characteristics. Just about as colorful as an ice cube on a snow bank in Antarctica.

Not remotely what she expected, Cassie thought dismally, as she sat in the back seat of the van gliding smoothly along well-paved highways. They ought to be bouncing along in an open truck with bad shocks across back country dirt roads. They should all be wearing khaki and safari helmets instead of jeans and T-shirts.

Erik sat up front with Fred and Griffin was in the back with her. She confided her disillusionment in a whisper to the scrivener, not wanting Erik to hear.

He smiled sympathetically. "I think you've seen one too many films about mummies."

She turned away to look out the window. They had to drive forty miles to Catal Huyuk which Fred explained meant "fork mound" in Turkish.

Hmmm. Not such an exotic name after all. It was located on the central Anatolian plateau where the terrain was flat, and most of it was planted in wheat fields. It was all so utterly ordinary.

The minivan slowed to pass through a gate with a barbed wire fence which protected several acres of hillside in the middle of nowhere. There were some guards in uniform, but nobody stopped them or asked them for papers or tried to pass them any suspicious relics wrapped in brown paper like the Maltese Falcon.

Cassie gave one last hopeful look out the window to see if there were any upper-class Brits in camp chairs writing field notes under canvas canopies while inscrutable houseboys served them tea. Nope. All she could see were a bunch of tourists in cross-trainers standing in a semi-circle around a tour guide.

"Romance is dead." She sighed.

"I beg your pardon?" Griffin gave her a startled look.

"I mean, where's the glamor in it?"

"Archaeology is far from a glamorous profession. A good deal of it consists of scraping dirt off the odd bit of crockery."

"Can I touch some of the objects they're digging up?" Cassie asked eagerly.

"No!" both Erik and Griffin shouted in unison.

"Do you have bat ears?" she asked Erik. "How can you hear all the way back here?"

"I hear the important stuff, and no you can't touch anything!"

"Why not," she challenged.

"Cassie, this dig site isn't controlled by the Arkana," Griffin cautioned.

"It isn't?"

"Nope," said Erik. "The Arkana has its own section of the dig separate from what's going on here, but the last thing we need is to call attention to..." he paused.

"Your special gift," Griffin finished tactfully. "We're only here to collect information from the trove keeper."

"I don't know why you guys are so twitchy about it," she grumbled. "I mean the people in charge have to know about the Arkana, don't they?"

"They actually don't," Fred called over his shoulder. "When we have to share a project with outsiders, we operate using front organizations that have respectable academic credentials. Staying off the radar is especially important when we're working on a government-controlled site like this one."

"But then you don't get to keep any of the artifacts you find," Cassie objected.

"Neither does anybody else," Erik countered. "It all gets turned over to national museums."

"But we do get a chance to see what's here in its original state," Fred explained.

"Why is that important?"

"Ah, there's many a slip twixt the cup and the lip," Griffin remarked sententiously.

Cassie sighed. "Do I even need to tell you to unpack that?"

Erik laughed. "What Sir Quipsalot is trying to say is that a dig site can get messed up by the people who are doing the digging."

"Quite so," Griffin agreed. "It's very common for objects at a site to be taken to museums before they've been identified in their original context. Not to mention some of the official interpretation given to the objects found."

"He's right," Fred concurred. "It's always better if we're around to see for ourselves without being treated to an overlord explanation of what it all means."

"I guess that makes sense." Cassie relented slightly. "So, no touchie?"

"Absolutely no touchie." Erik's voice was stern. "Just stick your hands in your pockets while we're here, OK?"

"And whatever you do, don't tread on any of the structures that have been unearthed at the dig site," Griffin advised.

"Is it OK if I breathe?"

"Only if it's through your nose." At least Erik sounded as if he were joking.

The minivan idled its way through the main parking lot past something called the Dig House. Again, Cassie's expectations were deflated. Instead of a tent, it was a long ranch-style building that housed exhibits. A handful of sightseers were milling around the parking lot waiting for the next tour to start. Off in the distance, she could see one of the actual digs. It was covered by what looked like a huge canvas tarp.

Griffin pointed toward some of the workers who were dumping multi-colored plastic buckets into a hopper next to a water-filled metal trench. "That's a quick way to filter the dirt for smaller, finer artifacts."

"Kind of like sifting for gold," Cassie observed.

"Precisely."

Fred drove past the central buildings to a higher section of the mound. Set off by itself was a short flat building near another dig site covered with a canopy. He pulled the minivan up to the building and switched off the engine. "We're here," he announced.

Cassie slid open the side door. "Where's here?"

Fred climbed out. "This is the Arkana's section of the dig. The building is our site office. It's where the trove keeper works whenever he's in the area."

Griffin stepped down and stretched his legs after their long confinement.

When Cassie turned to face the door of the building, she smiled. For the first time today, she saw something that looked exactly the way she thought it should.

An elderly man stood in the doorway. He stepped forward a few paces with the aid of a walking stick. Cassie noted that it was capped with a gold lion's head. Despite the hundred-degree heat, he was dressed in a brown suit and matching vest. His crisp white shirt was neatly pressed. The only concession to the weather was a straw Panama hat. He shook hands with the men, but when his attention turned to Cassie, he gave a little bow from the waist.

"My name is Aydin Ozgur. I am the Anatolian trove keeper, and I am deeply honored to meet the pythia." He spoke flawless English with only a hint of an accent.

Cassie resisted the urge to dip him a slight curtsy. Instead, she held out her hand. "It's very nice to meet you, Mr. Ozgur." She studied his face. His skin was brown and wrinkled as a tobacco leaf. He had a bushy white moustache that drooped at the corners of his mouth. She guessed he might be as old as Faye, but his brown eyes sparkled with curiosity.

"You have come a long way," Ozgur said. "I can offer you refreshments, but perhaps you would prefer a short tour of the site first?"

Cassie blurted out impulsively, "Oh, I'd love to see the site!"

"Remember, don't touch anything," Erik muttered under his breath.

The pythia smiled impishly. "Relax, Max." She wiggled her fingertips at him and then jammed them into her pockets.

They made their way along a narrow gravel path leading up to the dig. The visitors shuffled behind the trove keeper, trying to slow their pace to match his. Ozgur steadied himself with his walking stick as he picked his way through broken rock. He stopped when he came to a canopy on the edge of a large hole in the ground.

"Wow!" Cassie exclaimed.

Looking down into the wide depression, she could see the floor was divided by a series of low mud-brick partitions. It was almost like looking at an overhead floor plan of a house. The partitions were only a few feet high though the crew working below was digging down to expose more wall. Several people were on their hands and knees scraping away at the floor of the structure. They all had plastic buckets handy where they dumped the dirt they were excavating.

Cassie turned to the trove keeper. "Who lived here at Catal Huyuk?"

He smiled at her eager curiosity. "A peaceful people. They farmed and kept livestock. Their houses were made of mud brick which was covered in white plaster. The structures were all built next to one another. There are no streets."

"No streets," Cassie echoed in surprise. "How did they get around?"

Aydin chuckled. "They moved from building to building across the roofs. In order to enter a dwelling, one had to climb down through a hole in the roof using a ladder. Are you familiar with the pueblos in America?"

"I've seen pictures of them," the pythia replied doubtfully, "but I've never been inside one."

The old man nodded. "They are built in much the same way as Catal Huyuk. People liked living in close proximity to one another."

"Guess high-rise apartments aren't so modern after all," the pythia commented.

"That is true."

"What's that over there?" Cassie pointed to the opposite end of the pit where a small hollow mound of clay protruded from the wall.

"I believe that's an oven." Griffin glanced at the trove keeper for confirmation. "Am I right?"

"Yes, each house had an oven for cooking food. It also provided warmth and light since there were no windows."

"You mean the only light came from a hole in the roof?" Cassie was incredulous.

"And very little light even from that source," Griffin speculated. "In winter the hole would have been covered to keep out the snow."

"It's hard to believe it ever gets cold here." The pythia felt as if she were standing in an oven. "It has to be almost a hundred degrees."

"Quite possibly." The trove keeper still looked unflappably cool himself. "But I assure you the winters are harsh. A covering would have been required over the hole in the roof. Sadly, while it kept out the snow and wind, it would also have kept in a great deal of smoke."

"Great. They probably all had emphysema."

"Not likely," Erik chimed in. "They only lived to be about thirty in the good old days."

"Yikes. That means at my age I'd be an old woman."

"Way past your prime, toots." The security coordinator gave an infuriating grin.

Cassie turned her back to him. Her attention was immediately caught by a very familiar object on the floor of the dig site. "Is that what I think it is?" she asked Griffin excitedly.

He nodded. "Something very like it."

The pythia studied the short square pillar of molded clay. To each end of the pillar were affixed cattle horns turned in an upright position. "They look exactly like the horns of consecration we saw on Crete," she explained to Ozgur.

He didn't seem surprised by her comment. "Some of the recent DNA evidence suggests that the Minoans originally came from Anatolia. They would have brought their sacred objects with them. The bucranium is a very old symbol. It may have existed as far back as the Paleolithic era."

"And it's a good example of why we're here," Fred interjected. "The overlord explanation is that the people of Catal Huyuk worshipped bulls while all the goddess statues they found scattered around were simply fertility figures."

"How could they tell the horns belong to a bull anyway?" Cassie wondered. "I mean you can't tell gender from looking at its head."

"The horns from a bull might be slightly larger," Ozgur said, "but among the wild aurochs there was much overlap in the size of cow and bull horns."

"What's an aurochs?"

"It's a cow," Erik answered. "Only a lot bigger and meaner than your average Holstein. Aurochs were never domesticated, and now they're extinct. The last one died somewhere in Poland in the 1600s."

"But as far as overlord archaeologists are concerned, it's all bull," Fred quipped.

Everyone laughed.

"We have uncovered a mural in this building that may do much to overturn the thinking that all the cattle horns are representations of a male deity. Follow me, and I will show you."

The trove keeper stepped down into the site and Cassie was about to follow him when Erik grabbed her by the arm and pulled her back.

"Do I need to put you on a leash?" he cautioned through gritted teeth.

"Try it, and you'll lose body parts," she hissed over her shoulder. Spinning around, she asked, "What is the big deal about me walking down there anyway?"

"The bodies," Griffin said nervously.

"What bodies?" Cassie looked around mystified.

"The bodies under the floor," the scrivener added.

"What?" She stood anchored to the spot, staring at her two companions as if they'd lost their minds. "You mean like John Wayne Gacy crawlspace bodies?"

"Oh, Mr. Ozgur," Griffin called out to stop their host. "Mightn't we find another way round? It may not be the best idea to have Ms. Forsythe walking through the dig."

Ozgur turned to look up at his guests. It took several seconds before recognition dawned. "Yes, of course. I'm sorry not to have realized. Please come this way instead." He climbed up to the rim and led the party around its perimeter to the other side.

"What bodies?" Cassie persisted.

"It was common for the people of Catal Huyuk to bury their dead beneath the house," Griffin explained. "In fact, some of these raised platforms you see along the floor probably contain skeletons."

"Their houses must have reeked. I mean rotting corpses underfoot. Yuck!"

"They didn't let them decompose inside," Erik corrected. "You know about excarnation, right?"

"I remember Griffin telling me about it," Cassie recalled. "The bodies were exposed on a platform outside for vultures and owls to feed on." She shuddered. "Still sounds disgusting to me."

"Once the flesh was removed, the bones would be cleaned and prepared for burial. It was all quite sanitary, I assure you." Griffin seemed to feel the need to defend the practice.

By now they had made their way around to the spot where Ozgur stood.

He waited until they clustered around him. "I do apologize, Miss Cassie. It was thoughtless of me."

The pythia shrugged. "I probably would have been OK."

The trove keeper gave a humorless smile. "There is a legend about this place. The local farmers have never tried tilling the mound of Catal Huyuk or disturbing it in any way because they always believed there are ghosts here. The people of this ancient culture buried their ancestors as guardian spirits to watch over them. Apparently, those spirits took their duties seriously and hover around the place to this day. I would not wish to tax one as sensitive as the pythia by having her encounter a whole city of the dead. They may not approve of our presence in their homes."

"Better safe than sorry." Griffin sounded apologetic.

"OK, guys, I get it." Cassie conceded. "No touchie, no walkie. Now, what was it you wanted to show us, Mr. Ozgur?"

"Ah yes." The old man tapped his walking stick on a portion of wall directly below them. "I would direct your attention just here. We were speaking of the sacred bucranium. How a cow or bull head could be viewed as a symbol of the regenerative power of the goddess."

Fred jumped down into the dig site and stood by the wall. "It's pretty interesting. I don't know how mainstream archaeologists can explain it."

They all peered over the edge at the remains of a painting. It showed several stylized female figures in seated positions. An odd shape appeared in the anatomical place where a uterus and fallopian tubes should be. A cow's head and horns.

Cassie let out a low whistle. "I said it before in Crete, and I'll say it again. Holy cow!"

"Good one," Erik laughed approvingly. "I must have missed it the first time."

"That was back in the day when you thought babysitting the new pythia was tedious work, so you ditched us," she reminded him.

"Babysitting the new pythia might be a lot of things, but I learned it's never tedious."

The pythia examined the layout of the room where the mural was painted. Opposite the picture were three horns of consecration set into the floor. On the wall directly beside the painting was an odd sculpture that she couldn't identify. "What's that supposed to be?" She asked the trove keeper.

"It is a frog goddess. She is most frequently associated with the act of giving birth because of the posture she assumes. Observe the object below her." He pointed with his walking stick.

"It's a bull's head," Cassie said then corrected herself. "Or maybe a cow's head."

"The position of the bucranium directly below the goddess is another image of regeneration."

"What does all this mean when you put the images together? The painting, the sculpture, the horns of consecration?"

"This room is a shrine, and these are all symbols of regeneration. Resurrection, if you will."

Griffin spoke up. "To these people, this symbolic grouping would have been as familiar as an empty cross on Easter morning would be to a Christian. Remember where the dead are buried."

Cassie made the connection. "I'm assuming if your nearest and dearest are sleeping under the floor, it's a way of asking the goddess to restore them somehow."

Aydin nodded. "Yes, that is quite correct. A constant reminder that the goddess eternally regenerates life and that nothing is ever lost."

Cassie raised her eyebrows. "Those are pretty abstract ideas. It doesn't sound to me like the people here were all that primitive."

"They weren't." Fred climbed back up to the rim to join the others. "That's more propaganda. History books like to preach that Mesopotamia was the first sophisticated culture on the planet with the first cities. Overlord culture really likes to promote that idea because Mesopotamia's city-states invented chronic siege warfare. But Catal Huyuk was thriving four thousand years before Uruk was even built."

"How long have people been living here?"

"The site was occupied as early as 7000 BCE," Griffin replied. "It may have contained as many as ten thousand inhabitants."

"We've only scratched the surface in terms of what's here," Fred added. "And I mean that literally. Who knows what else we'll dig up over the next decade."

Cassie's eyes swept the entire site and the people working diligently at the bottom of the pit, scraping away debris in search of lost treasure. "What happened to them all? The people, I mean."

"They left," Erik said casually.

The pythia looked at him skeptically. "You're kidding, right?

"Nope."

"The mound was abandoned a few times in its history," Ozgur elaborated. "We think that the earlier evacuations had to do with a prolonged drought which made farming here temporarily difficult."

His assistant continued. "There's another dig site called Catal Huyuk West where they moved for a while before coming back here. And then they left for good in the mid-sixth millennium BCE."

"Around 5500 BCE, they just pulled up stakes?" Cassie paused as a thought struck her. "That date sounds awfully familiar." She stared at Griffin. "Isn't that when..." She trailed off.

The scrivener beamed at her as if she were his star pupil. "I just knew you were paying attention. Erik didn't think so, but I was sure of it!"

"The flood." She flashed back to their conversation overlooking the Bosporus. "Didn't you say the Black Sea flooded around 5600 BCE?"

"Quite right."

"There is a very strong possibility that a connection exists between the flood and the abandonment of the site," Ozgur concurred. "The Arkana is still trying to find evidence to support the theory, but it seems very likely that some refugees from the deluge wandered in this direction."

"Did your team find any sign that there was a battle here?"

"There is some evidence of fire at the topmost layer of the dig but nothing conclusive," the trove keeper replied.

"There's a lot more evidence of disruption at Hacilar," offered Fred. "That's another Neolithic settlement about a hundred miles southwest of here. We know that Hacilar was destroyed by fire and when it was rebuilt, there was a wall around it."

"Overlord invaders?" Cassie guessed.

"I believe it was a bit too early for that," Griffin countered. "More likely it was roving bands of refugees, looting and pillaging on a small scale just to meet their immediate needs. There was no indication of organized military activity until much later, but the Anatolian plateau definitely shows signs of destabilization around the mid-sixth millennium."

"For the first time, dead bodies which had suffered violence, mainly children, were found in the burned debris at Hacilar," Ozgur said softly.

"Whether it was overlord culture or not," Cassie observed, "it sounds like the beginning of the end to me."

Aydin Ozgur silently turned and led the others away from the dig site.

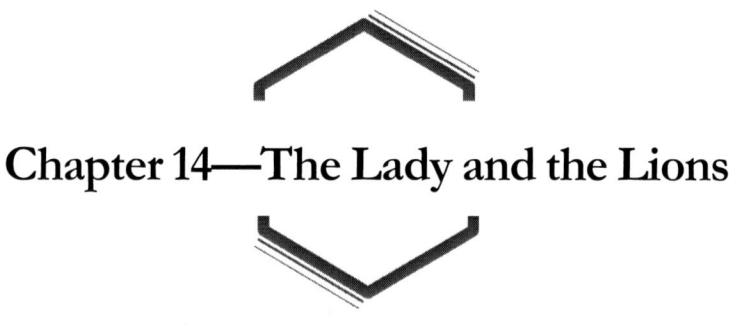

Chapter 14—The Lady and the Lions

THE TROVE KEEPER CAREFULLY retraced his steps along the rim and over the gravel path leading back to the site building. His companions followed in silence. When the old man reached the office, he motioned for the others to precede him inside. "Come in, please, and rest yourselves."

They filed in cautiously, not wanting to knock him off balance by rushing through the door. It was sweltering inside. Even though the windows were open, the only air flow was provided by a tired ceiling fan. The papers on Ozgur's desk wafted listlessly in the artificial breeze.

Cassie looked around the room. There was a desk, several chairs, and benches for visitors and metal filing cabinets everywhere. On the floor in the corners, boxes of rocks and other small objects were stacked.

"I'm sorry we have no proper reception room," the trove keeper apologized. "May I offer you coffee or tea?"

The three visitors drew chairs around the desk and waited patiently while Fred assisted Ozgur in preparing refreshments.

Cassie had asked for coffee, but she wasn't ready for the strong sweet concoction when she took her first sip. "Now I know why it's served in a tiny little cup. This carries quite a kick, doesn't it?"

Her companions grinned knowingly.

"Turkish coffee is very strong," Aydin agreed. "It is always brewed with sugar and cardamom."

"It's really good," Cassie reassured him, taking another sip, "but no refills for me, thank you."

Erik and Griffin had opted for tea which was served Russian-style in tall glasses instead of cups. They were all too polite to ask for something cold to drink.

"How are you getting on with the team that's running the expedition?" Griffin asked, blowing on his tea to cool it down.

Fred grimaced.

Aydin interpreted his look. "We don't rock the boat as you would say. A man named Percival who is on the lead team seems to be trying very hard to disprove the conclusions of James Mellaart, the original discoverer of the site. Based on what he found here, Mellaart believed that Catal Huyuk was a matristic culture which worshipped a female deity."

"Let me guess. Your buddy Percival isn't thrilled with that idea?" Erik asked sarcastically.

"He's doing everything but stand on his head to show that it was just your average overlord culture," Fred said in disgust. "I especially get a kick out of his interpretation of the bull horns."

"But surely, he's seen the mural you just showed us," Griffin objected.

"Nope, not yet." Fred gave a laugh. "We just finished cleaning it up yesterday. I can't wait to see the look on his face when we do."

While his assistant was speaking, Ozgur walked out of the room to retrieve something from the back-storage area. He returned with a figurine about as big as a man's hand and placed it gently on the front of his desk. It was a stone carving of a very obese naked woman seated on a throne and resting her forearms on the backs of two lionesses who stood on either side of her.

"That lady could use a tread climber!" Cassie exclaimed.

Erik chuckled.

"Fatness was once viewed as a sign of abundance," the trove keeper observed. "It would have been considered a desirable trait."

Griffin moved his chair closer to get a better look. "Oh, I say, she is remarkable."

"We found this statue in a grain storage bin in one of the shrine rooms," Ozgur said. "Many similar female figures have been found throughout the site, but the conventional theory is that these are fertility figurines."

"What's that supposed to mean?" Cassie was puzzled.

Fred raised his eyebrows. "That's what I'd like to know. Overlord archaeologists like Percival are falling all over themselves to say a bunch of horns are symbols of male divinity, but a statue like this gets explained away as a stone age lucky charm because it popped out of a cereal box."

"Oh, she's far more than that," Griffin said, turning the base of the object slightly. "The composition suggests she is a *potnia theron.*"

"I know you said *potnia* means something like lady or goddess," Cassie remarked.

"Very good," Griffin said encouragingly. "You see, Erik. I told you she wasn't hopeless."

"I didn't say that exactly," Erik demurred.

"No, I believe you said something about a brain like a sieve," the scrivener reminded him offhandedly, still entranced by the statue.

Cassie shot the security coordinator a reproachful look.

"Sorry, toots." His grin was almost sheepish. "I take it all back."

The pythia raised her chin defiantly and continued her earlier question. "Then what does *theron* mean?"

"*Potnia theron* would translate to something like Lady of the Animals or Goddess of the Wild Creatures," Griffin explained. "It's a concept that echoes all the way back to the Venus of Laussel some twenty thousand years ago. Gatherer-hunters worshipped the goddess as one who kept all living things in balance. She multiplied all life—both animal and human, hence her ample dimensions."

Cassie scrutinized the statue in puzzlement. "But why is she sitting next to lions? Isn't that a really odd choice? There aren't any wild lions in Turkey."

"Not anymore." Ozgur's tone was wistful. "They were hunted to extinction in this country in the 1800s. The Asiatic lion once roamed as far west as the Balkans. Now the few that remain are confined to a very small region in India."

"Overlords couldn't resist killing them," Fred interjected. "They didn't present that much of a threat to livestock, so it was mainly bragging rights over a trophy kill."

"That's disturbing," Cassie said.

"That's overlord culture," Erik commented succinctly.

Ozgur regarded the figurine closely. "While it is true that the idea of the *potnia theron* originated in the ancient past, this particular figure also persists well into historic times. Much as my colleagues try to deny that she is a deity, this little statue is the embodiment of the Goddess Cybele."

"Who's she?"

"The great mother goddess of Anatolia. During the classical age, she was the most significant deity in all of Asia Minor. You are, in fact, going to her principal place of worship on Mount Ida."

"But how do you know it's the same goddess?" Cassie persisted. "The classical age didn't start until thousands of years after this statue was carved."

"Because Cybele is always depicted with lions," Griffin jumped in. "She is either shown driving a chariot pulled by lions or seated on a throne between two lions. There are statues carved in Rome as late as the second century of our current era that show her in exactly the same pose as this figurine."

"The Romans, haughty overlords that they were, did not mistake Cybele for a mere fertility symbol," Ozgur observed. "To them, she was the Magna Mater. They respected her power and prayed for her assistance,"

"The Sybilline prophecy," Griffin said cryptically. "Of course."

Cassie and Erik exchanged a blank look. Erik shrugged.

Griffin continued speaking, half to himself. "When Hannibal was on the verge of invading Rome around 200 CE, one of the Sybilline oracles predicted that the only way the Romans could defeat their enemy would be to bring the goddess to Rome."

"How do you bring a goddess anywhere?" Cassie asked.

"Do you recall what I told you about baetyls? They are meteor rocks that are believed to be the seat of a deity. One such baetyl was housed in the ancient city of Pessinus. It was the largest iron meteorite in the known world. Over sixteen feet high and weighing several hundred tons, it was believed to be the personification of the goddess Cybele. The Romans negotiated to have the baetyl moved to Rome. They took the prophecy so seriously that they commissioned a magnificent temple to be built for it, right on the top of Vatican Hill."

"What!" Cassie felt shocked.

Griffin laughed. "That's right. Directly under Saint Peter's Basilica rests the remains of Cybele's temple. In fact, Bernini's *baldacchino*, a huge bronze canopy in the present church, is said to have been inspired by the design of the pagan structure."

"Cybele became the state deity of the Romans. She was venerated everywhere." Ozgur gave a slight smile. "Unfortunately, the Romans were less accepting of her devotees."

Cassie stared at the trove keeper blankly.

"He's referring to the *galli*," Griffin explained. "Cybele's transgender priestesses. Each year, in late March, on what was called the day of blood, men who wished to attain the rank of priestess castrated themselves and thereafter dressed as women."

"Hope they were drunk when they did it." Erik grimaced.

"In all probability, they were," Griffin agreed. "The cult of Cybele is a mystery religion which relies on ecstatic communion with the divine. Various hallucinogenic and intoxicating substances would have been a standard part of religious ceremonies."

"You were saying the Romans had a problem with these guys or gals or whatever?' the pythia asked.

"They passed laws prohibiting any Roman citizen from becoming a *gallus*," Ozgur explained. "Though in later years, a citizen could substitute the sacrifice of a bull and its genitalia for his own in a ritual called the *tauroboleum*."

"Craziness," Cassie commented, shaking her head in disbelief.

"Actually, most of the early goddess religions were quite tolerant of transgender worshippers," the scrivener pointed out. "Cross-dressing didn't become a problem until overlord cultures, and especially the Christian Church, actively persecuted such individuals."

"Why doesn't anybody know about all this?" the pythia asked of nobody in particular.

Ozgur picked up the goddess figurine contemplatively. "Once upon a time, everyone knew. Now we have forgotten and need to be reminded of just how ancient and universal the worship of this type of deity was. It echoes backward in time and spans countries around the globe. This image of a woman flanked by lions is repeated in myths around the world of goddesses so old that they are always referred to as the mother of the gods. In Egypt, it was the lion-headed goddess Sekhmet. In Minoa, it was Rhea. In Mesopotamia, it was Ishtar. In India, it was Durga who is called the Mother of the Universe. Even in remote Scandinavia, it was Freya whose chariot is drawn by two cats. This far-flung distribution suggests how very old this image of the goddess really is. Her presence is so all-pervasive that overlord mythology had no choice but to find a way to assimilate her."

"And in spite of all that, the archaeologists in charge of this dig are stumped by what this statue is?" Cassie felt incredulous.

Ozgur smiled. "You must remember that they are approaching this project like scientists with microscopes. Sometimes in the process of studying the details of a subject, one can lose sight of the larger picture. They have no context for understanding this image."

"I hope you set them straight," the pythia insisted.

"One day perhaps they will be ready to listen. For now, it's enough that we know what we know." He paused for a moment, considering something, then he held the statue out to Cassie. "Perhaps you could tell us more about her."

The pythia hesitated.

Griffin and Erik glanced worriedly at one another.

"Are you sure it isn't tainted?" Erik asked Ozgur.

"Not so far as we know," the trove keeper replied.

Cassie touched the pendant around her neck which Faye had given her. In case the object did have any disturbing associations, she would be able to ground herself. Wrapping her left hand around the pendant stone, she held out her right to receive the statue.

The room went dark. She was in a box, or she guessed that was how one of the Catal Huyuk rooms would have felt with walls and a roof overhead. The only light came from a fire burning in a corner of the room with its smoke funneling upwards through a hole in the roof. The atmosphere was so thick it almost made her choke. The air reeked with the acrid odor of smoke and unwashed human bodies. There were voices chanting behind her. They made a droning sound. Her consciousness settled in a thick-set, middle-aged woman who was kneeling in front of a freshly dug pit in the floor. Inside the pit, a small skeleton lay on its side in a fetal position. The remains of a child of about two. There were bracelets of blue stone around its wrists.

A little storage chest filled with grain rested on the floor by the woman's knees. She held the goddess figurine in front of her as she murmured a prayer for renewal. She placed the goddess inside the chest with the grain and closed the lid.

THE MOUNTAIN MOTHER CIPHER

Cassie could feel her invoking the goddess to transform the child who had been placed in the earth just as she transformed the seeds of grain into stalks of wheat. That which was planted would grow. This little one would change form in the body of the goddess and be reborn in the Otherland. The priestess sprinkled red powder over the bones. Then she sat back on her heels and bowed her head.

Cassie blinked. She returned to the present. The pythia laughed at the tense expression that her teammates wore. "Relax, guys. This one wasn't too bad." She then told them what she had witnessed. "I'm not sure what the red powder was though."

"It would have been red ochre," Griffin answered. "It was used in the burial practices of many ancient cultures. It symbolized the blood of life. The belief that the earth mother would give new life to the deceased."

"Transmutation? Resurrection? Hmmm. Seems to me that sort of power is a little beyond the paygrade of a mere fertility figure, don't you think?" Fred asked archly.

"Sure sounds like it to me," Erik concurred.

"Too bad we can't just trot out the pythia to end the great debate with Percival," Fred commented. "It could save a lot of time."

Ozgur gave a fleeting smile. "You must know he wouldn't believe her." He turned his attention to Cassie, and his expression became serious. "I am very grateful to you for the additional insight into our artifact. Thank you." He inclined his head in a slight bow.

Cassie blushed at being treated so respectfully. She gave a jerky little nod of acknowledgment. "I'm glad I could help."

Aydin lowered himself into his chair. Looking at each of his guests in turn, he asked, "And now what can we do to help you?"

Gloom settled over Griffin's features at the question. "Where to begin."

Erik gave a short laugh. "I think he means that literally. We don't know where to begin. We've got a riddle that tells us to look for a Minoan relic hidden someplace on Mount Ida, but that's all we know for sure."

"What is the riddle?" Ozgur settled back in his chair to listen.

Griffin recited the all-too-familiar lines. "You will find the first of five you seek, when the soul of the lady rises with the sun, at the home of the Mountain Mother, where flows the River Skamandros."

The trove keeper nodded. "Yes, it is clear the riddle refers to Mount Ida."

"But Griffin's having trouble with the second line," Cassie offered helpfully.

The old man stroked his moustache. "'When the soul of the lady rises with the sun.'"

"Do you have any notion what that might mean?" Griffin asked hopefully.

Ozgur shook his head. "Regrettably, no."

"Then perhaps you can recall seeing symbolic markings somewhere on the ruins that match our key."

"Your key?" the trove keeper asked.

"Oh, very sorry. I left it in the van. Be right back." Griffin hastened to retrieve the granite key from his knapsack in the car. When he returned, he handed it to Ozgur.

The trove keeper examined it briefly. "Some of these characters are Linear B. To find Linear B script anywhere outside of Greece would have been a major discovery. I should certainly have remembered."

"But you wouldn't have found the Linear B characters here," Griffin corrected. "You would have found the pictograms to which they correspond."

Ozgur examined the key again. "I'm sorry to be of so little help. No, I do not recall seeing any of these."

Griffin's voice held a note of despondency. "Well, no matter. I'm sure we'll pick up the trail somehow."

The old man seemed not to hear him. "'When the soul of the lady rises with the sun.' Since your riddle speaks of time, perhaps you should begin with the stone circles."

"What stone circles?" Erik sat forward.

"The megaliths on Ida."

"Megaliths?" Cassie echoed.

"Yes, large stones set in circles, like your Stonehenge in England. We believe the ancients used them as calendars to measure the seasons."

"That's brilliant!" Griffin exclaimed. "It makes perfect sense. If there's an event we're meant to witness, the most likely observation point would be a stone circle." He frowned as another thought struck him. "But we must be facing east. The riddle makes a reference to sunrise."

"It just so happens that one of the circles on the mountain does face east," Fred informed them. "I was part of a team that was checking overlord shrines on Ida. A lot of them were built over the ruins of goddess sites. While we were collecting Cybele artifacts, we stumbled across a stone circle."

Ozgur turned to his assistant. "Do you think you can show our guests where to find it?"

Fred nodded with assurance. "Absolutely. No problem."

Griffin could barely contain his elation. "That's wonderful. We may actually have a chance at solving this!"

The trove keeper smiled. "I am glad we were able to be of some small assistance. Fred will accompany you back to the Troad and guide you up the mountain. Perhaps fortune will be with you, and you will find the first of five you seek."

Erik leaned over and whispered to Cassie. "Better put on your size six and a half sneakers, toots. It sounds like you're gonna be tripping over some really big rocks."

Chapter 15—The Elephant in the Garden

TWILIGHT CAME AND WENT over Faye's cornflower blue farmhouse. An afternoon thunderstorm had left the summer air muggy. As the old woman opened her front door to let in a breeze, she found Maddie standing on her porch just about to knock.

"Come in, my dear, come in." Faye stood aside to let her enter. "I must say this is a surprise."

"I was on my way home, but I thought I'd swing by and give you an update." The operations director towered over her hostess as she stepped into the foyer. Her briefcase was bulging with papers.

Faye noted the portfolio. "Taking work home again?"

Maddie shrugged indifferently. "It's gotta get done somehow. I'm a little short-staffed just now."

"Shall we go outside and sit in the garden?" Faye suggested. "It's much too stuffy in here."

"Suits me. You wouldn't happen to have a pot of coffee made, would you?" Maddie asked wearily.

"Of course. In the kitchen. Help yourself."

The two women poured mugs of coffee and walked outside into Faye's immense backyard. It was densely planted with fruits and flowers and vegetables and trees old enough to pre-date Columbus, all of which muffled the sound of suburban traffic. They seated themselves under a pergola strung with miniature Chinese lanterns. The only other light was emitted by fireflies blinking on and off in their meandering flight over the lawn.

Maddie leaned back in her chair and let out a tired sigh. "What a day!"

"A particularly rough one, I take it?"

The operations director laughed humorlessly. "Lately, they've all been rough. This new relic hunt just added another layer of enrichment to my job."

They sat silently for a few moments. Their eyes adjusting to the semi-darkness.

"You haven't been around headquarters much lately." There was a hint of reproach in Maddie's voice.

"I don't like to... what's the word you young people use nowadays? Micromanage. That's it. I don't like to micromanage." She paused. "Besides, I have great faith in all my associates."

"Well, I suppose we're all experienced enough to know what we're doing," Maddie grudgingly agreed.

"Ah, but that isn't faith. To rely on you because of your demonstrated competence is simply a reasonable conclusion based on observable facts."

"You make it sound all clinical and scientific." The operations director smiled through half-closed lids.

Faye stared off into the distant darkness. "I don't much care for science myself. Trusting it has a tendency to limit one's possibilities."

Her companion made no comment.

"You had something you wanted to report to me, dear?" Faye prompted gently.

Maddie's eyes were now fully closed. It appeared as if she'd dozed off and not heard the question until she spoke. "I don't know what it is about your garden. Especially on summer nights. But it makes me feel like I'm falling backward into a dream pool where I can drift outside of time."

Faye chuckled. "Why Maddie, that bordered on the poetic."

The operations director yawned and stretched. "Yeah, I know. It doesn't sound like me at all, right? That's what I mean. This place makes me a little dazed in the head."

Faye took a sip of coffee. "On the contrary. I think the effect my garden has on people, you included, is to make them sane in the head."

"Maybe," Maddie conceded, sitting up straight. "A little extra sanity would be good right now. I've had a few updates about what's going on in the field. Leroy and that Nephilim they call Daniel have landed in Crete."

"We can only hope they aren't able to make heads or tails of the riddle too quickly."

"At least they're missing the final line." Maddie paused to light a cigarette. The tip burned red in the darkness. "That ought to buy us some time."

"Yes, it should," Faye agreed, but her tone indicated worry. "If only we knew why they want the Bones of the Mother so badly."

"That's a riddle in itself," agreed Maddie. "I'd love to get some intel from inside their organization, but they're awfully twitchy about who joins the ranks."

"An opportunity may present itself in due course," Faye observed. "At least for now, we can monitor Mr. Hunt. As long as he stays tethered to this Daniel person, we have some idea of what's going on."

"That's true," Maddie conceded. "We might not have much info, but we're getting the basics. As for our side, we're making a little bit of progress. I got some good news from Griffin today."

"Yes?"

"He said Ozgur was able to put them onto a lead about some calendar stones on Mount Ida."

"Calendar stones," Faye echoed. "Of course, I should have thought of that myself. Poor Griffin. He was in such a state before he left. I thought he was going to give himself an ulcer over that riddle."

"He is wound kind of tight," Maddie agreed. "I don't think I've ever seen that boy relax."

A breeze stirred lightly in the treetops releasing the scent of angel's trumpet into the air.

"Speaking of boys," said Faye, "has Erik been behaving himself? I know he had some reservations about working with Griffin and Cassie."

"If you'd asked me that question before they left for Crete, I wouldn't have given it a week. But from what Griffin tells me, it sounds like Erik's gotten used to the idea of cooperating with them. Then again, Erik's idea of cooperation is when he holds himself back from punching you in the face if you get in his way."

Faye laughed softly. "Are you still annoyed with him about that Venice retrieval?"

"Annoyed doesn't begin to cover it! An entire hotel room trashed." Maddie snorted in disbelief. "Who does that?"

"Someone who is determined to finish the task you sent him to do," Faye observed quietly. "No matter what."

"Yeah, maybe." The operations director crossed her arms and blew a puff of smoke. "But I'm not letting him off the hook with a smile and a 'Sorry, chief.' Not this time."

"Oh Maddie, you didn't," Faye protested. "Substandard accommodations again?"

"That boy's gotta learn that he's not ten feet tall and bullet-proof. Being reckless has consequences."

Rather than argue the point, Faye changed the subject. "And what about our new pythia? How is she faring?"

"It sounds like she wowed the Anatolian trove team with another great performance."

"I'm glad of that." Faye smiled and took another sip of coffee. "Each time she succeeds in bringing hidden information to light, her confidence in her gift will grow."

"She's doing great by all accounts." Maddie's voice struck a false note.

"And this disturbs you?" Faye peered through the darkness at her companion.

"No, it's not that. I'm really glad she's working out but..." She hesitated.

"But?"

Maddie ground out her cigarette in the grass. "Dammit! Why isn't anybody talking about the elephant in the room?"

Faye looked cautiously around her garden. "Well, for one thing, we're outdoors."

Maddie immediately lit another cigarette. "Don't play coy, Faye. Why isn't anybody talking about Sybil? I mean the kid lost her sister barely two months ago. Didn't just lose her. Saw her murdered, in fact. Yet she's perky and happy to be bouncing off on this relic hunt. That doesn't seem normal to me."

Faye studied the tips of her shoes for a moment. "You're right. It isn't normal, but nothing about Cassie's relationship with Sybil was normal."

"What do you mean?" Maddie turned in her chair to stare at the memory guardian.

Faye set down her cup and folded her hands in her lap. "When Cassie first came to me, it was obvious she was shattered by her sister's death, but I got the impression that it wasn't personal."

"How in the hell could it not be?" The operations director leaned forward. "Sybil was her last living relative."

Faye nodded. "Yes, Sybil represented family to her and her family was gone. For that, she grieved. But on a personal level, Sybil and Cassie were strangers to one another. Cassie never knew her sister at all." The old woman paused, lost in thought for a few moments. "If I'd realized it in time, I might have tried to intervene. I've always believed that the Arkana has no right to pry into people's personal lives. In this instance, however, it was a mistake. I should have done something."

Maddie remained uncharacteristically silent. An owl hooted softly in one of the ancient oak trees at the back of the garden.

"After their parents' death, Sybil became obsessed with protecting her sister—making sure neither one of them became easy targets for the Nephilim or any other artifact thieves. They moved constantly. Cassie never had time to catch her breath much less make a single friend while Sybil was bustling her around the country. When I first met her, the poor child was defensive and belligerent, betraying just how insecure she felt. Unfortunately, much of the blame for that distress belongs to Sybil. Our late pythia was so focused on her sister's physical safety that she forgot all about her emotional well-being. Cassie never felt safe anywhere or with anyone."

The operations director watched a lightening bug crawl onto one of the Chinese lanterns, adding a strobe effect. "For somebody who spends so little time at headquarters, it amazes me how much you seem to know about all of this," she remarked.

Faye gave a little shrug. "I don't need to spend much time at headquarters. The world has a habit of finding its way to my door as a matter of course."

"I'm not just talking about Cassie and Sybil. You seem to know exactly what's going on at the Arkana all the time. I bet if I asked you to tell me the last artifact reported from Japan, you could."

"It was the Jomon trove, I believe. A clay figurine of a mother goddess unearthed last week." Faye retrieved her mug and took another sip of coffee.

"You see!" Maddie exclaimed. "How do you do that?"

The old woman smiled. "Like most people nowadays, I have both a cell phone and a computer, dear."

"That's not what I mean, and you know it," the operations director challenged. "It's almost like you pull the intel right out of thin air."

"Perhaps I do," Faye replied cryptically. "Perhaps I'm tuned in, as the saying goes."

Throwing up her hands in exasperation, Maddie went back into the house to fetch the coffee pot. She returned and refilled both their cups. When she resettled herself, she changed the subject. "You know, it's kind of ironic."

"What is, dear?" Faye had lost the line of Maddie's reasoning.

"About Sybil, I mean. She spent her whole life fixated on protecting Cassie. And in the end, she couldn't protect either one of them."

"It was more than ironic. It was tragic." Faye grew silent as she contemplated a new idea. "And yet it's also true that Sybil's obsession, and the estrangement it created, may have helped soften the blow for Cassie when the end came."

"Huh?"

The old woman elaborated. "One can't miss what one has never had."

"You mean like a real relationship with a real sister?" the operations director asked archly.

"Quite so," the memory guardian agreed. "Once she passed through the initial shock of her sister's murder, Cassie adjusted rapidly. I suspect learning about us and her special place in our organization may have helped ease the transition for her."

"Sure. As long as she doesn't think about the fact that we're the reason her sister died in the first place. We might even be the reason why she never had a good relationship with Sybil when she was alive. Not to mention the fact that we're the reason her parents are dead too. When you put all those things together, it seems like she ought to hate us."

Faye shook her head. "But she doesn't. I believe she thinks of us in a positive way. We're the people who gave her a sense of belonging. A purpose in life. Perhaps it wouldn't be too high-flown to say we revealed her destiny to her."

Maddie scowled, unconvinced. "I wonder if Sybil would thank you for that. When she was alive, she moved heaven and earth to keep Cassie away from the Arkana."

Faye tipped her head to one side, considering the idea. "I wasn't the one who made Cassie a pythia. As for Sybil. She was the one who sent Cassie to us."

Maddie leaned back in her chair and gazed at the stars. "It is kind of strange. That chain of events."

"One might almost say it was Fate." The corners of Faye's mouth twitched slightly. "If one believed in such things."

Another owl hooted from the top of the pergola. Its mate in the oak tree called back.

"You must have spent a lot of time with Cassie to know so much about her."

"We met three times."

"All of three times?" Maddie turned her head to stare at Faye appraisingly. "You see. That proves my point. It's unnatural how much you know."

"Just call me a keen judge of character." Faye serenely finished the rest of her coffee. "One can't have lived as many years as I have without honing one's observational skills."

"Oh, I don't know about that," Maddie disagreed. "There are millions of people in nursing homes who couldn't tell you what they ate for breakfast. I think you're fairly unique."

"Then call it my special gift if you will. A certain economy of perception that frees up my time to pursue other interests."

"Like baking?" Maddie teased. "You sure do seem to enjoy spending time in the kitchen."

"Which reminds me. I just finished frosting a chocolate cake. Would you like to take some home with you?"

Chapter 16—Religious Inexperience

DANIEL PAUSED TO CATCH his breath. The altitude was making him light-headed. They had been climbing up a steep dirt path well above the tree line of Mount Ida. The mountain was now known as Psiloritis, the tallest peak on the island of Crete. In the distance ahead of him, the trail ended at a gaping hole in a solid wall of rock.

His companion Nikos panted as he caught up with him. "We are here, Brother Scion. This is the cave they call *Ideon Andron*—the childhood home of the heathen god Zeus."

The son of the diviner studied the landscape for a moment. He was surprised at the immense size of the cave entrance. It looked like a train tunnel. To complete the impression, iron tracks ran directly into the cave. Daniel wasn't sure of their purpose. The gauge was too narrow for a regular train. That was a minor mystery and not one he was here to solve. His purpose this day was to find the first artifact—one of the Bones of the Mother.

As he and his companion trudged the remaining distance to the cave entrance, Daniel felt the gloom of his predicament settle over him. What was he doing here? Returning to this dusty, rock-strewn country brought back some very unpleasant memories. During his last visit to Crete, he had stood by and allowed three people to die. And for what? To carry out his father's will. Since that time, he had disabused himself of the notion that God's will and his father's were one and the same.

So many things had changed in his world over the course of the past two months. He had seen more of the Fallen Lands than many of his brethren would experience in a lifetime. Though he could never tell his father this, the outside world didn't seem to be an unpleasant sort of place at all. Not the Sodom and Gomorrah he had expected. Certainly, the women adorned themselves more. They painted their faces and wore bright clothing. Even the men wore jewelry. Golden watches and rings and necklaces. Aside from vanity, the Fallen didn't display any obviously vicious or immoral behavior. They seemed, for the most part, friendly. Far less tense and worried than his own Nephilim brethren. Perhaps being damned carried certain advantages, he thought bitterly. There was no need to try. One who had no hope of entering the blessed kingdom could do as one pleased. For a single frightening second, he wished he was one of them. Then he smothered the thought. That idea was surely the devil's doing.

"Look here, Brother Scion."

Daniel snapped himself out of his reverie to see where Nikos was pointing. To the left of the cave entrance was an immense stone outcropping that had been shaped by human hands. It looked like stairs for giants. "What is this?" he asked.

"It was once an altar where offerings were made to the pagan god Zeus. See up there, on the topmost step."

Daniel looked upward to what appeared to be a rectangular stone slab. It was large enough to be a stage much less an altar. He turned his attention back to the entrance of the cave. "You understand what we are searching for?"

"Yes, of course." Nikos bobbed his head vehemently. "The same symbols you came to find before. I still have the photographs." He waved the snapshots in front of Daniel's face. "We are to look at the walls and ceiling of the cavern for these signs."

Daniel was about to advance, but Nikos laid a restraining hand on his arm.

"Please. You must take this." The young convert handed him a flashlight. "It will be very dark at the back of the cavern."

The scion nodded and took the flashlight. He glanced behind them down the trail. There were no other tourists about. Nor did he see any sign of the archaeologists who were reputed to be digging here. That was good. Daniel didn't want any curious eyes watching them. He was glad Leroy Hunt had decided to wait for them at the taverna at the bottom of the hill. He always tended to attract attention wherever he went because of his cowboy attire.

Since Nikos was a Cretan by birth, he seemed to feel it his duty to act as tour guide. "It was in this cave that the god Zeus spent his childhood. His mother the goddess Rhea gave birth to him in another cave on the island but moved him here to hide him better from his father Cronos who would have eaten him."

"Yes, I am aware of the heathen myth," Daniel commented. "I also know that the winged demons called Kouretes protected the infant. Whenever he cried, they would beat their shields and make enough noise to muffle the sound of his wailing. That way his father wouldn't know he was still alive." He had spent weeks researching the strange deities of Greece. The notion of a father devouring his own son might once have felt alien to him. It didn't now.

"There is something I have never understood about this myth," Nikos said. "If Zeus is called the father of the gods and all are descended from him, then how can he have a mother?"

Daniel raised his eyebrows. "I'm not sure."

"And also, the pagans say that he was born in a cave and each year he dies in a cave. If he is an immortal god, how can he die?"

The scion shook his head. "There is a great deal about the heathen religions that makes no sense. The ancient peoples had the minds of children. They did not use reason as we do."

Seemingly satisfied with that explanation, Nikos switched on his flashlight and moved forward.

The two men left the sunny afternoon behind and descended down a steep flight of stairs into the recesses of the Ideon Andron.

Daniel had learned much about the cave and its structure on the internet and in books. The main chamber of the cavern was approximately 150 feet wide with two horizontal chambers leading to an inner sanctum. He knew all the facts about the place, but nothing in his research had prepared him for the actual experience of entering it. He became aware of the dampness. Water dripping from the ceiling and trickling down the walls. The wooden viewing platform was slippery. Green moss grew from the stones high above his head.

From where he stood at the bottom of the central chamber, he looked up toward the cave mouth illuminated by a bright blue sky. As he stepped back a few paces, he felt a line of shadow cross his face. The darkness seemed to swallow him.

The side chambers had been blocked off because of the archaeological excavation. Since nobody was around, Daniel decided there was nothing to prevent them from investigating the inner recesses of the cave. The two men agreed to split up. Nikos would search one of the side chambers while Daniel searched the other. As the scion slipped past the gate and moved down the gallery, he could no longer hear Nikos' footsteps echoing off in the other direction. He became acutely aware of how still this underworld was.

Following the twists and turns in the tunnel caused him to lose his orientation. It grew increasingly dark. No brightness from the outside world reflected on the walls in here. Only the meager beam of his flashlight. The rock walls on either side were so narrow in places they seemed to fold in on him.

He trained his light toward the ceiling. Wavy curtains of stalactites pressed down from above, their bottom-most tips dripping with moisture. Looking up at them made him feel dizzy. He studied the walls for any evidence of the symbols from the key. The bare rock swirled and twisted into grotesque shapes. Daniel's mind began to play tricks. He saw faces in the stone. Lost souls feeling the torments of hell. Their mouths gaping in endless screams of terror.

He continued moving down the gallery searching the walls and ceiling as he went, but all he found were unnerving images from hell. By now, he knew he was far beyond the reach of the world above. With no warning, his flashlight faltered and went out completely. He shook it to reseat the battery but accidentally dropped it. He could hear it rolling down the slope in the tunnel floor.

He fought the urge to scream as a surge of panic shot through him. He felt the darkness like a living thing. It was pressing into his eyes and ears and nose. He lost all sense of spacial orientation. Everything seemed to be tilted at an angle. Which way was up? Which was down? He couldn't feel the dimensions of his own body. He tried guiding his fingers to reach for a wall, but his fingers weren't where he expected them to be. Nor was the wall. He flailed around in an absolute void.

He didn't like this underworld. He couldn't understand why anyone would choose such a place to worship a god. He was used to divinities who lived in the sky. Worship was conducted from a pulpit by a minister who told him what laws God expected him to obey.

There was no law here. There was no reason here. That had been left behind in a world of light and order and the works of man. Here there was only feeling. What kind of god might one meet here? Nothing in Daniel's religion had prepared him for an encounter with the deity of this place. He was sure it wasn't Zeus. Something older than time itself lived in the silence here, and it marked his presence. He remembered a word he had discovered while researching the heathen religions. Chthonic. Primordial deities that presided over birth and death. Womb and tomb seemed to fuse together in this place. The combination unsettled him. Weren't they supposed to be distinct? He felt his mind, his very identity, collapsing into the darkness.

He dropped to all fours. At least he could feel the ground. He knew which way was down. Groping around, he finally grasped the cold metal tube of the flashlight. He tapped it sharply against the stone and tried switching it on again. A feeble beam of light emerged.

Daniel scrambled to his feet and ran out of the gallery, afraid that the battery would fail for good if he lingered to complete his search. He shouted for Nikos and told him to come outside when he was done. Racing up the stairs toward the sky, he felt his legs trembling under him. He leaned heavily against a boulder at the cave entrance, commanding himself to calm down. For several minutes he did nothing but concentrate on breathing in and out. Slowly, by degrees, he felt the ordinary nature of the world returning. Even so, he couldn't shake the sensation that something—a shadow of something—had glided across his soul. Was it evil? The devil? He didn't think so. It hadn't felt either good or bad. It was simply a presence. A something alive inside the darkness.

He felt the need to climb high to shake it off. He turned to look up at the altar stone several feet above where he stood. He scaled the boulders until he reached the top of the stone table. From here he could see the Nida plateau below where the earth was blanketed in summer green. Small white dots speckled the landscape - sheep grazing peacefully. He took comfort in those ordinary sights. His shallow breathing finally relaxed. He sank down heavily on the altar, his feet dangling over the edge.

From this vantage point, his began to reconsider his strategy for finding the relic. He realized it had been a mistake to search the cavern on the mountain and not simply because it unnerved him. He thought of the words of the riddle. "When the soul of the lady rises with the sun." Surely, this referred to something in the sky and not in the ground. The eastern sky to be exact. This altar table where he sat faced east. From here he might see something dawning in the eastern sky. But what? The three clues were all a muddle that made no sense.

Daniel rubbed his forehead wearily as a disturbing thought struck him. How could he be sure he had the right translation of the riddle at all? He hadn't actually looked at the symbols himself. He had relied on the interpretation of the strangers that Hunt had killed. What if they had been wrong? What if they had translated the glyphs incorrectly?

He knew what he had to do and the thought of it upset him even more than the idea of encountering that thing in the darkness again. He would have to go back to Karfi. The place where three bodies were buried under an avalanche of rock at the bottom of an underground tomb. He would have to look at the carvings on the stone stele and decipher what was written there for himself.

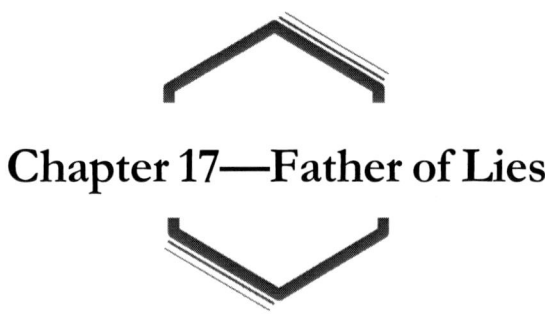

Chapter 17—Father of Lies

ABRAHAM STRODE PURPOSEFULLY through the door of the girl's dormitory. He glanced down the long row of vacant cots, the blankets all folded with the precision of a military barracks. On a bed at the opposite end of the room sat a lone figure. Her back was turned to him, and her head was bent.

She didn't look around to see who was coming even when his footfalls clicked loudly across the polished wooden floor.

"Hannah!" he barked.

She jumped up and spun around. "Oh, my goodness! Father Diviner." An object flew out of her hand and clattered to the floor.

Abraham bent down to pick it up. It was some sort of doll. About four inches long and carved out of a solid piece of wood. The figure of a woman in a long straight gown. Her arms were pressed stiffly against her body. An attempt had been made to give the carving some life with a layer of paint. The hair was yellow, and the lips pink against a cream face. The eyes and the dress were both painted blue though the color had been chipped and rubbed away in many places. The face itself was expressionless and discomfiting. Like a sphinx. The diviner found the entire effect grotesque. He turned it over in his hands. "What is this thing?"

"Oh, it's nothing," the girl said hurriedly, snatching it out of his palm. "I...uh...I've had it for as long as I can remember." She slipped it back into her apron pocket with shaky fingers.

He attempted a light tone. "Soon you'll have babies of your own and no need to play with dolls."

"Yes, sir," she agreed dutifully.

"Be seated," he instructed her.

She obeyed and flounced down on the bed.

He stood over her in silence for several seconds. He hadn't spent much time noticing her before. Too many other people around and too many distractions. She wore her thick blond hair braided and coiled around her head in the prescribed manner of a married woman, but her skin was far from matronly. It glowed with the freshness of a rose petal. Her body was far from matronly too. The girl's shapeless grey shift somehow managed to reveal graceful feminine curves. Her eyes were green, a curious almond shape. Almost like a cat's. Abraham didn't much care for cats. They were sinuous and slippery and had minds of their own. Willful, unruly creatures. Small wonder they were so often associated with Lucifer, that most insubordinate of God's angels. Still, the shape of her eyes held an exotic appeal. They were wide open in alarm at the moment.

"Calm yourself, child." He sat down on the bed next to her. "I had a few questions for you, but you weren't in your quarters. What are you doing here?"

She eyed him anxiously. "This is where I slept before I was married, Father. With all the other girls."

He gave a thin smile in an attempt to put her at ease. "But surely you must prefer to have a nice room all to yourself and your husband?"

She didn't meet his gaze. "It felt lonely there, so I thought I would sit here for a while."

"Of course," he patted her hand reassuringly. She recoiled from his touch and clasped her hands together in her lap.

Ignoring the gesture, he observed, "It's understandable. You miss your husband. I know he had to depart on his journey very soon after you were joined in marriage."

"That's not it," she said tremulously, her eyes misting with tears. "I don't think he likes me very much."

Abraham was taken aback by the comment. He drew himself up. "What do you mean he doesn't like you?"

"After we were married..." She hesitated. "He didn't stay with me on our wedding night."

The old man waited for her to elaborate but she offered nothing further. The girl sat silently on the edge of the bed, swinging her feet to and fro since her legs were too short to reach the floor.

"Can I please go now, Father?"

"Not quite yet, my child. I have a few more questions to put to you." Abraham was at a loss as to how to interpret this story. He was wary of accepting her words at face value. Women were liars by nature. What else could one expect from the daughters of Eve? Daniel's other wives had certainly lied about their relations with his son. They had all failed to produce numerous offspring, and now they wanted to lay their own inadequacies at their husband's doorstep. Could they have persuaded Hannah to join their conspiracy by fabricating this outrageous tale? The diviner scrutinized her face closely but couldn't detect any evidence of guilt in her expression. Just a pretty confusion. He tried another approach. "The day a girl becomes a woman is a very big day in her life, don't you agree? A very busy day."

She nodded uncertainly.

"You must have been very tired by the time evening came."

"I was sleepy," she admitted simply.

He placed a hand on her knee to still her swinging legs. She became dead calm. He squeezed her thigh lightly before letting go.

"When a person is tired, the mind can sometimes play tricks."

It was her turn to stare at him. "Play tricks?"

He smiled again. "Perhaps you don't remember everything that happened that evening. If you were very, very tired..." he trailed off.

She knit her brows in concentration. "I think I remember what happened and what didn't."

He pressed the point. "I'm sure everything happened just as it ought to have done."

The girl shook her head vehemently. "No, Father, it didn't."

He rose and stood over her. "Are you suggesting that I am in error?"

She gazed up at him in shock. Her mouth gaped open, but she said nothing.

"Answer me!" he commanded.

"No, Father. You're never supposed to be wrong."

"That is correct!" he asserted. "The diviner is given the gift of discernment in all things. You will believe me when I tell you that you are mistaken. Satan is deceiving you and has caused you to forget the events of that night."

Rather than hastily agreeing as he expected her to do, she tilted her head to one side and gazed up at him curiously. "He has? Why would he do that?"

The question caught him off-guard. Abraham paused for several seconds before framing a reply. "Because...because... he wishes to destroy our community from within, that's why! By sowing the seeds of error among the people."

"Oh." She didn't seem entirely convinced by his explanation.

Her obstinacy angered him. He raised his arm and pointed at the door. "Now go to your quarters and pray. Pray that God will cast out the demon who has tricked you. Go!"

She jumped off the bed and pelted from the room without another word. Abraham sat down heavily. This was worse than he had expected. It was enough of a trial that the Nephilim were assailed every day by the Fallen World outside their gates. But this? The greatest threat to his congregation now was the cancer springing up within its own ranks. Satan had found the perfect means to undermine Abraham's authority. Destroy the credibility of the scion. And the Evil One had chosen as his instrument this naïve child whose memory could be easily manipulated. The diviner was determined that the devil would not succeed. He would take steps to subdue the forces of hell. This delusion would spread no farther.

Chapter 18—Ida Ho!

CASSIE VENTURED OUT onto the wooden balcony of her hotel room. She took a deep breath of clear mountain air. It was shortly after sunrise, and everything felt fresh and very still. She was surprised by how piney this mountain was. She wasn't sure what she'd expected, but the waterfalls and jagged rock formations had surprised her. Except for the elevation and the fact that nobody was speaking English, she might have been staying at a lodge in Yosemite. They were, in fact, registered at a boutique hotel halfway up the slopes of Mount Ida or, as it was now called, Kaz Daglari.

The mountain ran all the way down to the Gulf of Edremit. That's where they'd started their journey the day before. Fred had arranged everything, acting as both tour guide and chauffeur. They'd left the concrete jumble of vacation homes lining the shore and headed upland. The foothills of the mountain were dotted with farms and miles of olive groves. They'd passed through a number of small villages that couldn't be described as anything but quaint or maybe even charming. Tiny hamlets of old stone houses, cobbled streets and village squares complete with bubbling fountains. The higher they ascended, the fewer the villages. Farms and olive groves gave way to pine forests, rushing rivers and cooler temperatures. Just when Cassie was sure they'd left civilization behind for good, they arrived at their destination. A four-star hotel complete with Olympic-sized swimming pool and gourmet cuisine. They gratefully piled out of the car to check in and get a good night's sleep. They would need it before tackling the summit of Gargarus which rose a mile above sea level.

Cassie took another deep breath of mountain air. A good night's sleep had certainly done wonders. She felt rested and ready to find the fabled calendar stones. She wondered what they would look like. Just then, her reverie was punctured by the blast of a car horn. Looking down into the hotel courtyard, she saw Fred waving at her. He was standing up in the driver seat of an open Jeep.

"Hello there, sleepyhead. Are you and your team just about ready?"

"Two minutes," she called. Sliding the patio door shut, she hastily left her room and sped down to the lobby.

Eric and Griffin were already waiting for her. Griffin appeared restless, alert. Cassie knew him well enough by now to recognize his inner relic hound. He was on the scent of something. It reminded her of a beagle just before a fox hunt. At least he wasn't barking.

"Down boy." She patted him on the arm.

"What?" he looked at her quizzically.

Eric gave a subdued chuckle. Apparently, he had noted the resemblance too. "Time to get this show on the road."

The trio emerged into the brightening day and climbed into the four-wheeler Fred had rented for their trek.

"A few roads crisscross the top of the mountain," their guide explained, "but the place I'm taking you is pretty far from any of them. Hang on. Some of these trails can get awfully bumpy."

Cassie gripped the roll bar above her head as the Jeep jolted to life. Once again, Eric was seated up forward with Fred while Griffin was doing the best he could to keep all his gangly limbs inside the back seat.

"Now this is more like it," Cassie said to the scrivener appreciatively, savoring the feeling of adventure.

"More like what?" he asked testily. "Trundling over boulders in a sardine tin?"

"You're really not a morning person, are you?" she teased.

He relented a bit and smiled back. "It is exciting, isn't it? By the end of today, we may be holding the first relic in our hands."

The pythia nodded in agreement. "That would be something."

The Jeep lurched and bounced over rocky trails, cut across fast-moving streams and wove its way through dense thickets of pine. The terrain was too uncertain to allow them to travel at high speed. Cassie settled in for a long ride.

"You know this mountain is one of the most famous landmarks in the classical world," Griffin began. "It's mentioned no less than forty times in the *Iliad*."

Anticipating a history lesson, Cassie cut him off. "Yeah, I know. The Trojan War and all that."

Griffin gaped at her in amazement. "You actually know something about Troy?"

Cassie glanced at his puzzled face and grimaced. "Close your mouth. You don't have to act so surprised. I occasionally know facts too. The *Iliad* was the last thing we covered in my ancient lit class before I left school. Let's see if I remember the story." She gave him a sidelong glance. "I just know you'll correct me if I'm wrong."

"Have at it," he prompted. "I'm listening."

"Well, it all started when the goddess of discord lobbed a golden apple into the middle of a wedding feast on Mount Olympus. It had an inscription that read, 'To the fairest.'"

She paused as a thought struck her. "The Greeks really had a thing about golden apples, didn't they? They have all these myths with golden apples in them. Didn't they ever hear of the fruit of the month? I mean, why not a nice kiwi once in a while for variety?"

Griffin sighed. "I know you're being deliberately outrageous just to annoy me."

"And I'm succeeding." Cassie grinned. "Back to the wedding feast. Once the apple started rolling around the floor, three of the goddesses pounced on it like cats on a ball of string. They all started arguing about who was the prettiest. Since nobody could decide, they asked Zeus's opinion. For somebody who claimed to be the king of the gods, Zeus was something of a weenie. He didn't want to get into the middle of that discussion any more than your boyfriend wants to answer the question, 'Does this dress make me look fat?'"

"I'm not gay!" Griffin protested indignantly.

"Relax. I didn't mean your boyfriend." She emphasized the word "your."

"I was just being generic."

"Perhaps you could confine yourself to gender-specific generalities," the scrivener sniffed.

"Fine." The pythia shrugged. "Anyway, Zeus didn't want to answer the question, so he sent the goddesses off to some hapless redneck tending sheep on this very mountainside who was appointed to judge the beauty contest." Cassie frowned in concentration. "I should remember the shepherd's name because it was a city. Was it London?" She paused, her eyes sparkling with mischief. "Maybe it was Detroit."

"Detroit?" Griffin echoed in disbelief. "It was Paris! The hapless redneck, as you describe him, was a youth named Paris. And the three female deities in question are the very famous Aphrodite—goddess of love, Hera—Zeus's wife and patron of women, and Athena—goddess of wisdom."

"Right. As I was saying, the three goddesses try bribing Paris to win the Miss Aegean beauty pageant, but he likes Aphrodite's offer best. She says if he gives her the title, she'll make the most beautiful woman in the world fall in love with him." Cassie turned to the scrivener for confirmation. "How am I doing so far?"

"Quite well if one overlooks the appalling cheekiness of your narrative style. Do continue."

She nodded. "After that, Aphrodite gets the apple and Paris sails off to Greece to collect his bride bribe." She chuckled at her own witticism. "Bride bribe. Get it?"

Her companion rolled his eyes.

"Anyhow, the prize is a queen named Helen. Of course, Aphrodite forgot to mention that Helen is already married to the King of Sparta. This little detail doesn't seem to bother anybody very much except for Helen's husband. When he finds out his wife has run off to Troy with a guy who likes spending quality time with sheep, he rallies all his cronies. They jump on their ships and sail off in hot pursuit. After a ten-year slug fest, lots of manly battles, much chest-thumping, and many big speeches, Greece wins. Troy gets burnt to the ground, and Helen gets bundled back home." Cassie grinned impishly. "What do you think? Did I get it right?"

"I'm speechless."

Erik twisted around in his seat and called over the loud growl of the engine, "What are you two gabbing about back there?"

"The Trojan War," Griffin answered. "Cassie has just managed to reduce the epic to the length of a sardonic soundbyte. If only Homer had been alive to hear her, it would certainly have killed the old sod."

"How upset can you get about my irreverent take on a long-winded overlord poem anyway?" Cassie objected. "I wasn't wrong about any of the facts, was I?"

"In essence, no," the scrivener conceded. "The facts are as you've stated them."

Cassie tilted her head, considering. "But maybe fact isn't the right word. Are they facts? I mean, did any of it really happen?" She peered around at her companions, waiting for an answer.

Fred remained silent, concentrating fiercely on navigating the Jeep up a steep slope.

Erik had hooked his arm around the headrest and was following the exchange in the back seat. "Some of it really happened," he said.

Cassie stared at him. "You mean gods sitting on top of Mount Ida waving pennants and rooting for their favorite team? Go Trojans!"

The security coordinator laughed. "No, not that part. But there really was a Troy. It's near the coast just a little northwest of here."

"And the archaeological evidence suggests the city was burned around 1200 BCE," added Griffin. "That timeframe is consistent with Homer's epic."

"It's odd though that the Greeks would pick a fight in this place," Cassie remarked. "Turkey used to be goddess-worship central."

"That's why the *Iliad* is so important a piece of overlord propaganda," offered Griffin. "The Trojan War wasn't about recapturing a stray woman. It was about capturing all women in legally sanctioned matrimonial alliances. The overlord Greeks fighting the matristic Trojans."

"Too bad it ended the way it did," Cassie commented gloomily.

"Cheer up." Griffin tried to comfort her. "Despite the Greek victory, this section of the Aegean remained a goddess stronghold for millennia afterward. In fact, there's an amusing story in the *Iliad* wherein Hera seduces her husband Zeus to distract him from the battle long enough to tip the scales in favor of Hera's team. Mount Ida was the home of the goddess, so Hera's power here was very strong. Even the all-powerful father of the gods couldn't win in this place."

"Still, she was rooting for the Greeks and their patriarchal new world order," Cassie objected. "What kind of crazy sense does that make?"

"Not sense," Erik replied. "Propaganda. It's always more effective when you can make it look like your former enemy has been convinced of the error of her ways and defects to your side. Hera used to be an all-powerful Mother Goddess. Another version of Cybele until she got demoted by the Hellenic tribes and had to marry the new guy in town. And she sure didn't want to marry him."

"So how did Zeus get her to agree?" Cassie asked.

"According to the overlord myth," Erik explained, "when he wasn't getting anywhere courting her, he disguised himself as a rain-soaked cuckoo. After she picked up the poor little birdie to take care of it, Zeus changed back into his old self and took care of business. Once he'd raped her, Hera was shamed into marrying him."

"What a prince," Cassie commented acidly.

"Zeus had quite a reputation as a seducer and/or rapist," Griffin said. "The conventional explanation is that as classical mythology evolved, the new deity was symbolically appropriating the original goddesses of the conquered peoples and incorporating them into the overlord pantheon." He paused. "But the more I think about it, the more inclined I am to believe that Zeus's antics mirrored what was actually taking place during the Kurgan invasions. Since the intruders tended to be roving bands of armed males on horseback, the quickest way to secure a local bride was through abduction and rape. In fact, the practice of bride abduction still occurs in the steppe nations today. Of course, nowadays the preferred getaway vehicle is an automobile rather than a horse."

"Please tell me you're joking about that." Cassie was incredulous.

Griffin's voice was grim. "I wish I were. Quaint local custom, don't you think? Not coincidentally, many of the countries that still practice this atrocity are located in the region where the horse was first domesticated and where Kurgan culture originated. The Eurasian steppes. There does appear to be a correlation between bride abduction and a fast horse."

Cassie was about to badger him with several more questions when the Jeep came to an abrupt halt.

"We made it," Fred announced. "And in one piece which, all things considered, is a bonus."

His passengers climbed out of the vehicle and dusted themselves off. Cassie shook her hair to dislodge particles of grit. The sun had risen high enough to make her notice the mid-day heat.

"Does it ever rain here?" she asked their guide.

Fred shook his head. "Not much at this time of year. Hot and dry is the weather forecast for the next couple of months." He pointed off in the direction of a narrow dirt trail that cut through the forest. "We have to walk the rest of the way to the calendar stones."

The group followed him wordlessly as the path twisted ever upward through the dim pines. After about a ten-minute hike they passed the tree line. The pines gave way to windswept earth covered with a thin layer of scrubby grass and the occasional boulder. They continued to walk to the top of a rise where they finally paused to catch their breath.

Cassie looked off into the distance at the panorama spread out before her. She could see a series of mountain peaks running off in a straight line to the east. "Wow!" she exclaimed. "What a view."

"It's pretty impressive," Fred agreed.

"Oh, I say!" Griffin exclaimed. His attention was focused on a section of hillside below the rise where they were standing. The ground leveled out into a small plateau. On this table of land, a series of stones had been arranged into a ring. The boulders were all approximately eight feet high and had been shaped into rectangles of a uniform thickness. Massive crosspieces rested across the tops of several of them. Some of the stones contained relief carvings of animals or birds and one held the figure of a human female. They had once been spaced evenly though time had marred the original symmetry. Some of the crosspieces had cracked and fallen to the ground. A few of the base stones leaned at odd angles, and several had toppled or been pushed over. Still, the ring shape was unmistakable.

"This is extraordinary!" The scrivener scurried down the hill until he stood in the middle of the henge which was strewn with boulders, broken rock, and weeds. To all appearances, the place had been abandoned for millennia.

The other three caught up with him and began to examine the formations, some of which ran almost to the edge of the plateau.

"Careful there," Fred cautioned as Cassie moved dangerously close to the edge.

She had been so intent on examining a megalith that she'd paid no attention to her precarious position. She cast a quick glance over her shoulder. "Yikes!" she exclaimed as a loose rock under her heel rolled down the decline and tumbled over the side.

Fred steadied her arm. "It's a sheer drop of about a hundred feet off the edge."

The other two men came to examine the cliff.

Cassie peered over the rim which dropped off a mere five feet from the base of one of the megaliths. "There's a little ledge down there," she noted.

The others looked to where she was pointing.

"Must be a great view for anybody who could get down there to sit on it," Erik observed.

"Actually, there is a way down there," Fred offered. "This cliff is honey-combed with hermit cells. You just can't see them from up here."

"Somebody held hermits prisoner here?" Cassie asked in disbelief.

"Not that kind of cell," Griffin objected. "Early in the history of the Christian church, certain reclusive souls abandoned the world for a life of spiritual contemplation. Many of them took to the mountains and hollowed out caves where they could live and pray in peace."

"But how could they get down there?" Cassie persisted. "Rope ladders?"

"There are tunnels through the mountainside," Fred explained. "Most of them were natural cave formations that were excavated and extended over time. You have to know where to look, but I've explored a few. There are trails below the tree line that will lead you directly through the mountain and out to the hermit cells in this cliff. You just can't get to them from up here."

"Fascinating," Griffin said. He took one more look over the edge of the cliff before retreating to observe a megalith several feet away.

The others followed him back.

"How long do you suppose these stones have been standing here?" Cassie asked.

Griffin was scrutinizing one of the bird carvings—a vulture. "It's difficult to tell, but I would hazard a guess that this site was already ancient by the time Troy was sacked. There are other megalithic formations in Turkey and Armenia that date back to 9000 BCE."

Cassie glanced at him in surprise. "But that's a couple of thousand years before Catal Huyuk, and I thought that was supposed to be ancient."

The scrivener gave her a brief smile. "I'm afraid we're all going to have to revise our definition of the word 'ancient' during the course of this relic quest." He transferred his attention back to the carving. "The depiction of this specific bird is significant. The vulture is a prominent figure in the excarnation rituals depicted on the walls of Catal Huyuk. In all probability, the ancestors of those people built this ring."

"Just exactly what are we looking for here?" asked Erik.

All three paused in their examination and turned toward Griffin.

The scrivener's exhilaration evaporated. He seemed to hesitate. "I'm not sure exactly. Megalithic formations have been found all over the world. They may have measured a variety of astronomical phenomena. It all depended on which planet or which star was important to a particular culture. Certainly, most of them would have taken account of obvious phenomena like the summer and winter solstice. Lunation cycles. Possibly even eclipses."

"But how does all of that work?" Cassie felt lost.

"The principle is quite simple really," Griffin replied. "Let's take something like the winter solstice. The ancients watched the skies on a daily basis in a way that most modern people would find incomprehensible. It was, in effect, their favorite television program. Over time, they would have observed the sun rising at a different point along the horizon as the seasons changed. In the case of the winter sun, they would have noticed it rising at a point farther and farther south as the days grew shorter. There would come a day when the sun had reached its southernmost point. The ancients would position a stone to mark that location. Every year thereafter, when they observed the sun rising above that particular stone, they would know that winter was over and the days were about to grow longer again."

"Cool. Which stone is it?" Cassie asked eagerly, looking around the circle.

"I have no idea." Griffin sounded nonplussed. "I might be able to calculate it based on the sun's current position on the horizon during sunrise, but there's no way to tell just by looking around the circle."

"Besides, we're not looking for the winter solstice," Erik corrected, kicking a small rock out of his way. He strode over to where the other two stood in the middle of the ring. "We're trying to figure out where the sun is when the soul of the lady rises."

"Yes, a much more obscure reference to be sure," the scrivener agreed.

"Look, guys. Maybe Griffin's original idea wasn't so far-fetched," Cassie suggested. "It's got to be one of these rocks, so why don't I just go around the circle and touch them and see if I can get any impressions."

The two men exchanged a skeptical glance. Fred came to stand behind Erik, listening to the conversation but offering no comment.

After a long pause, Erik asked Griffin, "You got any better ideas?"

"Sadly, not at the moment."

The security coordinator turned to Cassie. "Go for it, toots."

"OK, but one of you guys better follow me around in case I get a hit, and it knocks me off my feet. Remember what happened in Crete."

Erik nodded. "I've got your back." He obligingly trailed Cassie as she chose her first target.

"Let's start with this one." She selected a pillar that directly faced the mountain peaks in the distance. "Griffin, why don't you keep track of where I started."

Cassie braced herself, closed her eyes and laid her palms flat against the first megalith. Nothing happened. For the next half hour, she repeated the process with every standing stone in the circle and with the same disappointing result.

"No dice." She finally sat down wearily on a patch of dry grass. Her three companions joined her, looking equally depressed.

"What now?" Fred asked bleakly.

"I suppose we should go back to the hotel and regroup," Griffin suggested.

"The funny thing is that I know the Minoans were here." Cassie sighed. "I can feel it when I touch the surface of any one of those megaliths. It's almost like I'm wearing a blindfold and they're playing blind man's bluff with me. I just can't get a fix on their position."

"The fact that you were able to sense that much is comforting," observed Griffin. "At least we know we're looking in the right place."

"Yeah, but looking for what?" Erik lay down on the ground and locked his hands behind his head. "Thousands of years ago, some people came here to look up at the sky. There are a bazillion things they might have thought were important out there."

"Oh, come on. I'll bet it was two bazillion," Cassie joked weakly.

"Look, it's not over yet," Fred offered. "You guys traveled thousands of miles to end up in exactly the right spot. If you got this far, you're bound to figure it out."

"Yes, but not today," Griffin murmured wistfully.

"Nope, not today," Erik agreed.

Chapter 19—Through a Glass Darkly

IT WAS EARLY. STILL dark, in fact, and the compound was quiet. Abraham could hear no footsteps echoing down the corridors. No wailing babies. No whispering women. It was at least an hour before they would stir. Only the guards were awake. The old man's insomnia had caused him to join the vigil of those who kept a watchful eye on the sleeping flock. The wolves that inhabited the Fallen Lands were always prowling. Always hungry for souls. But the wolves were not the reason Abraham had tossed and turned for the past three nights. Nor why he had risen hollow-eyed and lethargic for the past three mornings.

He sighed and faced the bathroom mirror, intent on finishing his ablutions. Tilting his head, he shaved the side of his neck, but the final stroke nicked his skin. A few drops of blood spattered the sink. Abraham winced and jerked his hand involuntarily, causing the razor to clatter to the floor. Groaning at his own clumsiness, the old man stooped to retrieve it. As he bent down, his knees made a cracking sound in protest. He willed himself to stoop further despite an additional twinge of pain in his knee-cap. He was not about to give in to imaginary weaknesses. Especially not now. He would need all his strength for what lay ahead.

Abraham straightened back up, staunched the cut on his neck and appraised his haggard reflection in the glass. The cause of his sleeplessness was his last worrisome conversation with Hannah. She had opened his eyes to Satan's insidious plan to destroy the Blessed Nephilim from within. The sinking sensation in the pit of his stomach told him that Daniel's wives were only the beginning. Error always had a way of compounding itself so that what started with four might end with the corruption of all. If each of the women repeated the same story, rumors would spread that the scion was somehow deficient. This would inevitably lead to questions about the diviner's own lack of judgment. A crisis of faith might erupt that could shake the foundation of the brotherhood to its core. Although Abraham was more than prepared to fight Satan on the battlefield of the Fallen Lands, he never expected to battle that same unseen foe within his own sanctuary.

The diviner had no idea what course of action to take. He peered earnestly into the depths of the mirror. "Help me, Lord. Tell me what to do." He didn't know why, but he repeated the words over and over until they became a mindless chant. Five times, ten times, twenty times. He lost count but kept on chanting anyway. "Help me, Lord. Tell me what to do." The effect was hypnotic. On and on he went, growing hoarse from the effort until he heard a whisper bubble up from within his own consciousness. "You must save her soul."

Abraham stopped chanting. He stared dazedly at himself.

"You must save her soul."

He considered the instruction for a moment. The message must refer to Hannah. Daniel's other wives were older and too far steeped in their own corruption to be saved. But Hannah was young, hardly more than a girl. Malleable clay that could be molded to suit any purpose. There was still hope that she might be redeemed if she could be separated from the influence of her sister-wives.

Abraham straightened up and took stock of his appearance. Not so very old as all that, he thought. A few lines around the eyes but that was to be expected from a man of wisdom and experience. In his youth, he had been considered handsome. He turned sideways to regard himself in profile. Surely any woman of the congregation would count herself fortunate to be chosen by him. Any grown woman perhaps but would a girl think so too? The question made him drop his eyes briefly. He scowled and censored the thought. A patriarch of the Bible would have had no such qualms before taking a new wife.

He walked into the bedroom to dress. Carrying his tie back into the bathroom, he knotted it before the mirror. As he ran a comb through his thick silver mane, he noted with satisfaction that many men of his age worried about baldness. That condition would never trouble him.

"You must save her soul."

What better way to save her and set her feet on the right path than to marry her himself? It was true that she was currently wed to his son, but his son was often away from home doing God's work. Without Daniel to guide her behavior, she had already become an easy target for the devil. There was no telling what other trouble she might cause if left to her own devices. A beauty like hers could be dangerous—a sure occasion of sin. Better that such a temptation should be safely locked away in his keeping. He wasn't so very old as all that. His youngest wife was in her thirties. Not much more than Hannah's age.

Abraham warmed to the idea. The girl's future was bright indeed. To be elevated to the rank of diviner's wife at the age of fourteen. Rachel, his principal wife, had produced ten children. Given Hannah's youth, she could easily supplant Rachel by producing more and ascend to her title. The girl would surely be overwhelmed with gratitude once she understood the earthly benefits Abraham was about to bestow upon her.

The diviner switched off the bathroom light and crossed into the bedroom. He picked up his suit coat and dusted it meticulously with a lint brush. Inspecting the black fabric, he nodded with satisfaction and donned the jacket. It was settled. He would inform the girl this morning and make the announcement to the congregation in the afternoon.

Turning to leave the bedroom, he caught a final glimpse of himself in the cheval mirror and allowed himself to smile for the first time in days. This was the ideal solution. Abraham knew it was divinely inspired. Through his righteous influence, Hannah would become worthy in the eyes of the Lord. Satan would no longer attempt to cloud her thinking once she was the wife of the diviner and any further rumors about Daniel would be decisively quashed. Let her find fault with the outcome of her next wedding night if she dared.

He closed his eyes and whispered a final prayer. "Lord, I am ever yours to command. I shall wed this girl as you have directed that I might shape her into a consecrated bride worthy to enter your kingdom."

Abraham waited in silence for the reply which he knew would come from within.

"Well done, my good and faithful servant."

Chapter 20—Nomad's Land

THE DISPIRITED QUARTET of relic hunters climbed out of their Jeep and dragged themselves wearily into the hotel lobby. The search of the calendar stones had proven fruitless. They needed time to regroup and formulate a new strategy, but before they could cross to the elevator, they were intercepted. A compact middle-aged man launched himself out of an arm chair near the entrance and hurtled toward them.

He was dressed in a camp shirt, khaki pants, and hiking boots. Looking eagerly from one face to the next, the newcomer exclaimed, "I am so very glad you have arrived! I did not know how to reach you." He spoke with a heavy Slavic accent. Doffing his straw hat, he revealed a thinning patch of blond hair.

"Stefan?" Griffin asked in a puzzled tone.

"What are you doing here?" Erik mirrored his team mate's surprise.

Hurriedly dropping his duffle bag to the floor, the visitor energetically shook hands with the two men. "I have been trying to catch up with you for many days now. It has been very difficult. First, you are one place, then you are another. I am always, how you say, one step behind." He stopped abruptly and whirled to face Cassie. Clicking his heels, he gave a stiff bow from the waist. "You are Cassie Forsythe, no?" He peered intently into her face.

"No. I mean y... y... yes," the pythia stammered, bowled over by his energy.

"Allow me to introduce you," Griffin intervened. "This is Stefan Kasprzyk."

To Cassie's ears, the last name sounded as if it rhymed with wasp chick.

"He's the Kurgan trove keeper."

"Oh, how do you do," she held out her hand.

Stefan took it, bowed over it and clicked his heels again. "I am so very, very glad to meet you."

"And this is Fred," Erik added. "He works with Aydin Ozgur."

"Yes, of course, the Anatolian trove keeper," Stefan remarked, pumping Fred's hand. "I have met Pan Ozgur many times."

"Pan?" Cassie asked.

"I believe that's Polish for Mister," Griffin confided.

The introductions having been concluded, the five stood uncertainly in the middle of the lobby, eyeing one another.

"Perhaps we should go somewhere to talk," Griffin suggested.

"Yes, yes, of course," Stefan agreed readily. "I have much to discuss with you."

"How about over there." Erik gestured toward a deserted parlor adjoining the lobby.

The group followed him to the farthest corner where a couch, several chairs, and a coffee table were arranged before a large picture window. The seating afforded a panoramic view of the upper slopes of Ida.

Once they had settled themselves, Erik began. "Last I heard, you were in Kazakhstan."

"Yes, that is so," Stefan bobbed his head in agreement. "My team is still there. We are excavating a large burial mound. Here, I have brought some photos to show you." He opened his duffle bag and pulled out a thick album. Leafing through it, he selected a page in the middle and spread the book flat on the table in front of them. The first picture showed a grinning Stefan surrounded by a dozen other individuals standing in front of a sand hill in the middle of a treeless landscape.

"Kazakhstan, that's a plum assignment," Erik commented sarcastically. "Who did you tick off to get sent there?"

"I go where the kurgans are." Stefan shrugged philosophically. "Who knows? Maybe someday I find a burial mound on the Riviera."

"My friend, you are quite the optimist." Griffin chuckled wryly.

"Kurgans," Cassie piped up. "I remember Faye telling me about them. Overlord types, right? Liked to bury their leaders in big funeral mounds called kurgans?"

116

The scrivener looked at her in amazement. "Twice in one day, Cassie? First the Trojan War and now this. I may die of shock."

Erik tried to keep a straight face.

"That's right. Hell has officially frozen over," the pythia countered defensively. "I actually do remember what you people tell me."

Stefan looked from one to the next with a perplexed expression.

"Don't mind them," Fred explained. "They like to tease each other."

The trove keeper nodded politely and directed his next comment to Cassie. "The word *kurgan* is Russian. It means in English something like 'mound.' The name is used for all the tribes who buried their leaders in this way. The people who came before, the old Europeans, their funerals were different. They would burn the bodies or expose them for birds to pick the bones."

"Excarnation," Griffin added helpfully.

"*Da, tochno.*" Noticing Cassie's confusion, the trove keeper corrected himself. "I am sorry. I spend too many months in Kazakhstan where everybody is speaking Russian. Sometimes I forget. In Russian, I say *da, tochno*. In English, I say yes, precisely. Excarnation. That is the word."

"I think Stefan may hold the record among us for foreign language skills," Griffin commented. "How many do you speak?"

Stefan paused to tally up the number in his head. "I believe it is fifteen, but I am learning Hindi now."

"Why so many?" Cassie asked.

"Wherever I find a mound, it is better if I can talk to the people who live there in their own language. These Kurgan tribes." Stefan shook his head. "They move around too much. I find graves everywhere."

His listeners laughed.

The trove keeper flipped to another page in the album. "Look here. This is a better photo. It shows what is inside the kurgan."

Cassie leaned over the table to study the picture. A skeleton of a man with weapons arranged around his body. There were several other snapshots of grave goods. A gold lion brooch. A stone scepter carved into the shape of a horse's head. "Who were these people exactly?" she asked.

"They were tribes who inhabited the Eurasian steppes," Griffin said. "Pastoral nomads originally."

"That's a fancy way of saying they raised cattle, sheep, and goats," Fred interjected. "They also domesticated the horse."

"We don't know much about their original lifestyle," the scrivener added. "They remain something of a mystery until around 4500 BCE."

"What's so important about that date?"

"That's when they started moving out of their homeland," Erik said. "They came from an area north of the Caucasus Mountains in the Russian steppes. Eventually, they spread out in every direction. West into Europe, east into Asia, south into India."

"Wherever they move, we start finding kurgan burial mounds," Stefan explained. "And also things we wish not to find in a burial. Like this." He flipped a page to show more photos. A decapitated horse's skull. A female body buried in a crouched position at the feet of the male skeleton. The trove keeper pointed to the lower half of the skeleton. "Her legs have been broken before she was killed and put in the tomb."

Cassie laughed bitterly. "I thought Faye was joking. She told me the Kurgans sent their leaders into the afterlife with their wives and favorite horses to keep them company. Then these must be the original overlord bad guys, right?"

Erik paused to consider the question. "I guess you could call them that. When they came galloping out of the steppes, they either killed or exploited everything in their path. Yeah, I suppose that's fair."

"What do you mean exploited?" the pythia asked. "I thought they just liked to slaughter things."

"Not really," Erik demurred. "They actually liked to set themselves up as the ruling elite in an area. That's one of the reasons we call them overlords. They would build a hill fort where they could lord it over the locals. They forced the people to work for them, pay tribute, grow crops. Your average protection racket."

"Of course, it didn't happen overnight." Griffin picked up the thread. "It took two thousand years. What began around 4500 BCE was only the first wave of invasions. The third wave wasn't complete until around 2800 BCE."

"And when it was over, the kinder, gentler side of homo sapiens went with it," Fred added gloomily. "The matristic cultures were erased from history."

Cassie remained still, puzzling over the photo of the broken female skeleton. She briefly flashed on her telemetric experience at Catal Huyuk when she was immersed in the burial of the child. She remembered the attitude of the mourners. The death of a toddler held as much significance to them as the death of a warlord did to the Kurgans. There were no weapons in the child's grave. No strangled birds to keep it company in heaven. Only a prayer that the mother of all creation would give new life to the little one who had been lost. From what Faye had told her earlier, cultures all over the world would have treated their dead the same way. Why were these Kurgans different? She wondered what sorts of prayers they would have said over the body of their slain leader. Did they ask their sky gods to give the warlord new worlds to conquer? New people to slaughter and enslave?

Breaking out of her reverie, she asked, "How did they get to be so violent? I mean if everybody around the world up till that time was matristic, it's not like these guys rode out of the steppes with a completely new social agenda of mayhem and destruction. It didn't come out of thin air. There had to be some kind of trigger that changed them."

The men remained silent, pondering the question.

Stefan sighed. "That is, how you say, the crux of the matter. At the Kurgan trove, we are not only collecting artifacts of these tribes. We are seeking to trace all the way back to when they were like the rest of the world. Peaceful and not all the time killing."

"Good luck," Cassie said ruefully. "That's got to be one heck of a riddle to solve."

"It isn't as hopeless as all that," Griffin observed. "While we still lack a good deal of concrete evidence, we do have some fairly plausible theories as to why they became overlords."

"I'm all ears." Cassie sat back on the couch and folded her arms, ready for a long lecture.

Just at that moment, a young Turkish woman in an apron walked up to the group and asked in English if they would like something from the bar.

"Bar? What bar?" Fred turned to look around the parlor.

The waitress gestured toward the opposite end of the room. None of them had noticed the bar tucked away in a dark corner. At this hour of the afternoon, it was completely empty.

The group ordered various soft drinks, and the woman walked off to fetch their refreshments.

Picking up the thread of their conversation, Griffin said, "It's highly likely that in the beginning, the Kurgan tribes weren't very different from the rest of the world. They were most certainly goddess-worshipping and traced their family tree through the female line. The sexes would have been more or less equal. They moved about from place to place pasturing their flocks on lush grasslands. This state of affairs would have continued for a few thousand years until the climate shifted and the steppes began to dry out. It may have taken several centuries to notice a significant change, but eventually, there would have been less land suitable either for farming or for grazing. Water became scarce."

"A harsh landscape produces harsh people," Cassie observed. "Didn't you tell me that once?"

"I may have done," Griffin replied. "At any rate, it's true. Life on the steppes became more difficult. Resources dwindled. When such conditions occur rapidly enough, they foster a mental attitude of desperation and competition. To these nomads, taking by force what was needed may have seemed a reasonable option."

Erik continued the narration. "There's only one problem with stealing from the neighbors. They don't like it very much, and they tend to retaliate. This sets up a pattern where tribes are constantly skirmishing with each other either to defend their own stuff or to steal somebody else's. All of a sudden, battle skills start to get real important. You've got a bunch of people who spend most of their time practicing with weapons or actually using them to clean each other out."

"Dog eat dog. Sounds like a rotten way to live," the pythia commented.

"And it wasn't only the men who were trained in battle," Griffin added. He turned toward the Kurgan trove keeper. "Tell her, Stefan."

"That is so," Stefan agreed. "In the Kurgan homeland in southern Russia, many women warriors are buried with weapons. Their bones show battle injuries."

"Really?" Cassie sat forward, intrigued.

"Most certainly," Stefan continued. "Here is a very interesting picture." He hastily flipped through his photo album to a page at the front. The image showed a faceless mannequin dressed in leggings and a jacket embroidered with hundreds of small squares of beaten gold. The figure wore a tall conical hat. It stood in a museum display case.

Cassie looked up at Stefan quizzically. "I don't get it."

The trove keeper laughed. "This costume came from a rich kurgan grave in Kazakhstan that the tomb robbers missed. It is now in a national museum. Archaeologists have long called it 'The Golden Man.'"

"OK, so?" Cassie asked warily, sensing there was more to the story.

Griffin leaned toward the pythia and gave her a hint. "Remember the so-called Prince of Lilies on Crete?"

"You're kidding. You mean this is a woman?"

The trove keeper nodded energetically. "We are most sure it is. The grave contained weapons, and it used to be that whenever archaeologists found a grave with weapons, they automatically said it was a man buried there. Nobody bothered to look at the skeleton."

"Remember what I told you when I first showed you the vault?" Griffin interjected. "Mainstream archaeologists make assumptions about what they're seeing, and those assumptions are steeped in overlord cultural values."

Cassie studied the photo. "But how can you be sure this costume belonged to a woman? Did anybody examine the body?"

"The government does not allow us to look." Stefan sighed. "We were not there at the time the digging was done, and now it was too late." He brightened. "But the grave goods, they tell us the story. The earrings and jewelry that men do not wear. The polished mirror that is always found in the graves of shaman priestesses. The tall hat that is a sign of women of rank among the steppe peoples. No male grave has been found anywhere with these objects along with the weapons."

"It's very likely that she wasn't merely a priestess. She may have been one of the royals of her tribe," Griffin added. "This is a Saka costume, and the Saka culture had many queens. The Scythians and the Sarmatians, who were related to them, did also."

"Yes, the Sarmatians I know well," Stefan added eagerly. "They left their homeland north of the Black Sea, and the legend tells that they settled in my country of Poland a very long time ago. The women were very warlike. The tribe had a custom that a girl would not be allowed to marry until she had killed a man in battle."

"That's my kind of gal." Cassie laughed.

At that moment, the waitress returned bearing a tray of glasses and cans. She set it down on the table, and the group helped her pass around the order. They busied themselves with flipping tabs on cans and pouring the contents into glasses while they waited for her to retreat back into the lobby. When she was out of earshot, Griffin turned to Cassie and said, "Your kind of gal? I had no idea you were so bloodthirsty." He pretended to sound shocked. "Really, I'm appalled."

"Yeah, yeah," the pythia rolled her eyes. "Get on with the story."

The scrivener complied. "Stefan's evidence suggests that the steppe nomads were not rigidly male-dominated early in their history. They maintained many of the matristic customs of the cultures that surrounded them. While it's certainly true that the steppes were a harsh land that brought out the fiercest and most aggressive tendencies in humans, it would be safe to assume that those combative traits were not limited to the male sex."

"OK, I get the picture," Cassie said. "These tribes are hungry and thirsty which makes them mean and desperate. They get horses which makes them mobile, so they all mount up, charge out of the steppes, and start whacking everybody else."

The men exchanged looks.

"Well, not exactly," Fred hedged.

"What do you mean?"

"Not all of them left. In fact, most of them stayed right where they were, raiding and pillaging each other."

"But what about the flood of barbarians sweeping across Europe and killing everything in their path?" Cassie felt confused.

"You're thinking of Genghis Khan," Erik corrected. "That was thousands of years later."

"It wasn't a massive flood," Griffin added. "More like a slow trickle."

"Well, somebody trickled out of those steppes and changed history," Cassie challenged. "Tell me who they were."

The scrivener paused and considered a moment. "Do you know the story of Hengest and Horsa?"

Cassie gave him a withering look. "Excuse me. Have we met?"

Griffin smiled. "You were doing so well today I thought you'd like to try for three right answers."

"Nope, two's my limit. I wouldn't want to take away your job. Go ahead and tell the story."

"Ahem," the scrivener pointedly cleared his throat. "Hengest and Horsa were two brothers who belonged to the Anglo-Saxon tribes of Germany. They came to Britain in the fifth century to offer their services as mercenaries to King Vortigern who was having some difficulties with the Picts at the time. When the king asked them why they had left their homeland, Hengest answered that it was a custom among his people that when the tribe became too numerous, the leaders would summon all the fittest and bravest youths in the land. These would draw lots to determine who would have to leave the community in order not to become a burden on the resources of the rest. Those who were selected by the lottery would be expected to pack up their weapons, mount their horses and seek their fortune out in the world from that day forward."

"That means these guys were Kurgans," Cassie offered doubtfully.

"Very, very distant descendants of them, yes," Griffin replied. "A legend of twin brothers with equine names goes all the way back to the proto Indo-Europeans. The story is important because it establishes a historic precedent for the custom. It's quite likely something similar occurred among the steppe tribes. When faced with the problem of dwindling resources, the most able of them would be expected to leave. They would have chosen youths who had proven battle skills so that they could take care of themselves when faced with difficulties."

"But weren't they afraid of leaving themselves defenseless?" the pythia objected. "If they were surrounded by enemies, why would they send off their best fighters?"

"They didn't necessarily send their best fighters away," Erik weighed in. "The older, more experienced ones would have stayed at home. They sent away their most expendable fighters. Adolescent males mainly."

"Teenagers?" Cassie was shocked.

Fred joined the discussion. "Not teenagers in the way we think of them today. Life expectancy back then was a lot shorter, so kids had to grow up fast. These boys would have started training with weapons around the age of seven. By the time they were fourteen, they would have been on active raids. They were hardly defenseless."

"Almost like street gangs." Cassie was chilled by the parallel.

"And think about where they were headed," Erik added. "They had a huge advantage over the matristic tribes who didn't have horses or lots of experience with weaponry. It was all easy pickings."

"But the Kurgans must have been seriously outnumbered," Cassie objected.

Erik shook his head. "That wouldn't have mattered. They had a technological advantage. When Cortez conquered the Aztecs, who numbered in the millions, he did it with six hundred men, twenty horses, and ten cannons."

"Yikes!" Cassie exclaimed. "So basically, a pack of testosterone-crazed punks with fast horses and pointy weapons were turned loose on a tribe of lettuce farmers."

"Grim but accurate," Griffin concurred.

Boisterous laughter coming from the lobby caused them all to turn and look up. A party of German tourists had just arrived to check in. Their luggage carts were filled with hiking equipment. One of their number wandered into the parlor carrying a heavy backpack. He looked briefly around the room. Smiling and nodding toward the Arkana team, he strolled back into the lobby.

They paused in their conversation to see if any more sightseers would straggle in.

When the noise in the adjoining room quieted down, Stefan broke the silence. "There is one more interesting fact. It is very possible that not all the warrior bands who left the homeland were males."

Cassie stared at him uncomprehendingly.

"He's talking about the Amazons, toots," Erik prompted.

"But that's just a myth, isn't it?" Cassie turned to the security coordinator for confirmation.

"Nope."

"Actually, the theory that female warrior bands also migrated would go a long way toward explaining the Amazon stories," Griffin said. "Ancient chronicles described tribes of warrior women in the Ukraine, northern Greece, Bulgaria and even as far away as Libya in northern Africa. Conventional historians dismiss the Amazons as fanciful legends, but it's far more likely that they really existed and that they weren't a single tribe but many bands of female warriors migrating out of the steppes at various times."

"It is important to remember that all these things happened long before they were written down," Stefan added. "The first men who recorded stories of such women were living three thousand years later."

Cassie frowned at a troubling thought. "But why wouldn't the boy Kurgans and the girl Kurgans all migrate together? Didn't they believe in co-ed conquest?"

Griffin hesitated, seemingly to consider the question. "This is all speculation on my part you understand, but I believe that the female migrants represented a second wave. The males would have been the first group to leave a tribe whose supplies were already strained to the limit. Males are more biologically expendable. The survival of the tribe as a whole depends on the existence of females capable of giving birth to the next generation. A far smaller number of males are needed for procreation. However, let us suppose that a particular tribe is in such dire straits that even adolescent females represent a drain on its resources. If the males have already departed, then that leaves young women as the most likely group to migrate away from the homeland."

Cassie nodded, satisfied with the explanation. "I suppose that would be the reason why there were fewer female bands roving around looking for new territory and why they weren't traveling with males. They left as a last-ditch effort. But if that's true, then what happened to all of them? We know all about the male Kurgans, but it's like all the female warrior tribes went extinct."

Griffin smiled broadly. "That is an excellent question and one that brings us to the very brink of explaining the origins of patriarchy."

Stefan grinned. "This is where we are getting excited, yes?"

Cassie darted him an odd look.

Fred leaned over and whispered, "He means that this is the exciting part. The missing link."

Cassie nodded and smiled encouragingly at Stefan. "Yes, very exciting," she concurred.

Griffin was about to speak, but he cut himself short when the waitress re-entered the parlor to ask if they needed anything. Everyone politely declined and waited in silence until the echo of her footsteps faded across the lobby floor.

Cassie emptied the last of her cola into a glass. Then she turned to Griffin and raised a quizzical eyebrow. "You can start any time now."

"Very well. There is one distinct difference in the behavior of male overlords versus female overlords." He paused. "Females don't need to acquire females."

Cassie tipped her head and eyed him dubiously.

He continued. "Female overlords are already the means of their own reproduction. If they wish to have children to inherit their property, they can mate with any passing male and go on their way. They retain the children and have indisputable proof of lineage since they gave birth to them. Their matrilineal kinship system and inheritance remain intact. Unfortunately, their male overlord brethren aren't so fortunate. With no women in their band, they could no longer trace their descent through their mothers. Property would have to pass through the male line. If they wanted their children to inherit the wealth they acquired through conquest, they needed to be sure those children were theirs."

"Not so easy for the Kurgan boys," Cassie speculated. "Since they were all bachelors when they shipped out, they had to get wives from the local population."

"Precisely," Griffin nodded. "We're back to bride abduction which we discussed earlier."

"It may go a long way toward explaining the kind of misogyny that's typical of patriarchal cultures," Fred observed. "After all, if you slaughter a girl's family and then expect her to cozy up to you, you're always going to be sleeping with the enemy."

"Not to mention the laborious problem of having to control a wife's sexual activity in order to prove the offspring belonged to a particular overlord male," Griffin added. "Most matristic cultures were sexually free. Even those that practiced monogamy often allowed for other sexual attachments. How could a Kurgan male know his own progeny except by forcing his wife, or wives, to remain sexually exclusive? A virtually impossible task which the overlords solved by severely curtailing the freedom of women to move about in society. Females were restricted to living in harems or under house arrest."

"That's pretty grim, but what's it got to do with the extinct female overlords?" Cassie asked.

"Simple biology," Fred answered. "A female warrior gives birth to maybe five children over the course of her lifetime. A male warrior who practices polygamy can father fifty to a hundred children over the course of his."

"And don't forget the gender bias that is beginning to form among the male overlords," Griffin offered. "They are surrounded by foreign women who belong to the race of the conquered. These women are considered inferior and need to be controlled to guarantee paternity. Overlord men want sons to inherit their riches because sons can be taught to fight. Even though Kurgan women were good at defending themselves, the overlord men certainly aren't going to teach their indigenous brides battle skills, or they might turn around and kill their husbands. As a consequence, females become sexual commodities, lineage is traced through the father, and we're well on our way to patriarchal cultural norms. These male overlord cultures would eventually outnumber the overlord female territories and conquer them."

"But didn't they recognize they came from the same tribes as these female warriors?" Cassie objected.

Erik shrugged. "How could they know? It took thousands of years for all this to play out. In a space of three hundred years, how many African-Americans know what tribe their ancestors came from?"

"I see your point," the pythia conceded.

"The new world order simply engulfed and eradicated everything that came before it," Griffin said. "The current DNA evidence seems to bear out our theory. Mitochondrial DNA, which is obtained only from the mother, shows that the vast majority of female DNA in Europe is old European while a large amount of male DNA is Kurgan."

"Then the mothers were mainly from the conquered people, and the fathers were overlords?" Cassie asked uncertainly. "How's that possible?"

Erik laughed sardonically. "Simple. You kill all the men in a town you conquer, and you horde the available women. In a couple of generations, your DNA signature is all over the place."

"Ten guys on horseback could do all this?" Cassie still couldn't wrap her mind around the possibility.

"Think of them as prehistoric Hell's Angels," Erik commented. "Just like the modern version, those guys could tear up a small town in a matter of hours."

"And the rest, as they say, is history," Griffin summed up.

The group was silent for several minutes contemplating the implications until Stefan spoke up. "But that is why we are here, is it not? To tell the story that has been lost? I know that is why I am here."

Erik swiveled in his seat to regard the trove keeper. "Which brings us full circle. Just exactly why are you here?"

"*Pokażę ci, nie?*" With a gleam in his eye, Stefan reached into his duffle bag and withdrew an object wrapped in cloth. "You will see now." He furtively looked over his shoulder toward the lobby to make sure nobody else was around and then undid the wrapping to reveal a black stone knife with an antler handle.

Cassie had never seen anything like it before. She leaned over the table to study it for a moment. "What is that thing?"

Stefan grinned at her. With an arch look he replied, "Miss Cassie, I think maybe that is for you to tell me."

Chapter 21—Hope in Ruins

DANIEL STOOD ON A WINDSWEPT hillside and gazed off into the distance. To his left, he saw the two peaks curved inward toward one another like a pair of horns. He was back at Karfi. This time it was mid-afternoon on a bright, hot day. Not a cloud marred the endless blue of a Mediterranean summer sky. The hill sloped downward to his right. Mounds of bleached rock jutted out of the scrubby undergrowth. The *tholos* tombs of the Minoans.

Leroy Hunt was seated with his back resting against one of them. He had tipped his cowboy hat over his eyes and was indulging in a mid-day nap. He called it a siesta. Though he had insisted on accompanying Daniel up to the mountain refuge, he had no intention of aiding him in any other capacity than as a lackadaisical bodyguard. Daniel was on his own.

The son of the diviner had asked Nikos to remain behind. The young Cretan convert had not been part of the expedition on their last visit to Karfi and was unaware of the events that had happened there. Daniel saw no reason for involving him now. The scion wished that he, too, were as blissfully ignorant of what lay beneath the earth on this seemingly peaceful mountainside.

He cast a furtive look toward Hunt who was already snoring quietly. Scanning the area around the ruined tombs, he attempted to identify the one he needed. It was hard to tell. The last time they'd been here, it was pitch dark on a moonless night with only two flashlights to guide their way. They had depended on the lights of the strangers to lead them to their destination.

Daniel wandered around the cemetery, trying to find the right crypt. He remembered Hunt forcing the three strangers to climb inside the tomb. The ramp that led down to it had been choked with rock. Only the top half of the entrance had been open, and that was later buried completely by the earthquake that struck so unexpectedly. He remembered Hunt's joke following the quake that Mother Nature had finished the job of killing the trio for him. At the time, Daniel had been appalled by Hunt's callous behavior, but in retrospect he was more appalled by his own. He was the one who had stood by and allowed it to happen. Allowed three innocent people to be buried alive. It must have been a terrible way to die. He suppressed a shudder.

He skirted another *tholos*. Something about it looked familiar. He paused and walked back to the *dromos*—the ramp that led to the door of the underground crypt. It was filled with rock. The entrance was entirely blocked. He thought this might be the right one. How different everything looked in daylight. The spot itself was serene. His thoughts, unfortunately, were not.

Daniel directed a sidelong glance down the hill. Hunt was still dozing. How could he sleep so easily here, within fifty yards of the place where he had tried to commit murder? How could the man sleep at all given the things he had done in his life? No doubt, to a mercenary, it was all in the line of duty.

The scion felt a twinge as his own conscience reminded him what he, himself, had done in the line of duty. He was still carrying out his father's orders. Still engaged in this relic hunt which was tainted with the blood of at least four people—possibly more. Daniel distracted himself from going further down that road. He circled the tomb. The dome was intact. All the others surrounding this one had begun to crumble, leaving gaps open to the sky. He was sure the tomb he was looking for had been sealed. He walked back to the front again. There it was. The upright boulder with the strange markings. A lily carved at the top followed by two lines of pictograms and a niche in the middle of the stone.

He sat down on the grass in front of the stele and unpacked the computer he had brought with him. Unlike the British man who had done the translating on that terrible night, he was not going to rely on books. Daniel had learned a great deal about computers since he began this project for his father. David, the librarian who taught him, said he was a natural at it. The scion carefully fed the pictograms into a translation program. It took a few moments for him to copy them all. Now he would see for himself what sort of clues they provided. The translation came back in a matter of seconds:

"You will find the first of five you seek when the soul of the lady rises with the sun."

Daniel frowned in perplexity. The message was identical to what the British man had decrypted. Perhaps the third line would be different. He reached into his computer case and drew out the granite key. Once he fitted it correctly into the niche in the stele, another line of pictograms was revealed. He copied these into his software and hit the command button. The result gave him no consolation. The output read, "At the home of the Mountain Mother."

He sat back on his heels to consider. The results were identical in every particular to the information he already possessed. "You will find the first of five you seek, when the soul of the lady rises with the sun, at the home of the Mountain Mother."

Daniel rubbed his eyes. They were very tired from trying to see around corners. He blinked a few times and then something caught his attention. He stared at the base of the stele. It was almost imperceptible, but there was a tiny gap between the stone that rested at the bottom of the boulder and the standing rock itself. Almost as if it had been moved recently. He couldn't be sure if the ground around the stone had been disturbed or not. There had been too many people moving about that night and yet...

He crawled toward the stele on all fours. Keeping his face low to the ground, he examined the edges of the flat stone that rested in front of it. The seam of dirt that should have been piled up against the stele was missing. Someone had indeed moved this rock. Daniel began to formulate a theory.

He jumped up eagerly and circled the perimeter of the tomb again, searching. He shifted his attention briefly toward Hunt to make sure he was still sleeping. Halfway around the back of the dome, he thought he saw something. Crouching down he examined some cracks in the structure. Missing mortar. Rocks that might have been fitted back into place. His heart felt lighter than it had for months. A loose pile of brush had been stacked against the dome around this spot. Why? How did it get here? He began to smile to himself. They were alive. Somehow, they had managed to escape.

The smile froze on his lips as a far more disturbing thought occurred to him. If they had moved the flat stone in front of the stele after their escape, that meant they were still hunting for the relics too. In all likelihood, they were several steps ahead of him by now.

He raced back to the front of the tomb. "Mr. Hunt!" he shouted.

Leroy snorted and sat up. "Huh?" He tipped his hat to the back of his forehead, looking around in confusion.

"Mr. Hunt! I need your help!"

Hunt sprang to his feet. Reaching for his shoulder holster, he ran up the hill toward Daniel. "What you hollerin' about, boy?"

"Come here, please," the young man said excitedly. "I believe I've found something."

Relaxing his grip on the gun, Leroy sank down on the ground beside the diviner's son.

Daniel had already begun tugging at a corner of the flat rock in front of the stele. "Help me," he grunted with the effort. "I need to move this rock aside."

"Well, why didn't you just say so instead of scarin' a body half to death." Leroy wrapped his meaty paws around the other side of the stone and, with one jerk, slid it away from the base of the boulder.

"There! There it is!" Daniel pointed excitedly at the dirt-filled markings etched into the front of the rock.

"Well, I'll be." Hunt scratched his head in surprise. "Don't that beat all!"

Daniel barely heard him. He was busy copying the pictograms from the stone into his computer. He pressed the Translate button, and when the results appeared, his face lit up with a smile. "Ah ha," he said with satisfaction.

Hunt positioned himself behind Daniel, so he could read the output on the screen. "'Where flows the River Skamandros'? What the hell is that? Skamandros. Sounds like a disease if you ask me."

"Let's find out." Daniel opened another piece of software and began searching for references to the term. He read the data out loud. "Skamandros. Ancient name of the River Karamenderes which flows from Kazdagi (formerly Mount Ida) in Turkey."

The implications of the geography lesson weren't lost on even someone as obtuse as Leroy Hunt. "Oh, hell no!" he exclaimed. "You mean we been lookin' for this doodad in the wrong damn country?" He regarded Daniel with amazement.

The scion matter-of-factly began packing up his computer. "Apparently so. I'll contact my father immediately and let him know we're moving our search to Turkey." When he rose to go, Daniel deliberately steered Hunt away from the back of the tomb. He didn't want his bodyguard to notice anything out of the ordinary. The fact that the three strangers were probably still alive wasn't something Daniel intended to share with the mercenary, or with the diviner for that matter. If they were still engaged in the relic quest, then so be it. If they were destined to retrieve the artifacts first, then that would be for God, and not his father, to decide.

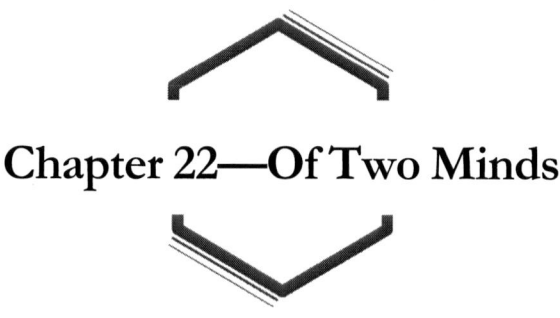

Chapter 22—Of Two Minds

ANNABETH SAT HUNCHED over a sewing machine, her eyes fixed in concentration. She fed the coarse grey cotton material past the needle, running a straight seam down the side of a girl's smock. This was the tenth she would finish today. Her shoulders and neck were beginning to ache from holding them tensed in this position. She raised her head and rotated her neck muscles to ease them. There were a dozen other women in the sewing room all engaged in the same work. Annabeth looked at the clock on the wall and sighed. Two more hours before supper in the refectory and afterward a brief chance to spend some time with her daughter. A flurry of motion at the door caught her attention.

Hannah stood there, wide-eyed and breathless. She seemed to be searching for someone in particular. When her eyes met Annabeth's, she rushed over and knelt beside her work table. "I need to talk to you, please!" Her tone was urgent.

Annabeth stared at her. "Now?" she asked in surprise.

The girl nodded vigorously. "It's important."

The older woman looked around at the other seamstresses who appeared to take no notice of the visitor's presence. They were all bent over their work. The clatter of sewing machines muffled the sound of conversation.

"Can we go someplace private?"

"But..." Annabeth cast around helplessly. What if somebody noticed she was missing? People would whisper. There could be trouble. She bit her lip, hesitating on the point of refusal.

Hannah tugged urgently at her sleeve. "There's nobody else I can talk to. Please!"

With deep misgiving, Annabeth stood up. "All right. We can go to my quarters."

The two women left without a word to anyone. They walked through the corridor in silence until they reached Annabeth's door.

When the older woman opened it, Hannah ran past her and threw herself face down on the bed. Without warning, the floodgates opened. "I don't know what I'm going to do!" the girl sobbed.

Annabeth hastily shut the door but kept her distance at the opposite side of the room. She wasn't sure what this odd behavior meant. "Hannah?" she asked cautiously. "What's happened?"

The girl buried her face in the coverlet. Her voice was muffled. "He wants to marry me!"

Annabeth's curiosity got the better of her. In spite of her wariness at this display of emotion, she took a few steps closer to the bed. "Who wants to marry you? You're already married."

"The diviner!" wailed the girl, still crying into the bedspread.

"What?" Annabeth sank down beside Hannah, not because she wanted to offer the girl any comfort but because she was too much in shock to remain standing. "What do you mean?"

Hannah rolled over and propped herself up on her elbow. She made an attempt to wipe her tears away with the hem of her apron. "The diviner... he... he... called me into his office. He said he had wonderful news for me." The girl struggled to sit upright, facing Annabeth. "He kept smiling. I hate it when he smiles!" She shut her eyes and shook her head as if to dislodge the image from her brain. "He told me the Lord had given him a revelation. That I was meant to be his wife, not Daniel's. He said he's going to make the announcement to the congregation this evening." The girl's eyes welled up again and spilled over. She looked at Annabeth in desperation. "Do you think he's right? Did God tell him to do this?"

Annabeth was taken aback. "It isn't for us to question," she protested. "If the diviner said this message came from God, then we must believe him."

"But he's so old!" Hannah exclaimed. "How can God want me to marry an old man?"

"With age, comes wisdom." Annabeth forced herself to smile reassuringly. "The diviner is a very wise man. He can guide you into the kingdom. Don't you want that? When Judgment Day comes, he can insure that you'll be welcome among the Blessed."

"I don't care about Judgment Day!" she girl cried. "I care about today and maybe a little bit about tomorrow. None of this feels right to me!"

Annabeth grew nervous at the outburst and tried to quell it. "Feelings can't be trusted. Would you set your impulses in opposition to the wisdom of the diviner and the will of God himself?"

Hannah looked uncertain. She remained silent.

The older woman pressed the point. "The diviner has been placed above us to correct our behavior, so we don't stray from the path. We must be pleasing in the sight of God, or He will cast us out of His kingdom. That would be terrible. Separated for all eternity from our families."

"I've already been separated from mine," Hannah said bitterly. "What more can He do to me?"

"You mustn't say such things!" Annabeth's eyes grew wide with alarm. "It's blasphemous. You'll go to hell."

"It feels like I'm already there," the girl replied in a small voice.

Annabeth was too appalled by the comment to speak. The two sat quietly for several moments.

"I was told I shouldn't talk to you anymore," Hannah finally offered.

"Who told you that?" The older woman felt a chill of dread run down her spine.

"The diviner."

Panic nearly made Annabeth faint dead away. She had been seen leaving the sewing room with the girl. What if somebody reported her to Father Abraham? What if he blamed her for speaking to Hannah? It hadn't been her idea. She hadn't known at the time that it was forbidden.

Hannah broke into her thoughts. "He said one of the reasons for taking me away from Daniel was because my sister-wives were a bad influence. That you were spreading lies about the scion. Father Abraham said that I was young and impressionable, and you had confused my thinking." She peered earnestly at the older woman. "No matter what he says, I know what didn't happen on my wedding night. You said it was the same for you too."

Annabeth jumped up and began to pace anxiously around the room. She clenched her hands into tight little balls. "I believe I was in error. Satan confounded me. He still confounds me. Sometimes I can hear his voice inside my head." She cast a terrified look toward the girl. "He's gotten into our minds and persuaded us to believe all sorts of things that aren't true."

The girl regarded her doubtfully. "How can you be so sure it was Satan?"

"The diviner told me." Annabeth nodded vigorously. "Oh yes. He knew, and he showed me what was happening to me. I have to pray all the time now because I get strange ideas."

"What sort of ideas?"

Annabeth laughed. Her voice held a note of hysteria. "Horrible things. Images that float through my head even though I don't want them there. I see myself picking up a knife and stabbing the diviner right through the heart. Other times I see myself swallowing poison. But if I really did those things I would be damned, and I would never see my little girl again in heaven." She dropped to the floor and began sobbing into her hands, rocking back and forth on her knees.

Hannah leaped off the bed and circled her arms around the weeping woman. "I don't think that's so crazy. Sometimes I get strange ideas too."

Annabeth stopped crying and gawked at her in surprise. "You do?"

The girl nodded solemnly. "Sometimes I imagine I'm running away. And I run and I run until I find my mother again. And then she takes me into her arms just like she did when I was little. And I feel safe and I know I'm where I'm supposed to be." Hannah paused. "Those ideas make me happy when I think them." She gazed at Annabeth earnestly. "Whatever is in your mind is yours to keep. Nobody else can know what you're thinking unless you tell them. I guess maybe that's the only place where anybody can really be free."

Annabeth gazed back at the girl with mixed feelings of fear and admiration. "I wish I was brave enough to want to be free," she said. Then she frowned as another thought struck her. "But my ideas are never happy. Just awful things. That's how I know they come from the devil and I can't trust myself any more."

"But you trust the diviner?" Hannah asked uncertainly.

"Oh yes! He knows what's best for us."

"He wasn't there! He didn't see how it was. But I was there and so were you. What makes the diviner right and us wrong?"

For one mad second, Annabeth felt an impulse to rebel surging up inside her. She saw herself telling the diviner exactly what he could do with his opinion about the state of her marriage. Then, just as quickly, the feeling passed. The devil was playing tricks with her mind again. She knew that disobedience was the first sin. Adam and Eve were cast out of paradise because of it. Lucifer was sent to the pit for disobedience and pride. Annabeth had no right to assume she knew more than the diviner. She looked at Hannah and shook her head. "Satan has the power to make us believe anything. Even something that seems very real to us. We have to be always on our guard." Hastily terminating the conversation, she stood up. The girl followed her lead.

Annabeth opened the door. She tried to give her visitor some final reassurance. Placing her hand on the girl's arm, she advised, "You must do as the diviner says. He won't lead you astray. Don't try to speak to me again if he says you mustn't."

Hannah gave a dispirited nod and left.

Annabeth leaned her head against the door, her mind racing to process a whole new set of possibilities. From her own perspective, Hannah's reassignment was far from bad news. She considered the implications. Perhaps she still had a chance to rekindle Daniel's affections. If she produced a second child, she would be elevated to the rank of principal wife. Then the diviner might look more favorably on her. She could hold her head up in the community as a person of consequence. She dared to give a little smile. Maybe this was a sign that God hadn't abandoned her after all.

Chapter 23—Relative Proximity

"I DON'T SEE HOW YOU can sit there so calmly and sip your tea!" Maddie protested. She had taken up a position on Faye's parlor sofa, with one arm slung over the camelsback while rotating a cigarette lighter between her fingers.

Faye raised a quizzical eyebrow. "I don't think it's time to hit the panic button just yet. There's a great deal we still don't know."

"Fine," sighed the operations director, tossing the lighter on the coffee table and folding her arms across her chest. "Let me recap what we do know. Somehow, some way, against all odds, the Nephilim have managed to dig up the critical missing line of the riddle and are ready to move on to Turkey."

"When did we get the information on this?"

Maddie consulted her watch. "About an hour ago. I figured this needed a face-to-face with you, so I didn't call first."

Faye nodded. "Of course, dear. I understand. You're distressed."

The red-haired woman let out a short bark of a laugh. "The fact that the bad guys are zeroing in on the right mountain doesn't distress me nearly as much as the way you're taking the news."

Faye allowed herself a brief smile. "What do you suggest I do?"

Maddie stood up and began to pace. "Something. Anything! We need to move fast on this. Call out reinforcements. Get our team out of the country."

The memory guardian set down her tea cup. Her eyes swung back and forth like a pendulum as she tracked her visitor's movements across the parlor rug. She allowed Maddie to tire herself out before speaking again. "I'm an old, old woman so you'll have to indulge me, dear. Give me all the facts and don't leave out any details."

Maddie stopped short and whirled to face her hostess. "Fine!" She flounced back down on the sofa. "I got a call from one of our operatives who had been keeping tabs on Leroy Hunt. Apparently, he and this Daniel character are trying to line up a Nephilim contact in Istanbul."

"What on earth would have made them want to retrace their steps to Karfi in the first place?" Faye mused.

"There was another call earlier in the week between Abraham Metcalf and Hunt. He told the old man that the boy had a hunch they were missing something. We didn't know exactly what that meant, until now."

"Indeed," Faye said. "A Nephilim who trusts his instincts is a rarity."

"One who trusts his instincts and totes around a computer is more than rare, he's dangerous," Maddie countered.

Faye reached toward the teapot on the table between them. Maddie declined a refill, but the old woman poured herself another cup. "I wonder how the Fallen Lands will affect him," she speculated.

"Huh?"

"Think about the way that Nephilim children are raised. No contact with the outside world. Minimal education unless it pertains to their scripture. And now we have this young man who is not only given the freedom to travel but unlimited access to computers and the internet. He's being exposed to all sorts of people and ideas that the rest of his cult will never know about. I'm sure it's going to change him in profound ways."

"Yeah, that's great," Maddie replied dismissively. "His quality of life really isn't the issue now."

"On the contrary, it may be the central issue." Faye raised her teacup to her lips and took a sip. "I suspect the more he learns of the outer world, the harder it will be for him to unquestioningly accept the dogma of the Nephilim. Harder still for him to accept his father's ruthless obsession to possess the Bones of the Mother."

Maddie paused to consider the idea. "Maybe so," she relented. "But how he changes over time isn't my main concern. Right now, I'm worried about how fast he's figuring out the clues to the artifacts."

"Have you gotten any recent updates from our own intrepid crew?"

Maddie sighed deeply. "As of this afternoon, they still hadn't found anything. They searched some calendar stones on Ida but so far no Bones.

For some reason, Stefan Kasprzyk showed up, and now he wants Cassie to tell him about an artifact he can't identify. The last thing they need is to get sidetracked now!" She paused to stare at the memory guardian in exasperation. "Oh, come on! Don't tell me you aren't worried. We're cutting the timing pretty close, don't you think?"

Faye smiled placidly. "Stefan has appeared with an obscure artifact that requires the assistance of the pythia? Hmmm. I wonder what this can mean."

"It means they're gonna lose valuable time talking to him when they should be out searching the mountain instead!" Maddie flared. "And pretty soon the Nephilim will be breathing down their necks. If Hunt hasn't already figured out our guys aren't dead, he's about to."

Faye didn't appear to have heard the comment. "The Kurgan trove keeper feels impelled to seek out the pythia at this most inopportune moment."

Maddie was too nonplussed by her leader's meandering thought process to speak for several seconds. She stared open-mouthed at the old woman. "Just what are you driving at?"

"Synchronicity. Odd coincidences that, in hindsight, seem to dovetail." She held a plate of lemon squares toward Maddie. "Are you sure I can't offer you one?"

The operations director waved the plate away irritably. "You picked a hell of a time to wax philosophical," she muttered.

Just then a knock was heard at the front door. It was actually more an insistent hammering following by an impatient jiggle of the doorknob.

"Are you expecting anybody?" Maddie sprang off the couch.

Faye shook her head, perplexed. "Please answer it, dear."

Maddie flung open the door to reveal a wiry teenage boy. He tilted his head to look up at the Amazon glaring down at him. His hair was blackish brown, spiked out with enough hair gel to make him resemble a porcupine. He wore a faded tee shirt and ripped jeans. A threadbare camo backpack hung off one arm. He gave Maddie a cursory glance and said "Hey" before sliding past her.

Dropping his backpack on the parlor rug, he threw himself unceremoniously on the couch. "How's it going, Gamma," he offered.

For the first time during the evening's conversation, Faye actually registered shock. "Zachary?" she asked uncertainly. "What on earth are you doing here?"

The boy sighed and rolled his eyes. "I can't stand it anymore. They're driving me nuts. You gotta let me crash here for a couple of days."

Maddie remained standing by the door, witnessing the exchange. "Who is this kid? Why's he calling you Gamma?" she finally asked.

The other two turned to her in surprise, apparently having forgotten her presence.

"Oh, I'm sorry dear. You don't know many of my relatives, do you? This is Zachary. Gamma is his special name for me. He started calling me that when he was two and still couldn't say grandma. Though technically I'm not his grandmother. He's my great-great-great... oh bother, I can't remember how many greats come before grandson, but he's—"

"Run away from home," the boy cut in. "Lemon squares. Excellent! You guys gonna finish these?"

Chapter 24—Twinkle, Twinkle

THE ARKANA TEAM SAT around a circular table eyeing the dagger in their midst as if it were a poisonous snake. No one made a move to touch it. It was very late in the evening. After a meal in the hotel dining room and a hurried telephone conversation to give Maddie a progress report, the group had adjourned to Stefan's suite. They wisely concluded that Cassie's telemetric abilities shouldn't be on display in the public areas of the hotel.

"I suppose we ought to begin," Griffin offered uncertainly.

"Can you tell me anything at all about this knife?" Cassie asked the trove keeper.

He shrugged helplessly. "Only that it is out of place where I found it. Such a dagger does not belong in a Kurgan burial mound. I know nothing more than that."

"What if it's a tainted artifact?" Erik challenged. "This could be bad news for Cassie."

"I cannot assure you that it is not," Stefan admitted. "Such a thing is used for killing, no? Knives do not generally have pleasant stories to tell."

Cassie sighed. "Look guys. Whatever it is, I think I can handle it. It's not like my head is going to explode and spatter my brains all over the carpet." She scowled and turned to Griffin for confirmation. "That isn't a possibility, is it? I mean you haven't heard of that happening to a pythia, have you?"

"Good grief! Of course not!" Griffin protested. "Just try to stay grounded as best you can. We'll all be standing by to assist you."

The pythia laughed nervously. "After that Vinca artifact nearly decapitated me, what have I got to be worried about?"

Her companions looked grim. No one spoke.

"Cassie, you don't have to do this," Fred reminded her.

She gave him a brave smile. "I sort of do. It's in the job description." She took a deep breath. Sitting forward in her chair, she reached around her neck for the pendant Faye had given her and grasped it tightly in her left hand. Then she stretched out her right. "OK, I'm ready." Stefan slid the obsidian dagger across the table toward her. She shut her eyes and placed her hand on top of the knife. "Gentlemen, fasten your seatbelts."

She went into free fall. She was nowhere and everywhere at once. This was unlike any trance she'd experienced before. Images strobed through her consciousness. The dagger was passing from hand to hand in fast rewind mode as one person after another grasped its antler handle. She didn't become any of them. The weapon was moving too fast though its impulse was always the same—to appease its rage with blood. She could feel flesh tearing, screams of pain, bodies falling to earth. Too many to count. Backward in time, the dagger traveled for thousands of years, leaving a mountain of corpses in its wake. Finally, the blade stopped moving and settled in the hands of a burly young man. Cassie touched down in his consciousness. She had scarcely caught her bearings before he leaned over a kneeling woman and, with one deft stroke, cut her throat. The woman collapsed on the ground choking. Blood streamed out and covered the snow around her body. The burly man snatched an amulet from her forehead. Fury churned inside of him like molten lava.

The blood in Cassie's veins felt polluted. Offal from a slaughterhouse. She tried to disassociate herself from the dagger. Pushing her awareness upward through a sea of gore. she gasped for breath, fighting a wave of nausea at the same time. Someone was calling her.

"Cass!" the voice reverberated inside her head. "That's enough. Come on, snap out of it!"

She blinked several times. Erik was kneeling next to her, shaking her by the shoulders. "Cass! Come back!" he urged.

"I... uh... I'm."

"Are you alright?" Griffin was beside her too.

She stood up dizzily, leaning on the table for support. "N... n... no," she finally stuttered. "No, I'm not." She ran to the bathroom and managed to reach the toilet just as another wave of nausea hit her. She vomited so violently that her head throbbed, and her rib cage felt as if it were broken. She nearly blacked out while one spasm after another shook her body. When she finally caught her breath, she could feel someone placing a warm washcloth on the back of her neck.

"You're going to be OK," another voice said soothingly. She thought it might have been Fred.

She became aware that a cold slick of perspiration covered her skin, causing her to shiver. Somebody had placed an arm around her shoulder and was guiding her back into Stefan's sitting room. It was Erik. In an uncharacteristically gentle voice, he said, "Just sit down here for a while and rest. I'll get you a glass of water."

She collapsed in a heap on the couch and concentrated on breathing in and out. Even her lungs hurt. When she finally blinked her eyes open, she could see four solemn faces peering down at her. The effect was almost comical. She chuckled weakly. "Guys, don't worry. Really. I survived."

Erik sat down beside her and handed her a glass of water. "Here, drink this."

The water helped wash the awful taste of blood and bile out of her mouth. The blood of all those people the knife butchered had oozed into her own veins. She'd been psychically poisoned if there was such a thing, and her physical reaction was just the same as if she'd swallowed something toxic. Her body acted decisively to purge away all that foulness. She wished her mind could purge the memories away that easily.

Erik scowled at Stefan in reproach. "That artifact wasn't just tainted. It was the granddaddy of all contaminated artifacts."

Stefan looked sheepish. "I am so sorry, Miss Cassie. I did not know."

She waved her hand weakly to reassure him. "Don't worry about it. Comes with the territory. What doesn't kill me makes me strong, right?" She gave a wan smile.

Griffin was standing over her looking skeptical. "A cold comfort that," he observed dryly. "You appear far from well."

She drank the rest of the water. Her head began to clear, and she sat upright.

"You're still cold." Erik had noticed her trembling hands. He hastened to the closet to retrieve an extra blanket. "Here, put this around your shoulders."

Cassie accepted the wrap and bundled herself into it like a cocoon before speaking again. "There's a lot to cover." She rubbed her temples.

"You can't possibly want to go over all of that now," Griffin objected.

"Oh, yes I do. I can't carry this bad energy around in my head. Better to get it out tonight so I can leave it behind."

The scrivener didn't argue the point. He settled himself on the arm of the couch while Erik seated himself on her other side. Fred and Stefan drew up two chairs. They waited in silence for her to choose her time to begin.

Cassie leaned her head back against the couch cushions. "This wasn't like any trance I've ever been in before. Blips and flashes of events, of people. Most of them dying on the sharp end of that thing." Her gaze traveled toward the table where the obsidian dagger rested so quietly. "I was being dragged backwards through its history, so I had to piece together a sense of what it all meant. It was like the knife itself had an emotion associated with it. Mainly anger and the only thing that quieted the anger was spilling somebody's blood. And then the emotion in the dagger got transferred to everybody who possessed it. It was used for rituals by this Kurgan tribe. Whoever wanted to be the leader of the tribe had to use that dagger to kill the competition."

"Although it's an appalling practice, such trial by combat is not uncommon in patriarchal cultures," Griffin commented. "Remember the Ottoman sultans who killed their own brothers to claim the throne?"

"But it wasn't only men," Cassie replied. "I don't think they were all that patriarchal at the time when this dagger was in play. Not all the leaders of this particular Kurgan tribe were males. Everybody had an equal chance to be vicious."

She laughed bitterly. "Once a leader died, the successor would be the one who was handiest with the dagger. The tribe passed it on from one generation to the next like some kind of unholy grail. It was a symbol to them. I guess you would call it a talisman. They believed that as long as they had that knife, it made them invincible."

"Excuse me, please," Stefan interrupted. "But this knife was found in a grave. It would not have been passed forward to anybody."

"That's because the last guy who had it ended up getting stabbed with it himself. Then all of a sudden, it was bad juju."

"Bad juju?" the trove keeper repeated doubtfully. "I do not understand this expression."

"Allow me to interpret," Griffin said. "I think I'm becoming proficient in Cassie-speak."

The pythia rolled her eyes.

"I believe she means it came to be regarded as unlucky. Its magic was broken. Better to bury it with its last owner than to pass it on."

"You know that female body you found in the grave with the chieftain and the dagger?" Cassie looked inquiringly at Stefan.

"Yes," he replied uncertainly. "She was most probably his wife."

"She was more than that," the pythia said. "She was also his killer."

The men all looked startled.

"I only got flashes of what happened, but it seems that he had already been wounded in some big battle and was recuperating. She'd been captured during a raid and didn't like being treated like prize livestock. While he was sleeping one night, she decided she would let him and his whole tribe know what she thought about the situation. She understood what a big deal the dagger was to them, so using it as the murder weapon was a way of giving them all a collective black eye. After she stabbed the chieftain, she ran off. Too bad she couldn't outrun a horse. They caught up with her and dragged her back. Broke her legs so she couldn't run away again. Then when they had the big funeral ceremony, they cut her throat and put her in the grave. I guess the tribe figured their chief would get a chance to punish her in the afterlife for what she'd done."

"What lovely people," Griffin remarked caustically.

"After that, the tribe thought the dagger was defiled. It had been used against them by someone they conquered—one of the so-called inferior tribes—so that's why it got buried." Cassie yawned wearily. "And that's where its story ends."

Fred handed her a fresh glass of water. "Which brings us back to Stefan's original question. How did that tribe get the dagger in the first place?"

Cassie took several sips before replying. "I think the guy who had it first was the founder of that tribe though he would have lived a couple of thousand years before its last owner. He was bad news, that one. Somebody should have forced him to take an anger management class. Except maybe 'angry' isn't the right word. It felt more like rage. The same kind of rage I could feel in the dagger itself."

"What was he enraged about?" Griffin asked.

The pythia paused to consider. "Everything. Everybody. It was almost as if he had a grudge against life itself for being the way it was. He didn't like being told no." She stopped speaking, trying to reach out into the atmosphere and pluck out the right phrase to describe what was wrong with him. "It's almost as if he thought he was God. And every time reality smacked him down to prove he wasn't, he got even madder." She paused again and closed her eyes, trying to recall the details. "He was traveling with a bunch of people who were all running away from a giant flood."

Griffin laid a hand on her arm to interrupt her. "Cassie, where were they? Could you see the surroundings?"

She nodded. "They were in some mountains. There was snow on the trail."

"Good heavens, do you know what you may be describing?" Griffin asked in wonderment.

Cassie stared at him. "No, what?"

"This young man and the people who were with him may have all been fleeing from the Black Sea deluge."

"But that would mean this knife goes back about seven thousand years," Erik speculated.

"Precisely," Griffin concurred. "Stefan, is there any way you could get this carbon-dated?"

The trove keeper nodded. "Yes, I think that is possible."

"Amazing," Griffin exclaimed. "This artifact may provide a direct link between refugees of the flood and the origins of Kurgan culture.

"How do you figure?" Fred asked.

"If these people were climbing into the mountains to escape a great flood, there's a very good chance they were fleeing directly into the Russian steppes. This may help broaden our understanding of the Kurgan tribes. Their warlike tendencies may have predated the dessication of the grasslands by thousands of years. Those refugees would have already been hungry and desperate when they arrived in their new homeland. Quite possibly they might have started preying on the indigenous peoples in the area. Remember what happened to the area around Catal Huyuk after the flood? Cities with fortifications. It stands to reason that these starving, predatory newcomers to the steppes might have entirely changed the cultural balance in that part of the world. This aggressive young man that Cassie has described would have been proto-Kurgan."

"He sure was brutal enough to be a Kurgan," Cassie observed. "He cut her throat like it was nothing."

"Who?" Erik asked.

"Sorry, I forgot. I'm getting ahead of myself. In my vision, this guy was ornery at the best of times, but he'd linked up with a tribe that was trying to get away from the flood. He was mad at the direction they were going. I think that was what set him off. He wanted to be in charge. But there was this woman. I guess she was the tribe's shaman, and she kept insisting that they go in a different direction. So, he took out his knife and cut her throat. That was the beginning for him. He saw that catastrophe with the flood as..." She paused to summon the right word. "As an opportunity. That's it. An opportunity for him to take over. He was a different kind of human from the rest. Maybe he was born different. The tribe he was traveling with—their leaders acted for the good of everybody. They all felt bound to each other. But this guy, he was disconnected. He really didn't care about the rest of the people or what was good for them. Only what was good for him. He wanted to be giving the orders. Wanted to be worshipped and obeyed. Some of the tribe followed him because they didn't know what to do and he acted like he knew where he was going. So, they went off with him and left the others behind." She shook her head ruefully. "What a psycho."

"Not psycho," Griffin corrected. "The personality you're describing sounds very much like a sociopath to me."

"It all fits," Erik added. "That kind of leader usually manages to show up whenever there's a culture in crisis. People get scared stupid, and they listen to anybody who sounds like he has a plan to get them out of the jam they're in. Overlord history books are full of his kind."

Cassie wasn't paying attention to their conversation. "There should be something else here." She was puzzled.

"Pardon?" Griffin stared at her.

She transferred her attention to the trove keeper. "Stefan, didn't you find something else with this knife? Something shiny buried right next to it?"

The trove keeper looked perplexed. "There was the sheath which you have already seen."

"No, not that. Can somebody get me something to write with?"

Fred walked over to the desk to retrieve some hotel stationary and a pen. He handed them wordlessly to Cassie.

She traced an outline on the paper. A five-sided geometric shape. Inscribed inside it was a five-pointed star. She held the picture out for Stefan to see. "It would have looked like this. An amulet made of metal, copper maybe. It had a star carved into the middle of it. The dead priestess wore it across her forehead. I got the impression it was the symbol for the goddess those people worshipped. Anyway, when the psycho cut her throat, he took it with him. It was handed down with the knife from one chieftain to the next."

"I have no knowledge of this." Stefan seemed bemused. "I am sorry to be saying I am sorry yet again."

"Oh well, it must have been lost somewhere along the way. But I think it was important to them. A trophy. The sort of thing you'd want to display in your den if you were a big game hunter. Like a moose's head."

"That's a pretty bizarre analogy," Fred commented.

Cassie made a wry face. "Give me a break. My head hurts, and all my bones feel like I've just been crunched by a boa constrictor. My communication skills are still a little off."

"On the contrary," Griffin broke in. He seemed oddly animated. "My dear girl, your communication skills are spot on."

"Huh?"

"The star amulet. A goddess symbol. It's given me an idea. A fantastic idea!"

By now they were all staring at him dubiously.

He jumped up and began pacing the room. "I'll have to get in touch with a few people back at the vault to run the calculations, but I believe we'll still be in time." He stopped muttering long enough to notice the reaction of his colleagues and hastened to explain. "Cassie's words jogged my memory about something. My theory may be far-fetched but if I'm right..." He was beaming now. "By tomorrow, I'll be able to tell you precisely when and where the soul of the lady will rise!"

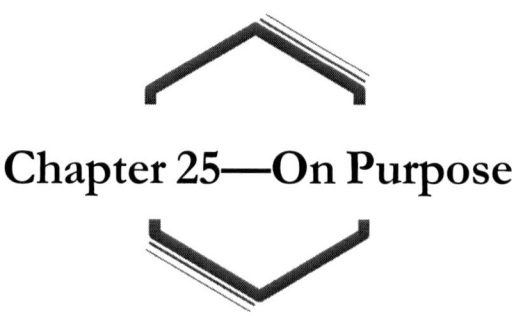

Chapter 25—On Purpose

"THANKS, GAMMA. I DON'T think I ate anything since lunch." Zachary wiped his mouth with a napkin and proceeded to lick up every last bread crumb on his plate.

The lemon squares had vanished into the boy's stomach an hour earlier to be followed by two sandwiches, several dill pickles and a bag of potato chips.

"I can make you another sandwich, dear," Faye offered. "Are you sure you wouldn't like some chicken salad instead of another mushroom burger?"

"Sorry, Gamma. You know I'm a vegan. Give me enough time, and I'll convince you to be one too. You wouldn't believe the way animals are treated in the meat and dairy industry. I could show you pictures that would turn your stomach. Worse than Auschwitz."

Faye regarded him dispassionately. "I take it you won't be wanting the chicken salad, then?"

Apparently deciding to proselytize another time, the boy replied, "Those portobellos were pretty good. I think I could manage just one more." Then he changed the subject entirely. "Sorry if I chased off your friend." He was alluding to Maddie's hasty departure. "Who is she, anyway?"

"Oh, just a neighbor." Faye remained intent on slicing two more pieces of bread. "She came over to borrow a cup of sugar."

"She didn't leave with any."

The old woman shrugged innocently. "She must have forgotten in all the excitement of your arrival." She placed another grilled portobello mushroom sandwich in front of Zachary.

He fell to devouring it without ceremony. "You'd think she'd be used to your great-grandkids popping over all the time," he said between mouthfuls.

N. S. WIKARSKI

"She isn't because they don't. My progeny is scattered all over the globe. Dropping by for a visit is reserved for major holidays during alternate decades. No, Zachary, your situation is unique. Your parents have the distinction of being the only relatives who live in close proximity to me."

While she was speaking the boy had managed to consume the rest of his sandwich and several chocolate chip cookies.

"Can I get you anything else?" the old woman asked.

"Got any soy milk?" he asked hopefully.

"I'm sorry, dear. Just cow's milk, I'm afraid."

"That's alright. I'm good for now." The boy stood up from the table and stretched contentedly. He wasn't more than five-foot eight, but he towered over Faye. "Just point me someplace where I can crash."

"You know this is only a temporary solution," Faye cautioned. "You'll have to deal with your parents sometime."

The boy rolled his eyes. "Yeah, but not tonight, OK? No lectures tonight."

The old woman chuckled. "I remember being a teenager."

"You do?" Zachary tried not to sound too shocked.

Faye gave an amused smile. "Yes, that long ago. Remarkable that my memory hasn't failed, isn't it?" She paused to recollect. "It was a time in my life when there seemed to be far too many rules."

"And all of them made by somebody else," her descendent muttered.

"Yes," Faye agreed quietly. "I believe that was the troublesome part." She exited the kitchen and gestured for Zachary to follow her. "I suppose the guest room will do. I just changed the bedding."

"Were you expecting company?" The boy trailed her up the stairs.

"I'm always expecting the unexpected," she said over her shoulder.

The second story floorboards creaked as she led him to a room at the far end of the hall. Switching on the light, she said, "You can put your things in here."

The bedroom was set under a dormer at the back of the house, so the ceiling was slanted. The room contained an old-fashioned brass bed, a nightstand, and an antique oak dresser. White lace curtains floated on the evening breeze streaming through the open window.

154

"Better than Howard Johnson's." Zachary tossed his backpack in the corner and flung himself across the mattress. The metal springs rasped under his weight.

Faye stood in the doorway with her arms folded, regarding him silently for several seconds.

Noticing her scrutiny, the boy sat up. "What?"

"Just tell me what triggered this urgent need for freedom."

"Gamma, do we have to go into that now?" His tone was wheedling.

"Twenty-five words or less."

"I wanted to do a summer internship with Greenpeace. The fascist dictators I live with said it was too dangerous. All I was going to do was hand out flyers in the city. It's not like I was trying to stop an illegal whale hunt or jump in front of a baby seal that was being clubbed to death." He threw his hands up in disgust. "When I save up enough money I'm gonna get a DNA test done. I can't be a blood relative to those people. I swear I must have been left on their doorstep by space aliens."

With a perfectly straight face, the old woman asked, "What color was the mother ship?"

"Metallic blue with white sidewalls."

"I'm not going to lecture you," Faye said softly. "But surely you know how worried your parents must be."

"They probably figured out where I went," Zachary offered grudgingly. He sat on the edge of the bed, kicking his legs back and forth. "I just took off, OK? It wasn't like I did it on purpose to make them crazy. I just couldn't take one more 'No.' For crying out loud, I'm not a baby. I'm sixteen!"

Faye smiled. "You're fifteen years and eleven months. Had you been sixteen, I'm sure you would have availed yourself of a driver's permit and hijacked one of your parents' cars to get here rather than hitchhiking. Am I right?"

The boy hung his head for a moment. "Busted." Then he gave his aged relative an appraising look. "How do you always seem to know stuff without being told?"

"Let's just say I'm very good at mathematics." She sat down on the bed next to him. "Being a parent is a tremendously hard job. They only want to protect you and keep you safe."

"Then they should just seal me up in a big damn plastic bubble and get it over with!"

"I'm sure there's a law against that. In fact, I read about it quite recently in the *Enquirer*."

Zachary did a double-take until he realized Faye was smiling.

"I wonder if they might get away with encasing you in a hazmat suit until you're twenty-one. Yes, that may be the better way to go."

Now he could tell she was joking. The boy grinned in spite of himself.

"In addition to remembering all the 'no's' when one is a teenager," she said, "I also remember how intense life can seem when one is young. I used to write some very lugubrious poetry at your age. Awful stuff!"

"Lugubrious?"

"Yes, it means melancholy. I had a perpetual case of the vapors until my early twenties. My own personal mauve decade." She smiled at the memory. "And I wrote some truly terrible poetry to commemorate my maudlin phase."

"I bet it was pretty good," Zachary observed. "You're the cool one. You're the only one in the family I'd ever admit to being related to."

"Why thank you, Zach. I'll take that as a compliment." She patted his knee. "But I can afford to be the cool one. I don't have to do the hard part. I can simply enjoy your company and send you packing whenever you become tiresome."

"Am I?" he asked anxiously.

"Are you what?" She brushed a breadcrumb off his shirt.

"Tiresome?"

She gave him a fond look. "No, my dear boy. Most assuredly not."

"But we are different from them, aren't we?" he persisted. "I mean you're the only one in the family who gets me. Everybody else is so busy trying to fit in. Be a solid citizen. I've got parents who make their living watching mold grow in petri dishes and a sister who wanted to be a lawyer before she was out of diapers."

"And what do you want to be?"

The boy paused and gave her a furtive glance. "I don't know exactly, but I want it to be something that isn't ordinary. Something that's going to change the world."

The old woman nodded understandingly. "I think most young people want to change the world."

"No, Gamma. I really mean it. I want to feel like my life makes a big difference. It's almost like I've got some kind of mission."

She raised her eyebrows in surprise. "A mission. Indeed. What sort of mission?"

He gave a frustrated sigh. "That's just it. I don't know. I can almost feel it out there calling me, but I don't know what it is yet." Zach paused to consider. "It's really weird, but I can feel it stronger whenever I'm around you." He peered into her face. "What do you think that's about?"

Faye returned his gaze. "I'm not sure, my dear. I do know, however, that people who feel a sense of purpose invariably find it when the time is right. Don't worry. Your mission will make itself known one day. Perhaps sooner than you expect." She kissed him lightly on the cheek and stood up to leave. "I'm going to speak to your parents now and ask them to allow you a one-week furlough. You may stay here for seven days but after that..." she trailed off.

Zachary hung his head in submission. "I know, I know."

"Tomorrow you will help me in the yard. My vegetable garden needs weeding."

"You're not gonna make me work, are you?"

Faye raised an eyebrow. "Were you under the impression that you wouldn't have to earn your keep? And in order to maintain your productivity, there will be no email, text messages, cell phones, video games, or other electronic gizmos to distract you from your chores."

"I get it." The boy laughed. "By the end of the week, you'll make me wish I was back home."

"You see right through me." The old woman chuckled. "Goodnight, dear boy. Get some rest. You're going to need it." She flipped off the light switch and closed the door.

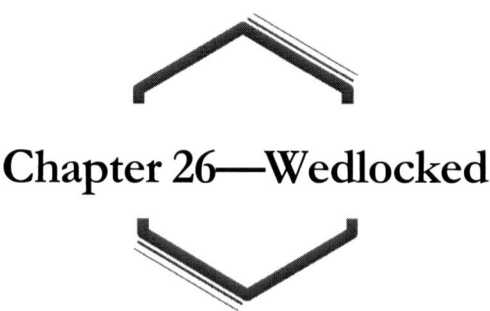

Chapter 26—Wedlocked

HANNAH UNCOILED THE braid wrapped around the crown of her head. She untwisted the rope of hair and ran her fingers through the curls, shaking them loose. It felt good to ease the tension in her scalp. She brushed her tresses slowly and methodically in front of the bathroom mirror, dawdling over the task. She wanted to postpone the inevitable as long as possible, trying not to think about what was waiting for her in the next room.

Today she had been married for the second time in as many months. The diviner's thirtieth wife. A large gaggle of sister-wives had clustered around to welcome her into their family. Many were old enough to be her grandmother. No one seemed to think it was odd that a man in his seventies had just wed a girl of fourteen. Not unlike the comments made after her other wedding, everybody told her how happy she must be. No one mentioned the whereabouts of her first husband or what he might be thinking about the annulment of his marriage to her. She was supposed to be happy. Everybody said so.

"Hannah?" a male voice called to her through the closed door. "Are you almost ready?" The diviner didn't sound commanding the way he usually did. His tone was almost cajoling.

"I... uh... I'll be out soon," she stammered. She peered at her reflection in the mirror to see if she looked any older than she had done on her first wedding night, but nothing had changed. The same slightly dazed and troubled face looked back at her.

"It's getting late, my dear," the voice hinted.

She gave her reflection one more anxious glance before opening the door and switching off the bathroom light. Hannah didn't meet her new husband's eyes as she scurried to the bed and slipped noiselessly under the covers.

He rolled onto his side, leaning on his elbow for support. She could feel his eyes on her.

She steeled herself and looked back at him with a blank expression. It gave her a start to realize he wasn't wearing a nightshirt. Loose skin hung slack over the muscles on his arms. The hair on his chest was white, and his arms were covered in liver spots. She guessed he was already naked below the waist and mentally cringed at the thought.

He regarded her for several more seconds with a doting expression. "You're very comely." He reached out to stroke her hair.

She lay still and said nothing.

He continued. "The Lord has great plans for you, Hannah. He commanded me to build up my celestial kingdom through you. As my progeny increases, so shall my heavenly estates increase. You will be the jewel in my crown and give me more children than any of your sister-wives. Do you know what that means?"

The girl shook her head slightly.

"As my fortune rises, so shall yours. You will be elevated to the rank of principal wife. Then you will have authority over all your sister-wives. I'm sure you'll like that." He beamed a sickening smile at her.

She noticed for the first time how yellow his teeth were and tried not to shudder at the sight of him.

"It is quite rare for a girl so young to attain so much," he said. "You will be the model for all consecrated brides. A shining example of what they too might achieve if they are dutiful and please their husbands well."

She knew he expected some sign of gratitude, but she simply couldn't bear the thought of thanking him. He had torn her family apart and separated her from everyone she loved. It didn't seem to occur to him that she might not want to help him reach a higher rank in heaven. It also didn't seem to occur to him that she might want something for herself that had absolutely nothing to do with him. She smothered the rage beginning to churn in her stomach, turning her face to the opposite wall. "Please put out the light," she whispered in a small voice.

"Very well." He nodded and did as she asked, too caught up in his own grand scheme to notice her lack of enthusiasm.

The room went thankfully black. No moonlight slanted through the single window in her bed chamber to illuminate that grinning, skull-like face.

"I trust you'll have no reason to complain about this wedding night," he said as he bent over to kiss her.

She didn't answer. As awkward as her first wedding night had been, she now wished Daniel were here instead of his father. Even though the room was pitch dark, she shut her eyes. She wished she could shut her nose to the leathery smell of his skin and shut her ears to the sound of his heavy breathing.

Her own breathing grew shallow and sharp. She couldn't seem to draw enough air into her lungs.

He began fumbling with her nightgown.

Panic-stricken, she knew there was nowhere to run. The sense of entrapment made her dizzy with fear. He began to whisper things, but the words were drowned by a roaring in her ears that sounded like the ocean. She didn't register anything he did to her after that because a funny thing happened to her mind. It flew to the ceiling and perched on top of the wardrobe in the corner, just like a bird. She became the bird, looking down on the room and the bed from a distance. Her mind perched and waited. The body experienced a brief stab of pain, but the bird took no notice. It perched and waited.

The other body wriggled and shuddered. It made a gasping sound, then rolled away and was still. The bird perched and waited. After a few more minutes, the other body fell asleep. Then the bird fluttered down and returned to its home.

Hannah lay on her back in a rigid posture, her arms pressed flat against her sides. She tried to take up as little space as possible on the bed. Abraham had turned away from her. He snored deeply like a man who had just gorged himself on a big dinner and needed to sleep it off.

She stared at the corner of the ceiling where the bird had been and thought about all the future nights that would follow this one. They would stretch into years, maybe decades, and this would be her life from now on. Hannah knew she was Abraham's favorite meal. He would glut his appetite until he was sick or until he developed a taste for a different kind of dish. That didn't seem likely to happen any time soon. She had a nightmarish vision of the diviner continuing to feed off of her for the rest of her life until there was nothing left to consume but bare bone.

The image horrified her. She felt like running down the silent corridor and screaming at the top of her lungs for help, but she checked the impulse. Nobody would want to assist her, and they wouldn't like it if she made trouble. Her mind flitted back to the compound where she had been raised. There was an older woman there who fell into fits. Some said she was possessed. The elders sent her away to a place where she was given medicine to make her quiet. She never came back. There were other wives too who became discontented, but they weren't sent away. They were given medicine at the compound. Whenever Hannah talked to one of these women, she always got the feeling that some part of them had left anyway. Maybe they had turned into birds too.

Her eyes welled up with tears of despair. She was sure they would freeze as they streamed down the sides of her face, so she made no move to brush them away. Her arms remained pressed against her sides. Hannah imagined she was lying in her coffin instead of a bed. It must be a coffin because she felt a deathlike numbness creeping over her limbs. She expected that in time the numbness would spread to her heart and extinguish the spark there. She could still feel it flickering now, but she wondered how long before the light would go out completely.

Could hell be any worse than this? She remembered Annabeth's terrified warning that she mustn't think such things. A new notion struck her. Could the Fallen Lands be any worse than this? She almost gasped at the boldness of the question and what it implied. If she tried to run, she would be entirely alone in the world. But wasn't she alone already? If she tried to run, she would surely be damned. Didn't she feel damned already? The numbness crept upward toward her heart urging her to choose the kind of hell that suited her best. She would have to decide soon before there was nothing of herself left to save.

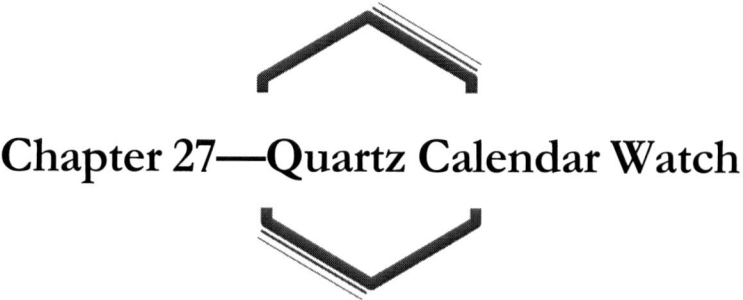

Chapter 27—Quartz Calendar Watch

"THIS IS RIDICULOUS," Cassie muttered, hopping on one leg as she tried to jam her other foot into a boot. It was still dark. More than an hour before dawn. She knew she was the last one up. Racing down the stairs, she caught up with the rest of the Arkana team, minus Stefan, in the courtyard. They were preparing to make the journey back to the calendar stones.

The pythia did a double-take when she looked at Erik and Fred. "Did you guys call each other up to decide what to wear today?"

The two men were both wearing blue jeans, yellow shirts, and white jogging shoes. Even though Fred was several inches taller than Erik, they were both blond. The effect was disconcerting.

Fred laughed self-consciously, but Erik chose to ignore the remark. The security coordinator addressed Griffin instead. "Now are you gonna tell us what this is about?"

"All will be revealed in time," the scrivener replied evenly as he climbed into the back of the Jeep.

For the past twenty-four hours, the Brit had been in constant communication with his staff at the Central Catalog. Most of what his teammates could glean from his telephone conversations consisted of gibberish. Numbers and dates flew back and forth in some sort of coded language. Whenever the trio asked for an explanation, their questions were met by a brusque, "No time now. I'll tell you later."

With nothing better to do, Fred, Cassie, and Erik loitered around the hotel grounds until it was time to bid Stefan farewell. The trove keeper packed his artifact and departed almost as abruptly as he had arrived. During this interval, Griffin emerged from his teleconference only long enough to tell the team they would be driving back to the calendar stones before dawn.

Now that they were actually in motion, Cassie felt as if she was riding a roller coaster inside a tunnel. Her queasiness after reading the dagger hadn't entirely subsided and bouncing along in the Jeep brought it rushing back. She fought off repeated attacks of dizziness and nausea as the vehicle trundled over rutted dirt trails in utter darkness. The headlights barely illuminated the road directly ahead of them much less the surrounding landscape. It was a good thing Fred knew where they were going. With no way to gauge their progress, Cassie lost track of time though they must have been traveling through the forest for over an hour. Just when her stomach was about to erupt in earnest, the vehicle came to a halt. Cassie breathed a shaky sigh of relief. They'd made it.

The pythia slid out of the truck and waited for the world to stop spinning. By the time it did, the others were already climbing the trail that led back to the megaliths. She scurried to catch up with the three flashlights bobbing ahead of her.

The team paused briefly at the top of the rise above the tree line. Now that they were out of the pines, Cassie could see a huge swath of stars twinkling overhead. A sliver of moon hung low in the sky, but its light was too weak to afford much help. Off to their right lay the plateau where the giant stones waited. Griffin trained his lantern on the megaliths and descended. The others followed in silence until he came to an abrupt stop in the center of the stone ring.

"Now what?" Cassie asked, bringing up the rear.

"Now we wait for the sun," the scrivener replied.

Orienting himself toward the mountain peaks that ran off in a straight line to the east, Griffin chose a grassy patch of earth and sat down. The others followed his lead. They set their lit flashlights down on the ground, so they could see each other's faces.

Cassie was relieved to be positioned anywhere that wasn't moving. Her stomach relaxed. "OK, Mr. Wizard. Let's hear it." She looked at Griffin reproachfully. "You've kept us waiting long enough."

He chuckled. "I'm sorry to have been so cryptic, but the calculations took a devil of a long time to sort out. They required my full concentration."

"Why are we here and why now?" Erik asked. His tone of voice suggested he was about to throttle Griffin unless the Brit provided an immediate explanation.

"Let me begin at the beginning," the scrivener replied.

"I hate it when he says that," Cassie confided to Fred. In a louder voice, she asked, "What's the matter? You never heard the expression 'cut to the chase'?"

"I have indeed heard it, but in this context, it would make no sense. If I were to cut to the chase, you wouldn't understand what we were chasing."

"Have it your way." The pythia sighed.

"Right then." Griffin forged ahead. "Do you remember that interesting clue you provided to me after reading Stefan's artifact?"

"You mean the star amulet?" she asked uncertainly. "It was in the shape of a pentacle."

"Ah yes, the ubiquitous pentacle." Griffin nodded sagely. "A bit overused in our current time, I'm afraid. I could go on about its symbolic associations ad nauseum."

"I'd prefer if you didn't," Cassie countered. "I'm still a little queasy."

"Sorry. It's not the historic symbolism of the pentacle that's important anyway. Your vision dates back to events that occurred in the sixth millennium BCE. Far earlier than the meaning which came to be associated with that shape in more recent times. Its earliest purpose was to represent a star."

"No surprise there!"

"But not just any star," Griffin cautioned. "The brightest star in the heavens. One which has been an object of veneration to peoples all around the world. I'm referring, of course, to Sirius in the constellation of Canis Major. Its name comes from the Greek word *seirios* which means 'the scorcher.'"

"Sirius is the dog star, right?" Erik asked.

"It's a binary star system actually which appears as one bright white light to the naked eye but, yes, it is often called the dog star. To this day, we refer to the dog days of summer without understanding the phrase's connection to Sirius. In the northern hemisphere, the star is most prominent during the hottest months. It's quite interesting how persistent the canine association has been. You know, of course, that the ancient Greeks and Romans referred to it as a dog. But so did the Assyrians, Chaldeans, and Akkadians. As far away as China, it was referred to as a wolf. American Indian tribes viewed it variously as a dog or a coyote. The Eskimos called it 'Moon Dog.' Such global consistency in the symbolism of the star suggests that it became an object of reverence at the very dawn of human consciousness. Most probably the first people to migrate out of Africa carried the myth of the dog star with them.

However, Sirius represented much more than a heavenly hound to the ancients. In some cultures, the star was associated with a specific deity. Consequently, it figured prominently in religious practices. The temple of Isis at Philae and the temple of Hathor at Dendera were both oriented toward the heliacal rising of the star."

"Back up for a minute," Erik instructed. "What do you mean by heliacal rising?"

"Based on the rotation of the earth and the season of the year, stars appear and disappear from the night sky. There inevitably comes a day when a star which has not been visible for some time reappears on the horizon just before sunrise. When a star's re-emergence coincides with sunrise that is called its heliacal rising. Heliacal, of course, comes from the Greek word *helios* which means 'sun.'"

"OK, great but why is this star rising such a big deal?" Cassie glanced at the sky. Billions of stars glinted back at her, some brighter than others. Who could tell what was what up there?

"In the case of Sirius, its first appearance at sunrise coincided with the flooding of the Nile which meant everything to the ancient Egyptians. Their crops, and hence their very lives, depended on the annual inundation of the river valley. The date also roughly coincided with the summer solstice, the longest day of the year. The Egyptians based their entire calendar system on its reappearance. Sirius held such great significance for them because they believed the essence of Isis dwelt in the star. It came to be called 'the soul of the lady.'"

"The soul of the lady," Cassie repeated. "Now where have I heard that line before?"

THE MOUNTAIN MOTHER CIPHER

"I don't want to burst anyone's bubble." Erik's voice was testy. "It's great that they called it the soul of the lady, but we're on the trail of Minoan artifacts, not Egyptian ones."

Griffin gave a slight smile. "The Egyptians were not the only civilization to mark the importance of Sirius. They just happen to have left us the best documentary evidence of its worship. Other cultures also believed that the essence of a divinity resided in the star. The Sumerians explicitly associated Sirius with their principal goddess Inanna. The Minoans revered it as the home of their *potnia*—their great lady. In fact, all the temples on Crete are oriented toward the heliacal rise of Sirius because that marks the first day of the Minoan calendar as well."

"So that's why we're here?" Cassie squinted off into the gloom. "To watch for Sirius on the horizon?" The sky was turning from inky black to a deep shade of grey. Fewer stars seemed to be visible now.

The scrivener shook his head. "Alas, if only that were true. It would be a wonderful sight to behold but the earth wobbles, you see."

Cassie turned helplessly to Erik. "Do you have any idea what he's talking about now?"

Erik snorted in exasperation. "Do I ever?"

"I think I know," Fred offered helpfully. "The earth spins kind of like a top. You know how when a top slows down the upper half will wobble while the bottom is still spinning on its axis."

Cassie and Erik both nodded uncertainly.

Fred continued. "Well. There's this thing called the precession of the equinoxes which means that the earth is wobbling on its axis, so the constellations don't appear in exactly the same spot in the sky that they used to. It takes about 26,000 years for the wobble to make one complete revolution and then all the constellations line up in their original positions. What that means for Sirius is that it doesn't rise with the sun on exactly the same date as it would have done a few millennia ago."

"Bravo, Fred," Griffin said appreciatively. "Couldn't have explained it better myself."

"No, you would have taken longer," Erik muttered in a surly undertone.

Ignoring the comment, Griffin pressed on. "So now you understand why I've been working frantically with my team back at the vault to find the day when Sirius would have risen at this latitude three thousand years ago. By sheer accident, we managed to arrive here at approximately the right time of year, but we only have a narrow window of time to hit it exactly right. Three thousand years ago, Sirius would have risen several weeks earlier than it does now. My team had to calculate the approximate date of its heliacal rising in 1000 BCE and translate that into our own calendaring system."

"But if we're not gonna see the soul of the lady rise with the sun, then why are we here?" Cassie was confused.

"Because Sirius won't point us to the artifact we seek. The sun will. The angle of the sunrise needs to be the same as it would have been for the Minoans when Sirius rose at dawn."

"You think the sun's going to cast a shadow across these stones some way that will show us where the artifact is buried?" Erik asked.

Griffin nodded hopefully. "That is my theory, yes."

"Guess we'll know pretty soon if you're right." Erik pointed toward the east. "Look's like it's almost show time."

They all focused their attention on the eastern mountain range. The sky was vaguely beginning to glow. Cassie pulled her jacket more closely around her shoulders. Even though it was mid-summer, the pre-dawn temperature on the mountainside was chilly, and the ground was soaked with dew.

No one spoke. It was as if they'd all been turned to stone. They seemed to fuse with their surroundings. The standing stones and the seated humans all waiting for something. But what?

Then it appeared. The first weak rays of sunlight shot over the horizon and began creeping toward them. The mountain peaks in the distance took on a rosy glow. The light seemed to crawl in slow motion, sliding up the side of Gargarus to the plateau.

At the eastern end of the circle, two megaliths stood close to one another. The giant stones on either side had cracked and begun to lean at odd angles. The sun cast oblique shadows around the other megaliths but shot straight through the center of the two pillars. The light advanced forward into the circle. The Arkana team scattered. They took up positions on the perimeter to allow the rays to move unimpeded. Across the grass, across the gravel, until the light illuminated a small boulder toward the rear of the circle that measured about three feet high. The rock was completely undistinguished.

No one had noticed it during their previous search. It contained no markings. It stood in a pile of rubble with smaller rocks strewn all around its base. The sun lingered on it persistently.

Cassie felt herself being pulled to the spot. She ran forward. Without knowing what she was doing, she began shoving aside the smaller stones piled at the base of the rock. Her efforts revealed a square flagstone recessed level with the ground. On its face was carved a lily.

"Guys! It's here," she called urgently. "I found it!"

The men scrambled to join her.

"Wait a minute," she cautioned. "I want to try something." The pythia stepped onto the carved stone and stood facing the sunrise.

It was an eerie sensation. She felt her consciousness split. Part of her was Cassie, standing on a flat stone watching the sun come up. Another part of her was an old woman wrapped in a shawl and surrounded by four companions. She was standing in exactly the same spot where Cassie stood and she, too, was watching the sun rise. But it was earlier in her time. Cassie felt as if time had rewound itself by three thousand years plus half an hour because the sun hadn't reached the horizon yet. The distant mountains were dimly backlit by the still hidden sun, but the sky was light enough that all of the stars had disappeared. All but one. A glimmering white dot could be seen just above the peaks. It hung suspended for perhaps ten minutes, glowing fainter and fainter as the sun's upper rays broke the horizon. When the first beams shot through the pillars and made their way to the boulder at her feet, the star disappeared completely against the brightening day.

"Wow!" the pythia exhaled. "You're right Griffin. That really was something to see."

"You had a vision? But you didn't fall down."

Cassie laughed. "I guess I'm getting the hang of this pythia business. Besides, I only fall down when I come across something awful. This vision was really, really nice. I saw Sirius."

"You mean you actually witnessed its heliacal rise?" He sounded flabbergasted.

The pythia nodded. "Yeah, I saw what it must have looked like to them when they planted the artifact here." She looked at each of her companions in turn. "And it is here. I'm one hundred and seven per cent sure that I'm standing right on it." She smiled. "And for the first time, I actually felt like I was connected to them."

"Them?" Erik repeated.

"The Minoans. There were five of them. The ones who buried the relic here."

"Did they give you a message?" Fred asked hopefully.

"No, it wasn't like that. They weren't talking to me. I was just standing with them. I got a sense that this was a sacred ritual for them. They had all taken some kind of vow to see this through. To hide all the artifacts until the time came for somebody to find them." She looked down at the stone beneath her feet. "I hope you guys packed shovels. We're gonna have to dig for it."

"I loaded some equipment in the Jeep," Fred answered readily. "I'll get the tools."

"I'll help you," Erik offered.

The two of them loped across the plateau and climbed the rise, animated by the thought that victory was so near.

Griffin stayed with Cassie. "I almost envy you your gift."

She laughed ruefully. "Bet you wouldn't have said that two days ago when I was tossing my cookies after that artifact of Stefan's."

The scrivener shrugged. "I imagine it was worth the price to be able to witness what you've just seen."

"It was pretty cool," she admitted. "I've lived all over the U.S. but always in cities. You never get to really see the night sky when you live in a city. Out here..." she trailed off, contemplating the mountains in the distance. "Out here, it's easy to understand why people used to think the stars were holy."

Griffin positioned himself beside her, so he could gaze across the same vista. "When I was a boy back home in England, I spent my summers in the lake district with my grandparents. They had a cottage in a small village near Windermere. In the evenings, after it grew dark, I would lie on the grass and look up at the Milky Way. I've heard people say how cold and distant the stars are. How they make one feel small and insignificant. But it wasn't like that at all for me. There were moments when I almost felt as if I could breathe them in. Drink them in. I would find myself getting lost in them."

Cassie stared up at the scrivener. "You?" she asked incredulously.

He shook himself out of his reverie and returned her glance. "Why do you find that so strange?"

The pythia shrugged. "I guess I've always thought of you as somebody who likes facts and statistics. But what you just said. It sounded almost..." She struggled to find the right word.

"Mystical?"

"Yeah, I guess that's it. Mystical."

"All of us who've joined the Arkana have a bit of the mystic about us." He looked over his shoulder. The other two were approaching. "Even tough-as-nails Erik."

"Not sure I buy that," Cassie remarked skeptically.

"Nevertheless, it's true," Griffin replied softly. "We've none of us lost our sense of wonder. Only someone who's come face to face with the numinous can say that."

Erik and Fred were now within earshot.

"Everyone grab a shovel," Erik instructed.

By now the sun was high enough to illuminate the task at hand.

"So, you think it's right under the lily rock, Cass?" Erik glanced at her for confirmation.

She stepped aside and nodded. "Positive. We'll have to be careful not to disturb the ground too much. If those Nephilim guys show up any time soon, we don't want this looking like a construction site."

"Understood," Erik agreed.

They all worked carefully to displace as little dirt as possible in moving the stone. Once they lifted it out of place, they were surprised to discover that it fitted like a lid over an underground storage box. Inside the box was a covered urn made of polished alabaster. And inside the urn was the object they had traveled five thousand miles to find.

"Wow!" Cassie exclaimed in admiration. "Will you get a load of that!"

Her teammates stared in amazement at the object for several moments.

"This has been buried here for three thousand years. Waiting," Griffin observed. "Waiting for us to bring it back into the light."

Erik snapped them all out of their collective trance. "Let's hustle people. We need to cover our tracks and get this intel to Faye and Maddie ASAP!"

Chapter 28—Duty Call

FAYE WOKE OUT OF A deep sleep to hear a sharp banging coming from downstairs. Disoriented, she looked at her alarm clock. It was five a.m. Zachary came skidding into her room.

"Gamma, who's that?" he asked, his voice filled with panic. "Is it my parents? Because you promised I could stay the whole week and I've only been here two days." He rushed to the bed and stood over her with accusation in his eyes. "Tell me you didn't narc on me. I trusted you!"

"Calm down, Zachary. It can't possibly be your parents. They agreed to your visit. It's probably one of my associates."

"Your associates?" the boy asked cautiously.

Faye caught herself. Grogginess had caused her to slip up. "Did I say associates?" She laughed lightly. "How odd. That must have come from the dream I was having. I thought I worked in an office in downtown Chicago."

The banging started up again.

"Be a dear and find out who that is while I get my dressing gown on." She shooed him downstairs and slipped on her robe. As she hobbled to the top of the steps, she heard two raised voices.

"Where is she?"

"Where do you think? She's sleeping. What do you want?"

Faye leaned heavily on the railing and made her way down to the landing where she saw Maddie, frizzy-haired and dressed in a jogging suit, glaring at her descendent. "Listen, kid. I didn't come here to get the third degree from you."

Zach wasn't about to be intimidated. He stepped in closer to the dragon lady and stared up at her. "No, you listen, Maisie..."

"It's Maddie!" she snapped.

"Whatever," he brushed the name aside. "Do you know what time it is?" He glanced at her wrist. "I bet you don't even own a watch. How about a sun dial? They're easier to read except, oh wait, the sun has to actually be up first!"

"Why Maddie, how lovely to see you." Faye smiled graciously as she descended the rest of the stairs. "What brings you round so early? Out jogging again?" She trained her eyes pointedly at Maddie's attire hoping the operations director would take the hint.

Maddie glanced down briefly at her sweat suit and hesitated. "Yeah, uh, that's right. I was out jogging. And I saw this really weird thing, and I tried to call you about it, but I couldn't get through."

"Couldn't get..." Faye paused. "Oh bother, my phone must be out of order again. The signal keeps fading in and out. I'll have to get in touch with the phone company.

"What about your cell?" Maddie pressed.

"I've had to lock up the cell phones during Zachary's stay to keep temptation out of reach. Sorry, I forgot to check my voice mails. I've become so distracted these days now that I have a house guest." She put significant emphasis on the last two words.

"I don't suppose you checked your email lately," Maddie persisted.

"Not since yesterday evening."

The operations director rolled her eyes.

Zachary had listened to this interchange in silence, but the suspicious look never left his face. "You sure do ask a lot of questions, lady."

"It's what I do. You'll get used to it."

"Well, I've got a few for you too," the boy pressed. "Do you make it a habit to come over and harass little old ladies in the middle of the night?"

"Middle of the..." Maddie was speechless. Her face began to turn an unhealthy shade of red.

Faye tried to forestall an explosion. "Why don't we go into the kitchen and I'll make some coffee."

"No time." The operations director shook her head. She glanced briefly at Zach, apparently realizing the need to come up with a plausible explanation. "Look kid. You may not know it, but this nice old lady is the head of ..."

Faye caught her breath, afraid that Maddie would divulge too much.

"The neighborhood watch," Maddie completed the thought. "I saw something really strange when I was out—" She swallowed. "Jogging this morning. I can't talk about it. Top secret stuff that might involve the police. Anyway, we need to call an emergency meeting of the watch, and your granny is the only one who has the authority to do that."

Zach looked at his ancestor with surprise. "Huh, go figure. Who'd a thunk it? Harmless little old lady by day. Scourge of criminals by night. Gamma, you're quite a character."

"You have no idea," Maddie murmured under her breath. She shifted her attention to Faye. "So anyway. We'd better get a move on. No time to waste."

"How come you don't have your meetings here?" Zach challenged.

Faye intercepted her associate's response. "We have a special meeting place."

"Like a bat cave?" Zach asked eagerly.

"My dear boy," Faye laughed. "What an imagination! Next, you'll picture me heading a secret organization to save the world or some such nonsense." She turned back up the stairs. "I'd better get dressed. Maddie, please make yourself some coffee in the meantime. I'll be with you shortly." She paused as a new thought struck her. Turning around, she asked, "Zach, will you be alright alone? This could take a few hours to sort out."

The boy snorted. "Gamma, I'm not retarded. I think I can manage by myself for a whole ninety minutes without falling down and drowning in the toilet or getting myself lost in the backyard."

Faye smiled. "Of course. What was I thinking?"

Zach smiled back, but there was a glint of something in his eyes that Faye found troubling. Was it suspicion? Curiosity? Those were both impulses that led to a desire for answers. She hoped this wasn't the day when she'd have to supply him with any.

Chapter 29—Sting Operation

"GIVE ME THE PHONE!" a disembodied voice demanded.

"No, me! Let me tell it."

The receiver dropped. There was the sound of a scuffle.

Maddie was seated behind the desk in her office while Faye sat in the visitor's chair. They were both staring at the speaker on Maddie's phone which emitted a series of scraping sounds.

Maddie drummed her long red fingernails impatiently for several seconds before deciding to take charge of the situation. "Hey!" she barked at the speaker box. "One of you pick up the damn receiver and say something useful right now!"

There was dead silence on the other end. After a few seconds, Griffin's voice emerged. "Very sorry about that. I'm afraid we're struggling with a low-tech environment on this end. Couldn't manage a video telecon since we're stranded in a dead zone on the mountain. I suppose we ought to count our blessings that there's a land line, but only one of us can speak to you at a time."

"Yeah, whatever," Maddie replied coldly. "You woke me up in the middle of the night to tell me you had urgent information for me and Faye, but you wouldn't tell me what." She regarded her superior with exasperation for a few seconds. "When I tried to reach Faye, she was incommunicado which means I had to jump in a car and drive to her house. This didn't put me in a very good mood, and that was before her great-great-whatever-grandson treated me to the third degree. That kid's got a great future ahead of him as a Rush Street bouncer."

"Faye had children?" The amazed voice was Cassie's. Apparently, they were all listening in on the single earpiece on their end.

"Another time," Maddie said curtly. "Now what's the big to do and I'm warning you it better be big."

"Oh, it is," Griffin hastened to reassure her. "We've found it!"

Faye sat forward eagerly in her chair. "Do you mean to say you've actually found the first relic?"

"That we have." Griffin couldn't keep the elation out of his voice. "I wish you both could see it."

"Yeah, it's really cool with all the little squiggly hieroglyphs on the wings. And shiny too after all this time," Cassie chimed in.

"Of course, we haven't had time to decipher the symbols, but I suspect they are clues that will lead us to the second relic. It's quite cunning how the Minoans—"

"Hey, can the chatter!" Maddie cut in abruptly. "You still haven't said what it is!"

Faye gave her companion a reproachful look. "Let them tell it in their own way, Maddie."

"Do you know how many minutes of actual sleep I got last night?" the operations director countered. "Notice I didn't say hours."

There was a pause on the other end as the receiver shifted to another person. "Nice going, chief. Now they're too scared to talk to you at all." The voice was Erik's.

"Then you tell me and keep it simple," Maddie demanded.

"It's a bee. A solid gold bee maybe three or four inches big."

"A bee," Faye repeated contemplatively. "The bee was one of the most sacred symbols of the Minoan goddess."

"Where did you find it?" Maddie asked. Now that her curiosity was satisfied, her anger seemed to abate.

"That was all Griffin's doing," Erik conceded. "Better let him tell it but don't yell at him, OK?"

"I won't." Maddie actually smiled. "Scout's honor. Put him back on the line."

The scrivener cleared his throat. "Yes, well, Cassie deserves some of the credit. If she hadn't pointed me in the right direction after reading Stefan's artifact."

Faye smiled knowingly. "Synchronicity," she whispered.

Griffin was still talking. "I came to realize the connection between the pentagram and Sirius." He then regaled them with an explanation of the star's heliacal rising and the shadow cast across the calendar stones.

"Very clever of you, my dear." Faye leaned forward to address the speaker box.

"We couldn't have found the right spot without Fred," Cassie chirped up again.

"Who's Fred?" Maddie asked. "Is he one of ours? Do I have to cover his expenses too?"

"He works for Aydin Ozgur, the Anatolian trove keeper," the pythia explained. "We sort of borrowed him to guide us up the mountain."

"Is he there with you?" Faye asked.

"He's right here." The scraping sound indicated that Cassie was passing the receiver to someone else. There was a long silence. In the background, they could hear her urging Fred on. "Say something! Don't be shy."

"H...hello?" A hesitant voice emerged.

"It seems we owe you a debt of gratitude." Faye addressed him. "Without your help, our hapless trio might still be searching in vain."

A brief pause. Fred swallowed hard. "Am I addressing the memory guardian?" he asked in a timid voice.

Faye smiled encouragingly even though he couldn't see it. "My dear young man, there's no need to stand on ceremony. My name is Faye, and you have my sincere thanks for the part you played in this retrieval."

"Y... y... you're w... w... welcome." Fred stammered. Apparently, the glare of the spotlight was too bright for his eyes because the receiver was being passed on to someone else. This time it was Griffin's voice which emerged.

"I'm afraid we don't have much time to rest on our laurels," he cautioned.

"Damn straight you don't," Maddie commented. "Last I heard, Daniel and Hunt were getting ready to move on to Istanbul."

There was an expressive sigh before Griffin spoke again. "Then it's as I feared. We may only have days to make the substitution."

"What do you need from us, dear?' Faye asked.

"We have to get an exact copy of the artifact made. It will have to match down to the last detail, and then we'll need to bury it in the box where we found the original. If we're very lucky, the Nephilim won't realize it's a fake.

If we're even luckier, we'll be out of the country before they stumble across it at all."

"That's gonna take some doing," Maddie muttered, half to herself.

"I don't get it." The voice was Cassie's, and she seemed to be carrying on a conversation offline with Griffin. "If you think those symbols on the bee are the clues to the next relic, why not just change some of them to throw the Nephilim off the trail."

The two at headquarters could now hear Griffin's muffled voice answering Cassie. "Because we actually want them to find the trail of breadcrumbs we're leaving for them. It's far riskier to give them false information that will misdirect them. It might cause them to cast a wider net. Might, in fact, lead them straight to the Arkana."

"Oh," the pythia replied simply. "I didn't think of that." Another pause and then Cassie spoke again. "But you've got to admit giving them accurate intel might mean that they get to the second artifact before we do."

"Then we'll just have to make damn sure that doesn't happen." The terse voice was Erik's.

Griffin took control of the receiver once more and spoke directly to Faye and Maddie. "Can you locate someone at the Anatolian trove who has the necessary metal-working skills? We won't have time to fly someone into the country from the Central Catalog."

"Don't worry, dear. Maddie and I will make arrangements immediately to get you the assistance you need."

After another round of congratulations, the call was terminated.

The two women at headquarters looked at one another in silence for several seconds.

Maddie raised her eyebrows. "Tick tock," she said archly.

"Tick tock indeed," echoed Faye pensively.

Chapter 30—Unmentionables

ZACH PROWLED THE HOUSE moodily for at least half an hour after his Gamma and her early morning visitor left. At that point, his stomach began to rumble, so he made himself some breakfast. He ate a bowl of cereal distractedly while he mulled a thought over in his mind.

Something was off. Of that much he was sure. The crazy lady with the frizzy hair was a smoker. He could smell cigarettes on her clothes. He doubted she could manage one lap around the block if her life depended on it. He didn't buy the idea that she'd been out for an early morning run. The story didn't wash. Then there was the first time he'd met her. Gamma said she'd come over to borrow a cup of sugar. For what? A neighborhood watch birthday cake?

He finished his cereal and rinsed the bowl in the sink. Then he wandered into the living room and threw himself down on the couch, still grappling with his mental dilemma. Absently, he picked up the remote and flipped on the TV. Basic cable! Nothing worth watching. Nothing to distract him from the idea that kept nagging away at him. He knew he didn't believe the story they'd told him, but he wasn't quite ready to take the next step. Was he really going to do this? Search through his own Gamma's stuff? Looking for what? A secret decoder ring? A sliding panel in one of the walls?

He knew nothing was going to make his suspicions go away. Nothing short of actually ransacking the house and finding that everything was absolutely normal. But there were things about Gamma that had never really been normal in the first place. Like the fact that she never seemed to look any older. Sure, she was ancient. But she'd looked that way when he was five. In the past ten years, he couldn't remember one more gray hair. Not one more wrinkle than she'd had when he was a toddler. Did people actually age slower once they got to be as old as she was? He didn't know.

And why was it his own parents didn't know how many "greats" came before grandma? Somebody on the family tree must remember. Nobody seemed at all curious about it. His parents, and their parents before them always referred to her simply as "Granny Faye." Why didn't anybody else seem to know how old she actually was? His whole family ought to be featured in Ripley's as the least inquisitive people on the planet. Absolutely unable to wonder or speculate about anything—except maybe how far you could push the expiration date on a carton of milk in the refrigerator.

He sprang up from the couch. He'd reached a decision. His parents might not be curious, but he sure was. He headed for the kitchen. He really didn't expect to find anything unusual there, but he had to take it in stages. He'd leave the upstairs for last because if she was hiding anything that was probably the place where he would find it. He almost didn't want to. In fact, he wanted to be proven wrong. Little old ladies were supposed to be harmless. They were supposed to live for their grandchildren and not have any other thought in their heads but coddling and spoiling the younger generation. He paused in the kitchen doorway. For the first time, it struck him how selfish that idea was. Why should anybody be expected to live for somebody else's convenience? When she was younger, when she was still Faye and not Granny Faye, what had she wanted for herself? He shrugged at the impossibility of guessing the answer. Maybe someday he'd ask her if she'd ever had any dreams of becoming a pirate captain. He grinned at the idea. She would love the craziness of it. She was that awesome.

He walked across the kitchen to the pantry. Gingerly opening the door, he started moving boxes and packages of cake mix aside, looking for something concealed at the back of the shelves. No luck. Everything was utterly normal though someday he was going to have to have a serious talk with her about refined carbs and what that did to a person's insides.

He moved on to the kitchen cabinets lining the walls. Nothing concealed in the upper shelves, nothing in the lower ones either. One of the drawers was locked though. He flashed on the moment two days earlier when she'd confiscated his cell phone and locked it in that drawer. She'd also thrown two cell phones of her own in there at the same time. What did she need two cell phones for? Maybe the second phone was a hotline for something? He almost laughed out loud at that idea. Yeah right. She'd be the first one contacted in case of a missile strike. Maybe he had too much imagination after all.

He shrugged and moved on to the dining room. China, crystal, crocheted table cloths. It was the epitome of little old lady land. So was the living room. He anxiously glanced at the grandfather clock in the hall. He'd been searching for about half an hour already. He didn't know how much longer she'd be gone or if he'd have the chance to get to the bottom of it all. He eyed the stairway with dread. There was no point in putting it off. He had to search the upstairs.

He trudged up the steps, turning aside at the first door on the right. It was a bedroom that Gamma had converted into a work space. There was a sewing machine, lots of fabric in heaps on the floor. There was also a roll top desk by the window. He thought it might contain important documents. He rummaged through every scrap of paper the desk contained, but there wasn't anything unusual. Just electric bills, phone bills. Business cards from eye doctors and chiropractors. He nervously peeked out the window and down at the street. He saw a few commuters leaving for the train station, but that was all.

He exited the workroom and looked down the rest of the hall. His room was at the far end, but he decided he would skip it. If she had anything to hide, she wouldn't have given him the one room in the house where she had concealed something. No, there was really only one logical place where she might hide something out of the ordinary. Her bedroom.

He sighed and moved toward the closed door across from where he stood. He turned the knob and furtively peered around the corner of the door. He laughed at his own hesitation. "Dude, get a grip!" he told himself. It wasn't like the place was going to be booby-trapped. He stepped inside. Morning sunlight flooded through the window. In spite of her hurried departure, she had made the bed neatly. The chenille bedspread didn't have a single rumple or a crease. You could have bounced a dime off it.

Something was wrong, said the little voice in his head. He stood still in the middle of the room, just absorbing the atmosphere for a few minutes. At first, he couldn't pinpoint what was bothering him, but the feeling had been growing ever since he finished searching the living room. Maybe it wasn't so much about what was in this room as what wasn't in it. He looked at the large mirror hanging over the double dresser. Didn't little old ladies love to tuck pictures of their grandkids into the sides of their mirrors? Didn't they love to plaster the walls of their houses with photos of drooling babies? Wasn't that, in fact, the trademark of grandmas everywhere? So, where were they?

Zach thought back to all the rooms he'd searched. There wasn't a single photo album, scrapbook or portrait anywhere. This room, this whole house, was almost impersonal. No mementos of her past. Didn't grannies all live in the past? Especially one as ancient as Gamma? What possible future could she have? It was all past for her but where was it?

He thought he might be on to something. Maybe he wasn't simply crazy or insanely suspicious. Emboldened by the idea, he felt ready to tackle the hardest part of this search. Her clothes. At least that was personal. He checked the closet first. Nothing but flowery house dresses which was practically Gamma's daily uniform. No secret panel in the closet wall. He moved on to the dresser. He'd deliberately left that for last. First, he glanced out the window again. He had to wrap this up soon because if she walked in now, he really couldn't explain what he was doing in here. He started with the bottom drawers. Lots of sweaters. Did she even own a pair of slacks? He doubted it. Probably before her time. He finally came to the top dresser drawer. The one he dreaded. Her "drawers" drawer. He turned his head aside, as he slid it open. The idea of old lady undies creeped him out. A wry thought occurred to him. His grandfather used to call them foundation garments. Maybe that would make it easier. Not panties and bras—foundation garments—like something you'd use to build a skyscraper. Still, even with the new terminology, the thought of rooting around inside the drawer made him feel like a real pervert. Stories he'd seen in the news about weirdos who liked to cross-dress flashed through his mind. He suppressed them.

He kept his eyes half shut as his fingers worked their way from the front of the drawer to the back. His eyes flew wide open when his hands touched something tucked into the very back corner of the drawer. It was a piece of paper, creased up and folded many times.

He drew it out carefully, replacing all the foundation garments he'd disturbed in his search. Then he sat down in the middle of the carpet and unfolded the sheet of paper. It was a letter. He began to read:

My Dear Little Sis,

I'm sitting here writing this and hoping that you never have to read it. The only reason you would come across this letter is if I'm gone. Maybe the danger will pass, and I can destroy this. Maybe not.

There are times when my work can be risky. This is one of those times. I've come across a find that has immense value to the people I work with, but it looks like somebody else wants this find too. Somebody who would be willing to kill for it. For the past week, I've gotten the feeling I'm being followed. It might be my imagination. In case it isn't and in case something happens to me, I want you to call the number I wrote on the back of this sheet. Ask to speak to Faye. Give her the packet. She can explain everything.

There's so much I want to say, but there isn't enough time, and maybe it only comes down to this. I love you and everything I did, even when you didn't understand it, was to keep you safe. No matter what you might have thought, I was always looking out for you.

Love,

Sybil

Zach looked up from the sheet. He could feel the blood draining out of his face. That must be what shock felt like. A cold, numb sensation. He stared back down at the page. One line leaped out at him. "Ask to speak to Faye. She can explain everything." He didn't know who the letter had been written to but whoever it was had been directed to find Faye. She supposedly could explain everything. Everything about this so-called find that somebody might have gotten killed over. His Gamma could explain a thing like that?

He laughed to himself bitterly as a new thought struck him. He'd often said, "Gamma, you're something else." For the first time, he realized the irony of that simple phrase. She really was something else. Something other than a grandmother. Something other than a harmless little old lady. But what?

He folded the letter and returned it to its hiding place at the back of the dresser drawer. He needed time to process all of this. Time to let it sink in.

N. S. WIKARSKI

He wasn't going to confront her right away. First, he needed to think. Then he would ask. He was already dead certain he wasn't going to like the answer.

Chapter 31—A Little Night Music

THE DRIVER SLAPPED on the brakes and jerked the steering wheel sideways. Two of the car's tires hopped the curb as he took a sharp corner. Daniel slid across the slippery back seat and slammed into Hunt's shoulder. The latter shrugged him off with ill-disguised contempt.

The driver yelled curses out the window in Turkish at a passing vehicle which he had nearly sideswiped.

Daniel was grateful he didn't understand what was said but was sure it somehow involved the unnatural use of a camel. "Brother Ilhami, perhaps we should slow down," he suggested tentatively.

"No, no!" The driver was vehement. "Is OK. Is all OK. We be there soon!"

He maneuvered the subcompact through the labyrinthine streets of a shabby Istanbul neighborhood. Loud music blared from the car's stereo. Daniel had never heard its like before. A quavering wail with heavy brass accompaniment. It sounded like nothing so much as a cat being stuffed inside a tuba. When he thought his eardrums could stand the assault no more, the racket ceased. The driver switched off the radio, eased into a very tight parking space, and turned off the engine. Daniel's ears continued to ring.

"We are here," the driver announced happily. He slid his bulky form out from under the steering column and bustled around to the back of the car to unload suitcases from the trunk.

Hunt got out and stretched his limbs. His eyes traveled up the hilly cobblestone street. Laundry was strung overhead from one building to the next. Women in headscarves called out of open windows to children playing ball below. "Nice," he said sarcastically. "It's got what you call local color."

Daniel watched as the driver dragged their luggage toward the dark entry of a three-flight walk-up. There was an iron grille over the door. All the street-level windows were covered by metal bars as well.

"We're staying here?" he asked in disbelief.

"Is OK!" the driver protested. "Is all OK! You follow."

Daniel and Hunt exchanged a puzzled look.

The mercenary shrugged philosophically. "Better do what the man says."

The stairs were ancient, rickety and dark. As they trailed their guide ever upward, Daniel could detect the odors of highly spiced food emanating from several apartments along the way. The clash of aromas made him slightly nauseous.

On the third-floor landing, the driver paused to catch his breath. "We go inside here," he panted, fitting a key into the door at the top of the stairs.

He ushered them proudly into a studio apartment with a small galley kitchen, a pullout sleeper couch and an open balcony overlooking the street. Immediately upon entering, the driver turned on the stereo which seemed to contain another cat in a tuba only this time both were encased in a bass drum. The speakers took up an entire corner of the room.

Daniel's head began to pound in time to the music. "Brother Ilhami!" He had to shout to get the man's attention. "Would you mind turning down the music?"

Their host looked at him blankly for a second as if the concept was entirely alien to his experience. "What you say?"

"The music!" Daniel shouted a little louder. "I'm sorry. I have a headache."

The Turk finally nodded and smiled. "You wait. I fix." He unceremoniously pulled the plug to the stereo system out of the wall. "Is better, yes?" he asked hopefully.

"Yes," Daniel exhaled thankfully. "Much better. Thank you."

Hunt stood watching the interaction, his hands in his jacket pockets and an amused grin on his face. "You sure do love your music, Brother Hammy," he observed.

"In Turkey, we say music is life!" the man replied.

"I expect it's gonna be the death of Brother Dan'l here." Hunt smirked. "Ain't that so, Brother Dan'l?"

The scion rubbed his brow bone and gave no answer.

"Here. You sleep here." Ilhami gestured to the foldout couch.

"Like fun, I'm bunkin' with you," Leroy muttered to Daniel under his breath. "We'll flip for it."

"You may have the couch, Mr. Hunt," Daniel answered wearily. "I'll take the floor."

"Well, all right then." The mercenary nodded his approval. "This is shapin' up better than I expected."

"You like something to drink?" Ilhami asked, looking from one face to another.

"That all depends," Hunt replied warily. "You got anything with a kick to it?"

The Turk smiled broadly. "Oh yes, I have raki. Very good. First rate."

The mercenary's face lit up. "Now you're talkin'. I do believe I'll have me a sip."

Daniel recognized the name of the beverage because Hunt had sampled some of Turkey's national drink on the plane on the way over. According to him, it tasted much like the ouzo to which he'd become addicted when they were in Greece.

Brother Ilhami looked quizzically at Daniel. "You like some too?"

The scion shook his head. The motion made his temples throb. "Nothing for me, thank you."

Their host bustled into the kitchenette.

Hunt leaned closer and asked in a whisper, "You sure he's one of yours?"

Daniel was as baffled as his companion. Unlike every other member of the Nephilim that the scion had ever known, Ilhami didn't wear the black suit and white shirt of the order. He was dressed in blue jeans and a striped polo shirt that bulged over his considerable paunch. While some order members wore beards, Ilhami sported a bushy black moustache and two days' worth of razor stubble. His entire appearance was scruffy and unkempt. When the man first approached Daniel at the airport, he couldn't believe the rotund little Turk was an emissary of the brotherhood.

The scion replied to Hunt's question in a low voice. "I was told he was a recent convert. The Nephilim have had difficulty establishing a presence in this country because of the large Muslim population. The nearest compound is in Armenia. It's obvious to me that no one in authority is nearby to regulate this man's behavior."

"Gone native, has he? Well, this ought to be interestin'." Hunt was all smiles as Ilhami returned with two glasses half full of a milky white substance.

Daniel noticed the second glass which he assumed was for Ilhami. "You also drink spirits?" he asked, slightly askance.

Their guide looked at him uncomprehendingly. "No spirits. Just raki. I like raki. Is good."

Hunt chuckled and slapped him on the back. "Well, well, Brother Hammy. I never thought I'd live to say this about any of you Nephilim, but I'm takin' a shine to you."

"We sit outside," Ilhami suggested. "Is hot in here."

This was one idea which Daniel supported enthusiastically. The tiny apartment was stifling on this summer evening, and the ceiling fan did little more than waft hot air into their faces. The French doors that opened onto the balcony offered the only relief.

They moved out into the open air and sat on folding chairs. There was barely enough room for the three of them on the tiny ledge that hung suspended above the sidewalk. Hunt's knees bumped against the wrought-iron railing.

The activity in the street below had subsided by now. The sun had set, and there wasn't a single parking space left. Cars were packed end to end as tight as sardines in a tin. Daniel concluded that it must be supper time since all the running children and shouting parents had withdrawn inside. The open windows in every tenement, however, effectively blurred the distinction between indoors and outdoors. Even though the music in Ilhami's apartment had been silenced, Daniel could hear the shrill wailing and head-pounding percussion of other stereos coming at him from several points in the neighborhood. Then there were the voices raised over dinner tables everywhere. Excited chattering female voices, fussy crying children. Authoritative male voices shouting to make themselves heard over the din. So many lives unconsciously exposed to his scrutiny. Nobody here seemed to care about privacy very much. They all seemed to revel in the communal racket.

Daniel thought of dinner time back home at the compound. A bell summoned everyone to assemble in an orderly fashion, and they all ate in a subdued manner. Conversations, such as they were, would be conducted in whispers. After curfew, the corridors were vacant and silent. To Daniel, Istanbul seemed like a roaring beast that never slept. He contemplated it with a mixture of fascination and fear. This city of the Fallen was disorderly and loud and teeming with life. The Nephilim compound, on the other hand, exhibited the perfect stillness of death.

"So how come you joined up with the Nephilim, Brother Hammy?"

Daniel cut his contemplation short when he realized Hunt was quizzing Ilhami about his origins.

The plump Turk took another swig from his tumbler before replying. "A man come to my door. He say I belong with Nephilim. He promise me many wives."

"Oh ho," Leroy said knowingly. "You like havin' lots of female companionship, do you?"

Ilhami nodded vigorously. "Koran say four." The Turk held up the requisite number of digits for emphasis. "No more." He frowned. "I no like."

Hunt finished the contents of his glass and held it out for a refill.

Ilhami wordlessly took the glass back to the kitchen along with his own.

When he returned with two brimming tumblers, he picked up the thread of the conversation. "Is like this raki. Koran say no, Ilhami, you no drink. But Nephilim man, he say OK. So I go with him."

Hunt chuckled. Directing his next comment to the scion, he said, "That's some recruiter you got in these parts, Brother Dan'l."

Daniel knew his face registered shock, but he tried to cover it. "I think perhaps something may have gotten lost in translation."

Brother Ilhami looked from one to the other suspiciously. "You say is no good to drink?"

Realizing that Ilhami was their lone contact in this part of Turkey, Daniel tried to repair the damage as quickly as possible. "No, not at all. Uh... don't worry about it. It isn't a problem."

"Boy, you slapped on the brakes so fast, I'm a mite surprised you didn't give yourself whiplash," Hunt murmured dryly.

"What you say?" Ilhami squinted at the mercenary.

Hunt patted him on the back. "Don't you worry your head over it, Brother Hammy. We got bigger fish to fry. Right, Brother Dan'l?"

He turned pointedly to the scion who stammered, "Uh... uh... yes. A... hem. Quite right."

The two men looked at Daniel expectantly. He sat up and focused on the matter at hand. "Yes, well, I think we need to discuss our strategy. I would like to visit any mosques, churches or shrines on the eastern side of Mount Ida. Are you familiar with the area?"

The question was directed at the Turk who gazed back at him with a puzzled expression.

Daniel clarified. "The mountain you call Kazdagi. Do you know it?"

At the mention of the name, Ilhami's face brightened. "Oh, yes. I know."

"Are you familiar with the terrain on the eastern side? The side where the sun rises?"

"Yes, yes. I show you. All churches. All mosques. I drive you there. I be very good guide. First rate."

"If y'all are drivin' like you did today, Brother Hammy," Hunt added, "I'd be much obliged if you'd pack me a couple bottles of raki to take along on the trip."

"And perhaps some aspirin?" Daniel added weakly, rubbing his forehead.

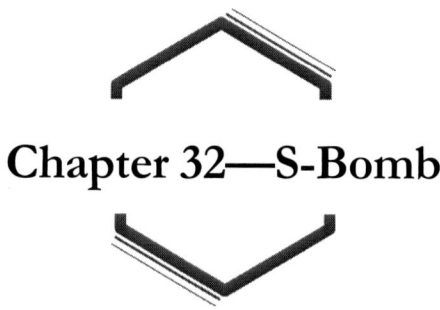

Chapter 32—S-Bomb

IT HAD BEEN A HECTIC week. Faye parked her station wagon in the driveway and got out. She'd had to make several trips to the vault to arrange matters for the team in Turkey. Many of those tasks might have been accomplished at home by phone if not for her house guest. Much as she enjoyed visits from Zachary, she felt some measure of relief at the thought that he would be leaving in a few days. His departure would make matters simpler in case any last-minute glitches occurred during the substitution of the false artifact.

She let herself into the house, but everything was silent. "Zach?" she called out tentatively. No answer.

She found him outside in the vegetable garden pulling weeds. She'd kept him busy with outdoor chores during his entire stay. That was partly because her yard needed tending and partly to tire him out enough to prevent him from getting into trouble. So far, the strategy seemed to have worked. By the end of each day, he was too exhausted to be inquisitive. In fact, he hadn't even asked her about the neighborhood watch business at all. Faye chalked it up to the short attention span of most teenagers.

"Hello, my dear," she greeted him with a smile. "I see you're hard at work. Can I fix you a snack?"

He stopped weeding and sat back on his heels, narrowing his eyes against the glare of the sun as he looked up at her. "I'd rather talk than eat if it's all the same to you."

"About what, dear?" she murmured absently, still thinking about her team overseas.

His voice was tense. "Who's Sybil?"

There it was. The moment she'd been dreading ever since he'd arrived. On some level, she'd rather expected it. It was bound to have happened sooner or later, and she'd always thought he might be the one.

"Sybil who?" she countered weakly, trying to buy time. His abrupt question had knocked her off balance, and she needed to sit down. Faye tottered over to a stone bench in front of her oldest rugosa.

Zach followed and sat down beside her, sliding to the far end of the bench as he did so. "I found a letter…" he trailed off and his eyes darted away.

"Found?" she inquired softly.

"OK, I didn't exactly 'find' it," he admitted. His fingers made air quotes around the word "find." She noticed how dirty his fingernails were from digging in the earth. He glanced back at her again. "I was snooping, alright? I know I had no business going through your things, but there's a lot of strange stuff going on around here, and I needed some answers."

"You might have just asked."

"Like you'd tell me," Zachary snorted. "I had to have some proof first that I wasn't crazy or paranoid."

"So, you read the letter?"

"Yeah, I read it, and it changed everything." He paused and sat silent for a full minute, distractedly picking dirt from under his fingernails. "Who are you?" he finally asked.

"You know me, Zach."

"I thought I did, but you've got a lot of layers. You're like a lasagna."

They both laughed. It seemed to break the tension.

"That may be an apt analogy," Faye agreed. "You're already familiar with the cheese topping. That layer would be your Gamma."

He grinned. "Cheesy, huh?"

Her smile faded. "I'm afraid the other layers are hidden for a reason."

He sat forward and stared at her intently. "Why don't you trust me?"

The old woman sighed. "Because, my dear boy, you're fifteen."

"I'm almost sixteen," he countered.

"You are still very young."

"Fine!" He folded his arms defiantly across his chest. "Just when will I be old enough to be let in on the secret?"

She gave him a searching look. "It isn't a single secret, Zach. It's an entire world of secrets. You asked me who Sybil was and I'll tell you this much. She's the tip of an iceberg. A small chunk of a much larger mass that remains invisible to the casual observer. To tell you any more about her would put other people's lives at risk. I can't confide too much information in you too soon."

He brightened as a new thought struck him. "You didn't say never. That means someday you'll tell me?"

She smoothed the creases in her skirt and turned the question over in her mind before replying. "I rather think I will."

"Yes!" Zach punched the air triumphantly.

Faye fixed him with a bright stare. "I wonder if you appreciate your singular position, Zachary."

That brought him up short. He peered at her uncertainly. "What do you mean, Gamma?"

"Nobody else in the family has ever shown the slightest interest in the secret layers of my life."

He registered surprise. "Really? Nobody?"

She shook her head. "Absolutely nobody."

"But how's that even possible?" he cried. "I mean somebody had to ask questions. Sometime."

She raised an eyebrow. "Would you consider curiosity to be a dominant trait in your family?"

He laughed ruefully. "Not hardly. I come from a long line of zombies."

"That lack of inquisitiveness goes back much farther than you imagine," she observed. "I suppose it began with my dear departed husband. He was the salt of the earth. Unfailingly kind but rooted as firmly in the ground as an oak tree. Not the least bit curious about anything unusual. He preferred to see what was directly in front of him and no more. At the time, his inattentiveness suited my purposes quite well. But after he was gone I thought perhaps someone in the family might show some curiosity. Might have the necessary spark to take a leap into the unknown. It became a test of sorts. I presented the opportunity for generation after generation to ask the right questions, but nobody ever did. Until you. You're really quite distinctive in the bloodline, Zach. An eccentric. A rebel. Inquisitive enough to want to get to the bottom of things. Most people sleepwalk through their lives. It takes an eccentric to see the world a little differently. It takes a rebel to question the facile explanations that authority figures so often give. In short, it takes someone like you. The more I think about it, the more I believe you'll be an asset to our organization. Yes indeed. You'll make a fine tyro."

"Huh?" His face was a blank.

Her mind was made up. She already began planning. "We'll go at it in stages. When I feel you're ready, your training will begin."

"Training? Tyro?" he echoed. "What am I getting myself into?"

"A whole new way of looking at the world. You said you wanted your life to make a difference, didn't you?"

"Yeah, but it all sounds kind of scary." His voice held a worried note.

"It's no use developing cold feet now, young man." She laughed. "You were in such a fret to get some answers. As the saying goes, 'Be careful what you wish for.'"

Chapter 33—Mercenary Considerations

ORVIS AKA CHOPPER BOWDEEN was trying to suppress a yawn as he sat on a dais behind the bearded fossil at the podium. He was waiting to be introduced to the fifty greenhorns sitting in the audience gawking up at him. Every last one of them was wearing a black suit and tie with a white shirt. Their mouths were all gaping open in the same surprised O. They looked like a school of guppies.

Bowdeen knew the reason for their wonder. They'd probably never seen anybody like him in their lives before. He was career paramilitary in a room full of nerdy little bible-thumpers. Maybe he scared them a bit. He wore his hair in a severe buzz cut and maintained his barrel-chested physique by bench pressing a few hundred pounds every day. But that wasn't what they were staring at. A deep scar that cut across the lower half of his face had lifted the right corner of his mouth into a permanent sneer. It put some people off. Given his line of work, he considered that an advantage.

He transferred his attention back to the one who called himself Father Abraham. The old coot sure knew how to give a stemwinder. He'd been at it for over fifteen minutes already. God's will, blah-blah. Everlasting glory, blah-de-blah-blah. Try as he might, Chopper couldn't keep his thoughts from drifting off-topic. This gig wasn't exactly what he had in mind when he came back to the states. He'd just finished a stint with a security operation in Iraq and decided to pick up a side job when old Abe contacted him. Leroy Hunt was behind the referral.

He and Leroy went way back. Two Bama boys who joined the service during the first Gulf War. Both found they had a natural talent for the military and liked the life. Chopper couldn't remember exactly when Leroy started dressing up like a matinee cowboy and talking like Slim Pickens, but he didn't really care either. Hunt always completed a mission with no foul-ups, and that was all that mattered.

Unfortunately, in their last conversation, Hunt had breezed over the details about who these Nephilim characters were. As a rule, Bowdeen tried to steer clear of religious types. He'd already gotten his fill of fanatics in the Middle East. They tended to make war a messy business when it ought to be cut and dried. He was a mercenary. He was willing to take a bullet for the right price, unlike those camel jockeys who were just itching to die for Allah to score points in heaven. He couldn't beat their price no matter how steeply he cut his own rates. This Nephilim bunch didn't seem all that different from their towel-headed brethren in the desert. Especially once Chopper forced himself to concentrate on what Abe was telling them.

The old man had worked them up into a fine lather by now. He was on a roll. "My sons, you are God's chosen, destined to play a vital role in the Lord's plan for this earth. He has commanded the Nephilim to lead the world out of darkness and you, my sons, will be at the forefront of that march. You are about to be trained in the skills of combat that you may become mighty soldiers of the Lord. You will take your place in glory alongside the great heroes of the past. With Michael who drove Adam and Eve from Eden with a flaming sword. With Joshua who destroyed the walls of Jericho. With King David who crushed Goliath in the Lord's name. Just as all these valiant ones live on in our memory so shall you, my sons. Your names shall endure forever, and your reward shall be great in the kingdom of heaven."

It was classic religious cliché. Pump up a bunch of losers with low self-esteem by telling them how important they are to the cause. How much glory they're going to achieve by becoming cannon fodder. Chopper had heard it a thousand times before, but as he scanned the faces before him, he could see them drinking it all in. Their eyes had the fiery, dazed look of the true believer. He didn't dismiss it all as holy smoke. Belief was a powerful thing. Sometimes Chopper thought of it as the ultimate weapon. If you could get a man to believe in something deeply enough, he'd be willing to commit any atrocity in its name.

Chopper sensed that the endless preamble was winding to a close. He stood up to take the podium and give these kids a lecture on basic combat skills. After that would come weeks of weapons training. Teaching somebody to fire a gun assumed the existence of a target. He wasn't sure who these Nephilim boys were supposed to be aiming at. He brushed the notion away. So what? He was a gun for hire. He'd never before questioned who the target was as long as he got paid. And he was being paid handsomely for this gig. What the hell did it matter who they wanted to destroy? As he stepped over to the microphone, an uneasy sensation in his gut told him that someday he might regret not asking that question.

Chapter 34—Sleight Change of Plan

CASSIE STOOD UP AND dusted off her hands. "Phew, that's a relief." She watched as Erik and Griffin moved the lily stone back into position.

"Any word on where our Nephilim buddies are at?" Fred asked, arranging smaller rocks around the perimeter to make their excavation less obvious.

"Last Maddie could find out, they were searching shrines on the eastern side of the mountain," Erik replied. He squinted across the plateau toward the mountain range in the distance. "I'd say that means close. They could get here any time now."

"Then it's a good thing we got the fake artifact in place first," Cassie observed.

Griffin consulted his wrist watch. "I know it isn't even midday, but I'd suggest we clear off. It could be rather awkward if we were to encounter them while making our exit."

"Got that right." Erik leaped to his feet. "The bait's in place. We don't need to wait for the rats to take it. Maddie is still monitoring Hunt's phone calls to Metcalf. We'll know the minute they dig it up."

The four teammates gathered their equipment and hiked the half mile back to the Jeep. They had just finished stowing their gear when Cassie picked up the jacket she had tossed across the hood. She reached into one of the pockets and gasped. "Oh no!"

The men all turned to stare at her.

"What is it?" Griffin asked.

"My room key! It must have fallen out of my pocket when I took my jacket off earlier."

"Your room key?" Griffin repeated. "Why on earth didn't you turn it in at the front desk?"

"I forgot. OK? I was running late this morning, and there was nobody at the desk anyway." She searched all her pockets again. "I thought I heard a clinking sound when I picked my jacket up off the ground. "Jeez! That means the key is sitting right out there in the open. Practically right next to the lily stone."

"That key has the hotel name and room number on it." Erik scowled. "If Hunt finds it and decides to check out who else was nosing around the megaliths, that key would lead him straight to us."

"Maybe he'd think it was just dropped there by a careless tourist." Fred laughed nervously.

"You want to take that chance?" Erik asked pointedly.

"I have to go back." Cassie was already jogging up the trail.

Her companions scrambled to catch up with her.

They trotted briskly up the path through the pines and climbed the rise toward the plateau when something stopped them dead in their tracks. The sight that greeted them was inconceivable. They'd been prepared to dodge the Nephilim, but this was an entirely different matter.

"Holy crap!" Cassie exclaimed.

"What are they doing?" Griffin asked in wonder.

"Guys, get down!" Erik commanded.

The four flattened themselves against the ground and peered over the rim of the hill toward the plateau where the megaliths stood. A trio of men were circling the place where the artifact was hidden. They appeared to be Turkish. One wore traditional attire—wool trousers, cotton shirt with rolled up sleeves, an open vest and a visored cap. The other two were younger, dressed in jeans and camp shirts. All three sported the typical bushy moustache of the region. The man with the cap stooped down to pick up an object that flashed in the sun.

"Dammit! That's my key!" Cassie whispered.

The trio seemed to be conferring about something. Then all of them bent down and began to dig around the base of the lily rock.

"How did they know something was there?" Fred wondered.

"They must have been watching us," Griffin replied. "They may have been here the whole time we were burying the false relic. Just waiting for us to leave."

Cassie inched closer to the top of the ridge to get a better look. "Who do you think those guys are?"

"Hunters maybe," Erik speculated. "One of them has a rifle. It's over there on the ground."

"They might be poachers looking for some illegal game," Griffin added. "Or worse. They could be trading in black market antiquities."

Cassie turned to Erik. "Where's that pistol you carry? It would come in pretty handy right about now."

"It's in the Jeep with the rest of the gear. I had it with me until you went running off after your key and we all ran after you."

"That's twice this has happened." The pythia glared at him. "You know what I'm going to buy you for Christmas? A holster! A freaking holster so the next time the bad guys have guns, you'll actually have one too!"

Erik was about to offer a biting retort when Griffin held up his hand. "Shhhh! Look!"

Their whispers ceased. The four of them watched in consternation as the men below slid the lily stone aside. It took only a moment for them to locate the alabaster urn and dump out its contents. They laughed and patted one another on the back, passing the golden object from hand to hand.

"Bloody hell!" Griffin exclaimed.

"We have to get it back," Erik growled.

"But it's a fake," Cassie objected.

"They don't know that," the security coordinator countered. "Fake or not, it's solid gold, and that makes it valuable to them. Besides, we don't have time to get another copy made and bury it before the Nephilim get here. For all we know those guys down below would dig that one up too. No, we need to make sure they stay the hell away from here."

"Just how do you propose to do that?" the pythia demanded.

"I don't know yet." Erik raised himself to a crouching position. "Right now, we need to move back into the woods. They're getting ready to leave. We have to follow them."

As soundlessly as possible, the Arkana team backed away from the rise and ran for the cover of the pines. They waited out of sight until they saw the Turks enter the woods by another path.

"Let's hope they don't have a car," Erik muttered.

"I didn't hear the sound of a motor the whole time we were up there," Fred observed.

"Then that means they must live nearby," Cassie speculated.

"I don't know whether that's a good thing or a bad one." Griffin sounded troubled. "If they live nearby in one of the villages, that may mean they have allies."

"Guess we'll see," Erik said curtly. "Now everybody shut up, or they'll hear us."

The Arkana team advanced stealthily through the woods. Luckily, the three men were talking loud enough to cover any stray noise. They spoke excitedly in Turkish, joking and laughing with each other. They were clearly elated by their windfall.

Their pursuers quickened their pace to close the gap when the trio went into a ravine that was hidden by undergrowth. Cassie came around the bend first. She almost yelped in surprise when she saw the men had stopped and were standing directly below them. She backed up. Unfortunately, Griffin chose that moment to trip over a tree root and stumble into her. The pythia lost her balance and fell forward. She tumbled down the hillside directly into the path of the relic thieves. The scrivener was about to lunge after her when Erik pulled him back.

"No! Wait!" he hissed. "We need a tactical advantage. You rush in now, and you'll get her killed for sure."

Cassie landed on her backside with a thud.

The three astonished men stared at her for a moment. Then the one with the rifle pointed it at her face. He gave commands in Turkish and gestured with the barrel of the gun for her to get up.

She raised her hands warily above her head and stood up. "Ooops!" she said.

Chapter 35—Lyrical Interlude

DANIEL DREW OUT A HANDKERCHIEF to mop his forehead. He felt exhausted from fighting the heat and the altitude. They'd been searching for days, working their way methodically through the villages that dotted the eastern slope of Mount Ida. Climbing ever higher. Mosques and churches and shrines. They'd covered every inch of the interior and exterior facade of each structure.

Hunt was clearly growing tired of the quest though he hadn't lifted a finger to help. Today his principal occupation had been to locate a fresh supply of raki once he'd emptied the bottle that Ilhami had brought along in the car.

Daniel walked up to the exterior of yet another obscure shrine which their guide had selected to show them.

"Here, you come inside here, please!" Ilhami beckoned to the scion insistently.

Hunt trailed absently in their wake. Now well into his second bottle of liquor, his gait had become a trifle unsteady.

Daniel wasn't impressed by the structure that confronted him. A small round building, windowless with a single arched doorway that stood open to the elements. Erected of rustic grey stone and mortar, it seemed to have sprung from the rocky terrain underfoot.

"This is church of Aiya Anastasia," Ilhami informed them. "Very old. Nobody come here now."

The Turk stepped aside to allow Daniel to pass. Daniel knew that Aiya meant something like "saint" in Turkish. He walked into the cool, dim interior. There was nothing to see. One stuccoed room with a flaking, faded fresco of what appeared to be an angel. In front of the fresco stood an iron votive stand with several dozen glass candle holders. No one had come here to pray for a very long time. He could tell by the thick layer of dust that coated the tops of the burned-out candles.

The scion lit his flashlight to inspect the ceiling and walls. As he expected, there was nothing to be seen. No lily symbol that would guide him to the artifact his father so desperately wanted him to find. He sighed as weariness overtook him.

Stepping backwards out of the little stone church, he walked around its perimeter, followed closely by Ilhami. He looked first at the rounded roof and then at the foundation. There were chips and irregularities in the surface of the stone but nothing that seemed to be a distinct mark of any kind.

As Daniel came back around to the front of the shrine, he noticed another car climbing up the dusty trail. A young couple got out. They appeared to be in their twenties. Perhaps newlyweds on vacation. The man held a video camera.

"Hello," the woman greeted them. Her accent was American.

"Hello," Daniel replied.

Ilhami bobbed his head.

Hunt tipped his cowboy hat but said nothing.

The three men moved several yards away to allow the couple privacy as they toured the shrine. They were deeply engrossed in a guide book that gave the history of the site. The woman was reading aloud from it while the man filmed the church.

Hunt had a calculating gleam in his eye as he leaned over to whisper in Daniel's ear. "Hey, what say I get 'em to clear out in a hurry?" He opened his jacket to briefly reveal the gun resting in a holster beneath his arm.

The scion grew alarmed. "Mr. Hunt, you can't be serious!"

The mercenary shrugged. "Ain't nobody around to tell on me. This trip's been mighty dull so far. How about I stir things up a bit? Throw a scare into 'em."

Daniel gripped Hunt's wrist. "You'll do no such thing! I'm afraid I must insist."

Hunt raised his eyebrows, shaking his hand free. "You gonna insist?"

For a split second, Daniel thought the man was about to strike him.

Then the mercenary broke into a lopsided grin. "Aw shucks, can't you tell I'm just pullin' yer leg? When you gonna learn to take a joke, boy?"

Daniel only relaxed by a hairsbreadth. Hunt's face was flushed, exhilarated. There was liquor on his breath. Despite his protests, Daniel wondered if Hunt might not have been serious about terrorizing the young couple. He seemed to like to scare people. He also seemed to like to kill people when the opportunity presented. If he thought he could get away with it, Hunt might have shot the couple for sport.

Shaking off the chilling notion, Daniel said, "Mr. Hunt, why don't you sit down in the shade of that tree for a while. I won't be much longer."

Leroy gave Daniel a sour look and wandered off to take a seat on the grass. He opened his bottle again.

Ilhami tapped Daniel on the shoulder. "Back here is cemetery. You come look here."

Strewn across the green hillside were a series of headstones. Unlike the neat, orderly rows of a modern cemetery, the rocks were scattered haphazardly Many were sunken into the ground.

Hunt called out, "Brother Hammy. Y'all come on over here and set yourself down for a spell."

The guide looked questioningly at Daniel.

"Go with him," the scion suggested, secretly glad to be rid of the duo while he inspected the rest of the site.

The Turk happily ambled over to the tree in whose shade Hunt was reclining. He sat down cross-legged on the ground and took a long draught from the bottle which the mercenary held out to him.

By this time the young couple had departed. After filming the exterior of the shrine, they got back into their car and headed down the mountain.

Daniel turned upland to inspect the markings on the headstones. Even though he tried to ignore the conversation of his companions, it was impossible.

Hunt was apparently in a jovial mood fueled by too much raki and the fantasy of killing innocent tourists. He put his arm around the Turk and said, "Brother Hammy, how'd you like to learn a song?"

"I like American songs." The guide smiled amiably.

"Well, this ain't like no song you ever heard before. In fact, it's about somethin' that happened right here in your own backyard."

"Here?" Ilhami asked doubtfully.

"Yup, it happened a long time ago when you all was fightin' the Russkies. During the Crimean War."

"Crimean?" The guide repeated the word carefully. "What this means?"

"It's that little spit of land that hangs out into the north side of the Black Sea. A lot of big battles got fought there, so that's why the war got named after it. Anyhow, this here song is called 'Abdul The Bulbul Emir.'"

"Emir," Ilhami repeated. "I know this word, and Abdul is man's name."

"That's right," Hunt nodded encouragingly. "So this fella Abdul is Turkish, and he gets into a tussle with this Russian dude who steps on his toe, and they end up killin' each other."

Ilhami's face was puzzled. "They die because one man steps on toe of other?"

"It's supposed to be a funny song, see, but there's two versions of it. The clean one and the dirty one. I learned the dirty one a long time ago when I was in the army. You're gonna love it." Without further prelude, Hunt launched into the song.

Daniel paused in his search to listen. The mercenary's voice was a passable baritone. The tune was catchy until Daniel actually started to realize what the song was about. After hearing the first two stanzas, he scampered as far away from his companions as possible. The lyrics were filthy. There were many slang words which Ilhami didn't understand. Whenever the Turk seemed puzzled by a line, Hunt obligingly paused in his performance to explain its meaning in salacious detail. Even though the scion hiked to the outer boundary of the cemetery he still couldn't get out of earshot. He tried to distract himself by inspecting a particularly interesting headstone. He pored over the single cross chiseled into the rock as if it contained the entire book of Genesis and all the prophesies of the diviners besides. Daniel remained fixated on his task until he could hear Hunt's voice subside. By this time, Ilhami was rolling on the ground with laughter.

As Daniel came back down the hill, he saw the Turk sit up eagerly.

"Now you teach me. Is good song!"

The scion groaned inwardly. Ilhami's morals were already questionable without Hunt corrupting him further.

Daniel interposed himself between the two men. "It's getting late," he suggested mildly. "Perhaps we should be moving on."

"Whatsa matter, boy?" Hunt asked thickly. "Air gettin' a little too blue fer you?" He shook his bottle disappointedly, realizing it was empty.

"The day will be gone soon, Mr. Hunt. We don't want to be stranded up here after dark, do we?" Daniel turned to Ilhami. "Where should we look next?"

The Turk regarded his doubtfully. "Is all."

Daniel squinted at him. "I'm afraid I don't understand."

Ilhami shrugged expressively. "Aiya Anastasia. Last place to look on mountain."

Daniel felt the color drain from his face. "You mean there are no more?"

"Where we are is very high up mountain. No more churches above this."

The scion slumped down on the grass and buried his head in his hands. "I just need to think for a few minutes."

"Take yer time, boy." Hunt leaned back against the tree trunk and dipped his cowboy hat over his eyes.

Daniel conjured a mental image of the lecture his father would give him if he returned home empty-handed. There had to be something he had overlooked. But what? He turned to the guide. "Are you quite sure there's no place else? Think very hard."

Ilhami screwed up his eyebrows in a look of intense concentration. After several seconds of facial contortion, he gave Daniel a sheepish smile. "Is all churches. No more here."

Daniel rose with a heavy heart.

The guide added in a small voice, "Maybe we go to big rocks, yes?"

The scion whirled to stare down at him. "What big rocks?"

Ilhami was taken aback by his intensity. "Long time ago before sultans. Somebody put big rocks in circle."

"You mean a stone ring of some sort? Megaliths?"

"Just big rock circle. You want we go look there?"

"Does it face east?" Daniel asked eagerly.

Ilhami nodded doubtfully. "On same side we are. Yes. Only up high. We have to drive long time."

Daniel looked at the position of the sun overhead. "Can we get there today and still have time to drive down the mountain?"

The Turk nodded. "If we go now."

Daniel roused the dosing Hunt with the toe of his shoe. "Then we go right now!"

Chapter 36—Captivating Companions

THE TRIO OF RELIC THIEVES held Cassie at gunpoint while they conferred unintelligibly in Turkish about what to do with her.

The pythia took stock of her situation. Surprisingly, she didn't feel afraid. She flashed back briefly to the moment when Sybil had first broken the news that their parents were dead. She'd been plenty scared then. A scared, confused little kid. And when Sybil herself died, Cassie felt like a slightly older but equally scared and confused kid. Then the Arkana entered her life, and everything changed. Faye and Maddie and Erik and Griffin were her people now. She thought of them and felt a grim resolve she hadn't known she possessed. Nobody was ever going to screw with her or her people again. Not ever! She had an idea.

"Hey! Any of you guys speak English?"

They stopped chattering abruptly. The two younger men gaped at her.

"I speak little bit," the man with the cap answered. "Where your friends?"

"They aren't here," she lied. "How do you know about my friends?"

The man laughed. "We see what you do. You bury something in ground. Why you bury gold like that?"

Cassie shrugged, appearing innocent. "It was a joke. A joke we were playing on some people we know."

The man gave her a shrewd look. "We play different kind of joke. We take gold things out of ground and sell them. We not put things in ground." He glanced back briefly at his companions. "Except sometimes people. We put them in ground if they take from us."

Cassie maintained a stony expression. Animals could sense fear. These guys weren't that much farther up the evolutionary ladder.

"Where your friends?" the man with the cap asked again.

The pythia brazened it out. "They're waiting for me at the Jeep. I had to go back to the stone circle because I dropped my room key."

The Turk fished in his vest pocket. "This your key?" He held it out for her to see.

"Yes, that's right. Can I have it back?"

The Turk chuckled. "I keep for now." He placed it back in his pocket. "Why you follow us?"

"To get my key back, of course."

The Turk didn't appear convinced. "You think you take key back from us by yourself?"

Cassie gave a little shrug. "Well, I wasn't going to rush you if that's what you mean. I just wanted to see where you went and then I was going to get my friends and have them take it back."

The man said nothing.

"My friends are waiting for me." She tried to sound bold now. "If I don't get back to them, they'll come looking for me."

The man smiled grimly. "They not find you."

Cassie couldn't believe her own composure in the face of the threat. She felt nothing but an absolute stillness at the core of her being. It helped her keep a clear head. She took a step forward. "I'm worth more alive than dead."

The Turk paused to consider. "What you mean?"

There it was. He was interested. She pressed her advantage. "I mean ransom. For me and the golden bee. I work for an organization that will pay you."

The Turk ogled her, walking around her in a slow circle.

She read his thoughts and nipped them in the bud. "And I mean intact. You don't get to sample the merchandise. If you touch so much as one hair on my head, the price goes down."

That stopped him short. Apparently, money trumped lust. His two associates were whispering to each other trying to understand what was being said in the foreign tongue.

The man with the cap rubbed his chin thoughtfully.

The pythia slowly lowered her arms. "Name your price. My people can afford to pay you twice what you'd get on the black market for that artifact."

"Plus, they pay extra for you," the man corrected her.

"Absolutely!" She nodded and folded her arms across her chest. Cassie thought about her teammates standing above and hearing every word she said. She spoke a little louder for their benefit. "Now take me someplace where I can write a ransom note. It has to be in my handwriting, so my friends will know it came from me. You should enclose the room key with the note as extra proof. One of your men can take the message to the hotel where we were staying."

The Turk's face took on a crafty expression. "If you play joke on us, we bury you. Maybe you not dead when we bury you. Then we have good joke."

Cassie returned his stare without flinching. Animals could sense fear. In a humorless voice, she said, "I'm not joking. You deliver me to my friends unharmed, and you'll get the money just like I said."

The Turk turned to address his companions. After a lengthy and very heated conversation, they fell in line and headed down the forest path. The man with the gun nudged Cassie forward.

THE ARKANA TEAM LET out a collective sigh of relief as they watched the party disappear around the bend.

"That chick must have brass ovaries!" Erik's voice was filled with admiration.

"You usually refer to her as a kid," Griffin reminded him.

Erik grinned. "No kid would have had the brains or the raw nerve to do what she just did. She's definitely been upgraded in my book."

The three of them rose to follow at a safe distance.

"Game faces, guys," the security coordinator told the others. "Time for us to save a kick-ass damsel in distress."

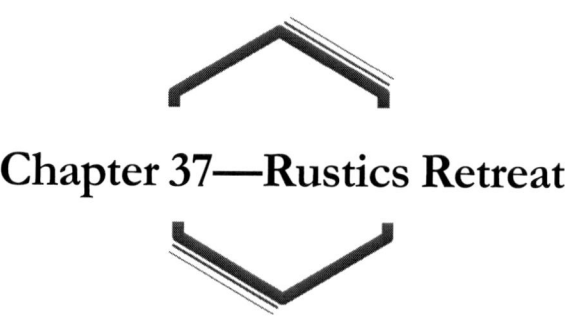

Chapter 37—Rustics Retreat

THE SUN WAS WELL PAST its zenith by now. Its beams slanted downward to the forest floor. The Turks and their captive traveled in silence for about a mile. They followed a single well-worn trail though several other paths crisscrossed theirs along the way. Eventually, they came to a small stone cottage hidden among the evergreens. It was a single-story building with a low-pitched roof that hung over a wooden porch. The structure was run down. The stucco was grayish and cracked in many places, exposing the stone wall underneath. Broken terra cotta tiles had slid off the roof and lay scattered around the foundation.

The man with the cap pushed the weathered wooden door open. It wasn't locked.

The Turk with the rifle shoved Cassie through the entrance. She looked around as her eyes adjusted to the dim interior. The whitewashed walls were as gray as the exterior. Black streaks from innumerable cooking fires ran up the wall above the hearth. There was a central room with two deeply recessed casement windows. The glass was so grimy it afforded very little light. A pair of doors led off to other rooms which Cassie guessed to be bedrooms or storage areas. The house smelled musty as if it had been abandoned decades before.

"You live here?" she asked the man with the cap.

"Sometime we stay here," he replied cryptically. "Now you sit." He gestured toward one of the chairs drawn up next to a rough plank table in the center of the room. This might once have been the kitchen though there was no running water or electricity that Cassie could see. An unlit oil lamp sat in the middle of the table.

The man with the cap walked over to a cupboard and began rifling through drawers and shelves. After a few minutes, he returned with the nub of a pencil and a torn piece of paper.

"Now you write," he commanded, handing Cassie the objects.

His two companions stood looking over the pythia's shoulder as she formed the unfamiliar characters on the page.

The Turk named an outrageous sum of money for the ransom. Cassie and he haggled over the price until the pythia convinced him to ask for something reasonable. She thought that agreeing to his terms too readily might make him suspicious. He settled for a smaller sum which she dutifully copied down on the page. She guessed that her companions must be somewhere outside by now. Again, she deliberately spoke in a loud enough voice for them to hear.

"Are you sure your friend knows where the hotel is?" She tried not to shout.

The man with the cap conferred with the member of his party who didn't have the gun. The fellow nodded.

"Yes," The Turk replied. "He know where."

"He must ask for a man named Erik," she instructed.

Once more, the Turk translated for the benefit of his associate.

Cassie folded up the ransom note. "Here, wrap this around my room key."

The man with the cap didn't argue. He took the key out of his pocket and folded the note around it several times. He then handed the packet to the messenger.

The younger man took it wordlessly and left the building.

"It's a long way," the pythia observed. "How will he get there?"

"We have truck." The Turk didn't choose to elaborate on where the vehicle was hidden.

"This could take a while," Cassie noted.

"Yes," he agreed. "Now we wait." He ambled over to the shelf above the fireplace and took down a pipe, filled it and struck a match. Then he took a seat across the table from Cassie and smoked in silence. His remaining associate dragged a chair over by the door and stationed himself there, cradling his rifle.

About fifteen minutes passed, though to Cassie it seemed much longer, when their silent vigil was shattered. A thumping sound came from the back wall of the building as if something heavy had been thrown against it. They all jumped to attention. The Turk with the gun was on his feet. He tried peering through the grimy windows without success.

The man with the cap spoke rapidly. The other man nodded and warily opened the door. Nothing was moving outside. At the urging of the older man, he went out to investigate, shutting the door behind him.

"Maybe your friends come looking for you," the man said.

Cassie stared at him in what she hoped was an expression of blank surprise. "How could that be? They thought I went up to the stone circle. How could they find me here?"

The Turk shrugged and puffed on his pipe. "If they come, we give them surprise, yes?"

The pythia frowned. "Well, you better not shoot them if you hope to get your money."

For some reason, the man found this remark funny. He slapped the table and laughed out loud.

Five more minutes passed, and the man with the gun still hadn't returned. The Turk with the cap rose from the table and attempted to peer out the filthy window. Then he walked slowly to stand behind Cassie.

"I think he come now," he said.

Cassie could hear footsteps outside, running across the gravel by the front door.

In one deft move, the Turk pulled her out of the chair and drew out a hunting knife which flashed under her chin. He positioned them both facing the front of the house.

Seconds later, the door burst open to reveal Erik pointing the rifle, flanked by Griffin and Fred.

The Turk had backed against the far wall of the cottage, holding Cassie in front of him as a shield. He pressed the knife close against her throat. "You put down gun or she die!"

Erik hesitated for a split second.

It was all the time Cassie needed to raise her leg and grind her foot down on the man's instep as hard as she could. He lost his balance, cursing in pain as a bullet whizzed past his cheek and grazed his earlobe. He dropped the knife, putting up a hand to stop the flow of blood. Cassie flew out of his grasp and ran across the room toward her teammates.

Erik handed the gun to Fred. "Cover me," he commanded before springing across the room. He grabbed the Turk by the arm and twisted it behind his back.

"Listen you!" he growled. "This has already been a bad day on a cosmic scale, and you're not gonna make it suck any worse. Do you know who we are?"

The Turk shook his head, too rattled to speak.

"We belong to an organization that's got enough resources to hunt you down and kill all of you if you meddle in our affairs. You understand what I'm saying?" He twisted the man's arm harder for emphasis.

The Turk nodded, wincing.

"And if you or your crew go anywhere near that stone circle again, I will rain down more vengeance on your heads than Keyser frigging Söze! You got that?"

For the first time, the Turk looked confused. "I do not know who is this. Who is Keyser Söze?"

For a second, Erik was too speechless to reply. "Oh, give me a break. We're in Turkey for crissake, and you don't know who Keyser Söze is?"

The man with the cap shook his head nervously.

"Hey, Hollywood," Cassie called from the doorway. "Give it up."

"OK, fine." Erik appeared completely nonplussed. He searched for an alternative explanation. "How about this. You or your crew go near that stone circle again, and you won't live to tell about it afterward." He twisted the man's arm once more. "Did you understand that sentence?"

The man nodded vehemently.

"Good, looks like we've come to an agreement." Erik scanned the room. "What's behind that door?" He gestured toward a small door in the far corner.

Fred went over to investigate. "It's some kind of storage room."

"Does it have a lock? I can't see from here."

"Yup. One of those old-fashioned key locks."

"Good." Erik dragged the Turk over toward the storage room.

"I found this outside." Griffin held out a coil of rope. "I thought it might prove useful."

"Cass, why don't you help us tie up our friend here," Erik suggested.

"With pleasure," the pythia replied.

"Time to drag in those two other guys we knocked out earlier."

The Arkana team retrieved Cassie's room key and bound the three Turks before locking them in the storage room.

"That won't hold them long," Cassie commented as they exited the cottage and hurried up the trail that led back to their Jeep.

"It won't have to," Griffin said. "We'll call for sweepers when we get back to the hotel."

"Sweepers?" Cassie repeated. "You're going to tidy up the cottage for them?"

"It's a special unit we have," Fred explained. "Sometimes we run across black market types who interfere with our work. We have a sweeper squad that secures them and turns them over to the authorities. Those guys will be cooling their heels in a Turkish jail for quite a while."

"Yeah but they didn't steal anything," the pythia objected.

"I'm guessing they've already built up a track record," Erik countered. "Either way, they'll be busy with the police long enough to stay out of our hair." He shifted the rifle to his other shoulder where he had already slung the extra coil of rope from the cottage.

"What's with the rope?" Cassie asked.

"You ask me that after the kind of day we've had? Consider it an insurance policy."

"That was absolutely brilliant of you, Cassie," Griffin said. "The way you handled those thieves. Though I do think it was risky to step on his foot. He might have knifed you."

"I figured I had the advantage. I was wearing steel-reinforced hiking boots. He was wearing loafers. Besides, I got to the point where I was more angry than scared. I am totally sick and tired of being the patsy."

"Patsy?" Fred repeated blankly.

"Yeah, the dame, the skirt, the frail."

"Now who's seen too many movies," Erik interjected. "Sounds like you binge-watched an entire noir marathon."

Ignoring the remark, Cassie continued. "I mean, first it was Leroy Hunt sticking a gun to my head. Then this joker with the knife. I've absolutely had enough. I figured it was time I put my foot down."

"Literally." Griffin laughed.

"The next guy who messes with me is going to lose some teeth." Cassie paused and glanced at each of her teammates in turn. "Still, all things considered, I'm sure glad you guys showed up to save the day."

Erik shrugged nonchalantly. "You're worth saving, toots."

Cassie did a double-take. She wasn't sure she'd heard him right. Maybe she'd have her ears checked when she got back to the States.

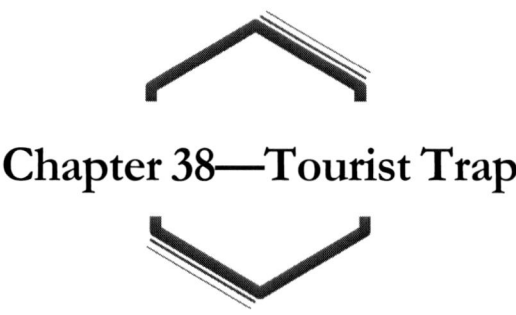

Chapter 38—Tourist Trap

IT WAS MID-AFTERNOON by the time the Arkana team threaded their way through the forest and arrived back at the Jeep. They stowed the gun and the rope and were on the point of climbing in when Fred paused. "Quiet," he whispered urgently.

His companions stared at him.

"Can't you hear that?"

They all listened intently.

"Is that an automobile engine?" Griffin sounded tentative.

"That just tears it!" Erik muttered. "Could this day possibly get any worse?"

"What?" Cassie looked from one to the other, uncomprehending.

"It's the Nephilim," the security coordinator explained. "Has to be."

"How can you be so sure?"

"Who else is likely to be driving up here?"

"It might just be tourists," she objected.

"Gee, why don't we stand here and wait to find out," Erik snarled back. "Even if I'm wrong, we'd be crazy not to assume a worst-case scenario. Luck hasn't exactly been on our side today. We've got to do something."

"No time to move the Jeep," Fred told them. "We're boxed in. The only trail that leads out of here is the one they're traveling. We'd run straight into them."

Erik rubbed his face distractedly then eyed the contents of the truck. "I've just had the mother of all stupid, dangerous ideas but it may be our only chance. Come on. We don't have much time."

DANIEL AND HIS COMPANIONS bounced along the rutted trail up the eastern slope of the mountain. They were approaching the end of the tree line now. Ilhami assured them that a set of megaliths was to be found close by. The scion wasn't in an optimistic mood. Even if they did, by some miracle, find the standing stones, there was no guarantee the relic would be hidden among them. He sighed. They had nearly reached the summit of the mountain. This was their last hope. Daniel dreaded the thought of his next telephone conversation with his father.

Ilhami stepped on the brakes abruptly, snapping Daniel out of his reverie. The scion blinked. There was a Jeep parked at the end of the trail.

"What on earth!" he exclaimed.

"Probably tourists," Hunt said matter-of-factly as he checked the clip of his pistol.

"There will be no need for that, Mr. Hunt," Daniel cautioned him.

Leroy grinned. "Aw shucks, boy. You aim to ruin my fun again?"

Daniel thought back to the tourist couple whom Hunt had threatened to shoot earlier in the day. He hoped the mercenary wasn't about to have another opportunity to indulge his violent streak. It unnerved Daniel to contemplate such a possibility, but he expected Hunt knew that.

"We go up this way," Ilhami was already out of the truck and gesturing toward a narrow trail that cut through the trees. "No more driving. We walk now."

Leroy holstered his pistol. He fell in behind Ilhami leaving Daniel to bring up the rear.

They trudged upward through the pines for half a mile before breaking out into a desolate open landscape of rocks and scrubby grass. The air was thinner and a bit colder now. They climbed a rise where the ground dipped unexpectedly onto a flat table of land. On the plateau beneath them were the standing stones. A lone figure of a man stood in the middle of the circle. For some reason, he looked vaguely familiar to Daniel. He seemed startled to see them and backed away to the far end of the megaliths, hiding behind one near the edge of the plateau.

"Somethin' don't smell right here," Hunt said. He hastened down the hill to investigate the spot where the man had been standing. Daniel and Ilhami scurried after him. The mercenary paused to scrutinize a small boulder. He kicked something beside it with his toe.

When Daniel arrived at the spot, his mouth fell open. A flat stone with the lily insignia lay on the ground before him. His excitement turned to horror when he shifted his focus to what lay beside it. An empty alabaster urn and a gaping hole in the earth.

"S... s... somebody has taken the relic," he quavered.

"Not somebody," Hunt replied. "Him!" He pointed across the circle to the man peering at them from behind a megalith on the far side.

"Hey, you!" Hunt challenged.

"Don't come any closer," the man warned.

Despite the command, the newcomers stepped a few paces nearer. As the gap between them closed, Daniel understood why the man looked familiar. God in heaven! It was one of the Fallen from Karfi. A young blond man in his mid-twenties. It had been dark that night, but even at the time, Daniel had been struck by this handsome youth's face. He tried to suppress his elation. He'd been right. They were alive after all! They hadn't died underground. He felt a burden lift from his heart. His conscience was clear once more

Hunt squinted at the man in the distance. "I know you, boy?"

"You might say that," the stranger replied.

"Mr. Hunt, he was one of the people at Karfi," Daniel reminded him. "They were sealed in the tomb after the earthquake. Don't you remember?"

Hunt stared at the stranger until recognition dawned. His face wore an exasperated expression. "How many times I gotta kill you, boy? Back in the day, when I shot somebody, they stayed dead. The world's in a sorry mess if everybody just starts resurrectin' themselves all willy nilly without permission."

"Technically, you didn't kill me," the stranger retorted. "You were about to."

"You say tomato," Hunt grumbled. "Where's the other two was with you that night?"

"They didn't make it out alive," the man answered.

"Well, that's some comfort to a body, at least," Leroy huffed.

While this conversation was transpiring, Ilhami looked from one face to the next, totally lost. Daniel didn't feel inclined to enlighten him. The stranger's last words were like a new dagger through his heart. His guilt hadn't been expunged after all.

"Your friends didn't survive?" he asked hesitantly.

"No, they didn't thanks to you," came the resentful response.

"I wouldn't be all hang-dog if I was you, boy," Hunt observed. "Seems to me you got the whole pie to yourself now. Don't need to share it with nobody."

"I would have if you hadn't shown up to ruin things," the man countered.

"So we did. Game's over." Hunt advanced a few paces.

"You take one step closer, and I swear I'll throw it over the cliff," the man warned. He held up his palm. He was holding a golden object. Daniel couldn't get a close look at the shape of it, but he was sure it was the relic.

"That's the artifact we've been seeking!" he exclaimed.

"Damn straight," the stranger confirmed. "If I throw it over the edge of the plateau, it's a straight drop down the side of the mountain and no way for you to get down there to search for it."

Daniel put a restraining hand on Hunt's arm. "Mr. Hunt, no." He turned to address the young man. "Surely we can come to some agreement."

"The agreement is this. I give you the relic, and you let me leave here alive."

Hunt fumed in silence.

"That is acceptable to us," Daniel assented readily.

"Oh, hell no, it ain't!" Hunt countered. "You let him go, he's gonna keep on huntin' them doodads, and maybe next time we won't be so lucky. Maybe he'll get there first."

"No, I won't." The stranger grinned impudently. "Scout's honor. Cross my heart."

"And hope to die." Hunt drew out his pistol.

"Mr. Hunt, no!" Daniel screamed.

The stranger was still concealed behind the standing stone so Daniel couldn't see what happened clearly, but he could hear it. He heard the scrape of gravel as the stranger took several paces back and lost his footing. He saw the stranger's arms flailing. The gold object flew out of his hand and clattered to the ground in front of the megalith. Then he heard the scream as the stranger went over the side of the mountain.

All three men stood frozen for several seconds. No one had expected such a thing to happen and they didn't react immediately. They were still fifty feet away from the spot where the thief had fallen. The trio scrambled forward. Hunt stopped short to scoop up the artifact first. Only then did they peer over the edge of the plateau.

The stranger had been right. It was a sheer drop over the edge of the cliff. Not a toe-hold anywhere to be seen. Two hundred feet below them, on a tiny ledge that was scarcely wide enough to support it, lay the body of the stranger, sprawled face down.

"We have to do something!" Daniel cried in anguish. "We can't just leave him there."

"Can and will," Hunt replied decisively. "Ain't no way to get down there even if I was inclined to try which I ain't. The vultures'll find him before anybody else thinks to look there. Let them clean up the carcass."

Hunt stood up and dusted off his sleeve. He held out the golden object and dropped it into Daniel's hand. "Congratulations, son. You got your first doodad. Your daddy's gonna be right proud."

Daniel stared at the exquisite golden bee. To his mind's eye, it appeared to be covered in blood.

Chapter 39—Installment Plan

LEROY HUNT STOOD ON the balcony of Ilhami's tiny apartment and surveyed the street below. Everything was dark and quiet. He figured it must be around three o'clock in the morning. Brother Hammy was sleeping under the stars tonight. He'd strung two of the folding chairs together into a makeshift bed. His head lolled over the back of one of the chairs, and he was snoring to beat the band. That boy sure liked his raki. Too bad he couldn't hold it worth a damn.

Hunt felt a surge of satisfaction. They'd done it. They'd actually gone and found it. The old man wasn't crazy after all. With all the holy smoke Abe had been blowing up Leroy's butt, the mercenary had begun to doubt that there was a pot of gold at the end of the rainbow. But lo and behold, here it was. He held the shiny bee in the palm of his hand and studied it, captivated by its delicate design. Pretty little thing. Probably worth a fortune on account of it was so old. The thought gave him a warm glow in the pit of his stomach—like half a dozen shots of tequila.

He walked back inside and cast a furtive look around the apartment. Daniel lay huddled fast asleep under a mound of blankets on the floor. Good. No way Hunt was going to share the sleeper couch with that weirdo. He couldn't prove it, but he had a deep suspicion the kid was batting for the other team. Probably didn't even know it himself. Hunt chuckled and wondered what the boy's wives thought about that. Probably nothing. Four silly gals who'd spent their whole lives shut up in that tomb of a compound. Likely too dumb to figure out anything was off with weasel face. Leroy could never understand the attraction holy rollers had with virgins. He'd take a whore who knew stuff any day of the week over ten giggling morons who were no damn good in bed.

The mercenary glanced down at the golden object in his palm once again. He slipped it into his pocket and padded barefoot to where he'd left his shoulder holster slung over a chair. He checked the clip on his pistol and attached a silencer. Pay day had finally come around.

The streetlight outside cast a yellowish glow over the lump sleeping on the floor. Easy pickings. Leroy aimed for where he guessed Daniel's head to be. He lingered a moment, savoring the thought of finally parting ways for good. He'd be well rid of the whole lot of them with their undertaker suits and hangdog faces. He took aim, but at the last second, something stopped him from pulling the trigger. He hesitated as a new idea came flying out of nowhere and hit him smack between the eyes so hard that it gave him a headache.

Leroy lowered the gun. A troubled frown crossed his face. Generally, he avoided thinking whenever possible because it was hard work and made his skull cramp up. He preferred to shoot first and never ask questions. But this time he decided to risk burning up some grey cells over the matter. He rubbed the back of his neck distractedly as more thoughts crowded into his head. There wasn't room for them all.

Hunt resisted these strange new notions because, in addition to disliking cogitation, he was a creature of habit. He preferred the safe, familiar routine of shooting folks and getting paid for a job well done. It was simple and straightforward, and he liked it fine the way it was. But his thoughts were rapidly haring off into uncharted territory.

"Leroy, you're too smart for your own good." His momma's words jostled with the multitude that was already occupying his brain pan.

"No, ma'am, I ain't. I'm just smart enough to make it pay." But was he?

He ground his teeth in annoyance. He was just spoiling to shoot somebody tonight because of the way he'd been thwarted earlier in the day. He flashed back bitterly to that blond Ken doll playing hide and seek behind the boulders. He'd tried to kill Kenny once before and been interrupted, and just when he was on the point of finishing the job proper, the fool went and tripped over his own feet and slid off the side of a mountain. Leroy didn't credit himself with an overabundance of brains, but even he wouldn't have done something that stupid. Prancing idiot! The whole episode left him with an itchy trigger finger. He felt an urge to go back up the mountain and shoot Kenny's corpse just for spite. Too far out of range to hit him though. Damn!

Leroy drew his attention back to the question at hand. What to do, what to do? For the moment, he put his pistol back in the holster, set the bee on the table beside it and lay down on the sleeper couch. He laced his fingers behind his head and turned the problem over some more. Ordinarily, he would have just shot his two bunk mates and taken off with the bee. Not that he had anything personal against Brother Hammy. In fact, he liked the little dung ball. The Turk had what the Frenchies called panash which meant he knew how to have a good time. It endeared him to the mercenary, but this wasn't Brother Hammy's lucky day. He was in the wrong place at the wrong time. Fortunes of war and all that. Now Daniel was a horse of a different color. Leroy would have loved to put a bullet in that pasty-faced bastard's head just on principle. His holier-than-thou crap made Hunt like to puke. But he restrained himself. There was more at stake here.

He thought of his cowboy heroes. He'd patterned his entire life around their exploits on the silver screen. What would Ramon Navarro do in a situation like this? He scowled. Maybe that was the wrong caballero to ask. What would Eli Wallach or Lee Van Cleef do? They'd take the money and run. That's what they'd do. After kicking the crap out of Clint Eastwood first, of course. Leroy shook the image out of his head. He didn't think either the white hats or the black hats had an answer for him this time. Sure as shootin', he was on his own.

He stared at the ceiling for what seemed like hours and pondered the topic some more. It all boiled down to one of two choices. He could collect his payday now, or he could wait. The mercenary rolled his eyes in frustration. He hated to wait for anything, but maybe this one time it would be worth his while to rein himself in. That little gold bee was proof positive that a treasure existed. He wasn't sure what the other doodads were like, but they would probably fetch as much as the bee. Maybe more.

He sat up. He'd reached a decision. He was going to stay in it for the whole game. He'd stick with Daniel until the kid had sniffed out all the relics. Then and only then would Leroy cash in his chips. When that day came, as a special reward to himself for being patient, he'd blow the kid's brains out *gratis*. But not today. He sighed deeply with a sense of fleeting disappointment. Nope. This wasn't the day.

Leroy lay back down and drew the covers around his shoulders. The sun would be up soon. They had an early flight back to the states in the morning. There wasn't any more to be done tonight. With stolid composure, he settled down to catch forty winks before dawn.

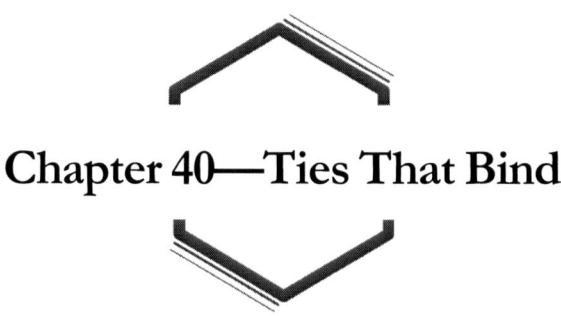

Chapter 40—Ties That Bind

ZACHARY AND FAYE SAT facing one another in the parlor. The boy's backpack rested on the floor next to his feet.

A car motor could be heard outside and then a gentle rap on the front door.

Faye rose to answer. When she swung the door open, she was greeted by a woman and a man—Zachary's parents. The woman was about forty with black hair pulled so tightly into a bun that her eyebrows seemed to be permanently lifted in surprise. The man was tall with a sallow complexion. He wore a drab brown suit that matched the color of his eyes and hair.

"Marta, Bill, please come in." Faye stepped back to allow them to enter.

"Granny Faye!" Marta exclaimed and swept the tiny old woman into an embrace. "So good to see you."

Her husband followed her lead and bent down to give Faye a peck on the cheek. "Hello, Granny," he murmured.

The couple's demeanor changed the minute they set eyes on the boy on the couch.

"You have a lot of explaining to do, young man!" the woman said sharply.

Faye interposed herself between mother and son. "Don't be too hard on the boy, Marta. He's been a model house guest while he was here."

Zach gave Faye a furtive look of thanks. He apparently wasn't sure if his brief career as a burglar was going to be a topic of discussion.

"I certainly hope so!" his father exclaimed. "Do you have any idea how many decades you're going to be grounded?"

"I believe I've punished him enough already." Faye gestured for her guests to seat themselves. "He's actually been working quite hard during his visit."

"Yeah, and I've got the battle scars to prove it." The boy held out his hands for inspection. His fingers and palms were covered in blisters. "Staying with Gamma was kind of like being on work release."

"Good!" his father said. "Maybe you'll think twice next time before taking off and worrying us half to death."

Zachary looked down at the carpet but said nothing.

"Bill, I do think he's learned his lesson." Faye tried to forestall any more scolding by changing the subject. "Where's Sally? I haven't seen her since last Christmas."

"She's home studying," Marta replied. "Just like Zach should be."

"Gimme a break," the boy moaned. "It's summer!"

"Sally is taking extra credit courses." The woman glared at the boy. "Just like you should be."

Zach rolled his eyes but kept silent.

"Can I offer either of you some refreshments?" Faye asked tentatively.

"No need," Marta replied. "We'll only be staying a few minutes. Just long enough to collect this one."

"Are you ready to go?" his father asked.

"All packed for the gulag," Zachary muttered under his breath. He stood up and slung his backpack over his arm.

Just then, an assertive knock was heard on the front door.

"Gracious me, who can that be?" Faye speculated.

Before she could rise, Zach darted over to the foyer. "I'll get it," he volunteered. He grinned when he saw who the new visitor was. "Now how did I know it was you?"

Maddie looked startled. "Haven't you left yet?"

Zach turned back to the occupants of the parlor. "Mom, Dad, allow me to introduce you. This is Gamma's friend Maisie."

"Maddie," the visitor growled through gritted teeth. "You know my name is Maddie."

Zach's parents looked bemused. "Very nice to meet you," they both said in unison.

"I'm glad Granny Faye has somebody in the neighborhood looking out for her," Marta commented.

"Oh, it's better than that," Zach offered impishly. "They're both on the neighborhood watch together." He gave Maddie a sly glance, daring her to offer a plausible explanation.

"The neighborhood watch!" Marta gasped. "Why Granny, don't you think you should leave that to the younger generation?"

Faye looked at Zach archly. "I've been thinking about that very subject quite a lot lately."

Maddie looked from Zach to Faye, her face registering both confusion and alarm. "I... I... uh... didn't mean to interrupt a family gathering. I can come back later."

"No dear, it's quite alright. Come in." Faye gestured for her to enter.

"We were just leaving," Bill volunteered. He stood up decisively as did his wife. The couple frog marched their son to the door with Faye toddling behind.

"Zachary has expressed an interest in coming to visit me on a regular basis," the old woman said.

Bill paused to regard his son. "Has he? Good. He needs to be around someone who won't stand for his moon bat ideas. A grown-up who's practical and down to earth."

Faye and Zachary exchanged a meaningful glance.

"I think Gamma's just the guy for the job," Zach declared, giving her a hug. "Til next time."

Faye tousled the spikes in his hair. "Come back to visit me after your next birthday. Then we'll have a nice long chat."

"You can count on it." The boy grinned.

His mother gave him a searching look, apparently trying to fathom the strange rapport that had developed between her son and his ancestor. "Thank you for keeping an eye on him, Granny Faye." She hugged the old woman and then nudged the boy outside.

Faye waited until the trio was safely in their vehicle and down the street before she shut the door.

"What the hell was that about?" Maddie asked, mystified.

"The consequences of curiosity," Faye murmured cryptically. She didn't elaborate.

The operations director took a seat on the now vacant couch. She appeared distinctly grouchy. "Do you ever answer your phone anymore? Maybe I should just buy a house down the street given the number of times I've had to drive over here during the past week!"

"I am sorry for the inconvenience. Now that Zach is gone, things can get back to normal."

Maddie scowled. "Maybe, maybe not." Her tone was ominous.

Sitting down in her purple arm chair, Faye leaned forward, "What is it, dear?"

"We may have a situation."

"A what?"

"Griffin called for sweepers to be sent to a location on Mount Ida. Apparently, our guys had a run-in with some local bandits."

"Oh dear." Faye felt a growing uneasiness. "Did you speak with him? What happened?"

Maddie shrugged helplessly. "I haven't been able to reach any of them. I only found out about the sweepers because the Anatolian Ops Division contacted me for authorization." She paused. "But that isn't the worst of it. I just got a transcript of Hunt's last phone call to the Nephilim."

"Yes?" Faye asked guardedly.

"Hunt and that Daniel character were getting ready to leave Turkey. He said they got the relic."

"But that's good news!" Faye exclaimed. "Apparently they aren't suspicious that it's a fake."

"No," Maddie's gloomy expression didn't change. "That part went OK. But Hunt said they had some trouble recovering it."

"You don't think they encountered our team, do you?"

"I don't know if it was the whole team. I can't confirm anything from our end because I haven't had a report for days. I'm hoping it's because they're already on their way back home. When I called the hotel where they were staying, all I was told was that their party had checked out."

"Then what on earth is the matter, dear? You look positively stricken." Faye wasn't used to seeing the operations director appear quite this worried about anything. The image alarmed her.

Maddie rubbed her eyes wearily. "Hunt said he ran across one of the people from Karfi. One he thought he'd taken care of before."

"Good heavens! That means he spotted Griffin or Cassie or Erik and knows at least one of them is alive!"

"That's just it. He said he tied up that loose end. From the physical description he gave Metcalf, I think he meant Erik."

Faye was too shocked to speak.

Maddie sighed. "I hope to goddess this is bad information but, if it isn't, Erik may be dead."

Chapter 41—Swap Meet

"COME IN, MY BOY, COME in!" Abraham's face was beaming.

Daniel stepped tentatively over the threshold of his father's prayer closet.

Unexpectedly, the old man wrapped his son in an embrace. He held him for several moments before saying, "This is my beloved son, in whom I am well pleased."

Daniel winced at the unexpected contact as well as his father's choice of scriptural text. Obviously, he fancied himself to be the voice of God now. Flustered, the young man stepped back a few paces and cleared his throat. "Ahem, yes, well...Thank you, Father."

"This is a day of great rejoicing for the Nephilim. Come, sit down and tell me all about your travels." He indicated the two chairs drawn up to the small table under the dead diviner's portrait.

To Daniel's mind, the portrait seemed to be glowering less fiercely today than usual. Not that the thought gave him any comfort. His head was still too full of other images. A golden bee flying through the air to land at his feet. A young man flying off the edge of a cliff to meet his death.

He sat down as instructed and drew a small wooden box out of his coat jacket. "Here it is," he said simply. He pushed the box across the table to his father who fell on it eagerly.

With trembling hands, the old man opened the lid. He seemed overcome with deep emotion. Daniel thought he saw his father brushing tears out of his eyes.

The diviner gazed hungrily at the golden bee. "So long, so long," he murmured. "I have waited many years to behold this sight." He took the object out of its wrapping and held it up. Even in the dimness of this heavily draped room, it gleamed.

Abraham looked up in surprise as a new thought struck him. "Where is Mr. Hunt?"

"He accompanied me to the gates of the compound and then instructed the driver to take him back to the city. He did say he would contact you later about his fee. I got the impression that the prayerful atmosphere within our walls upsets him."

Abraham nodded sagely. "It is often the case that the Fallen are uncomfortable in the presence of sanctity. No matter. I understand he acquitted himself admirably during your trip, did he not?"

Daniel hesitated. He wanted to say that Hunt acquitted himself as befitted a cold-blooded murderer, but he bit back the words. "He insured that we recovered the artifact without hindrance. There was a young man. He—"

"Yes, I heard about that." Abraham cut him off. "Mr. Hunt did the right thing under the circumstances and afterward escorted you out of the country before any entanglements with the law might arise. All quite satisfactory." The diviner was smiling again. Almost grinning in fact. Even the thought of collateral damage couldn't suppress his elation, it seemed. He turned the bee over in his hands, noting the script on both sides of its wings. He peered up at his son. "Have you translated this yet?"

Daniel shook his head. "Not in any depth. I ran into some difficulty with my computer program and didn't have all the necessary reference material with me in Turkey to resolve the problem. I have copied down all the hieroglyphs from the artifact, and I should have the full translation in a day or so."

The old man studied his son's face for several seconds. "Never mind that for now, my boy. You need rest."

The diviner must have noticed Daniel's haggard appearance. What he attributed to fatigue, Daniel attributed to an increasingly guilty conscience.

"You should spend some time with your wives and children." Abraham stopped short. "That reminds me. There is another matter we need to discuss."

Daniel was only half paying attention, so his father's next words caught him completely off guard.

"I've reassigned Hannah."

"What?" Daniel wasn't sure he'd heard his father correctly.

The diviner turned his eyes to the far wall. In a casual tone, he said, "She began to have delusions about the state of your marriage."

"Delusions?" the scion repeated uncomprehendingly.

"Yes, delusions." Abraham's tone remained casual. "Absurd lies that your union had not been consummated." He didn't bother to ask Daniel to confirm or deny the statement. "I knew it for what it was. The work of the devil. An attempt to demoralize the people by raising doubts about the scion."

Daniel found himself on the horns of a dilemma. If he leaped to Hannah's defense, he risked exposing his own problematic behavior. Instead, he asked, "You didn't punish her, did you? After all, she's only a child."

Abraham nodded in agreement. "That is why I reassigned her to a man who can keep her vagaries firmly under control. One who can bring her around to a proper way of thinking."

Daniel hadn't even formed the question before his father answered. "I am the only man strong enough to grapple with the demons who are attempting to possess Hannah's soul."

"You!" Daniel echoed, trying to keep the shock out of his voice. Although he had been raised with the practice of older men taking younger wives, a sixty-year age difference was obscene. The thought of his father coupling with Hannah made his flesh crawl. "And is Hannah happy with this new arrangement?" he asked tentatively.

Abraham seemed surprised by the question. "Why shouldn't she be? As the wife of the diviner, she will have many advantages."

"But did you ask her what she thought about the reassignment?"

The old man's puzzled expression remained. "There was no need. She hasn't complained."

Daniel gave a weak smile. "Then I'm sure everything is alright," he lied.

His father took his words as a sign of consent. "I am glad, my son, that you see the wisdom of my decision. I confess I should have been distressed if you were going to make some difficulty about the situation."

"No Father, not at all." While Daniel was glad to be relieved of the burden of a superfluous wife, he felt nothing but sadness for Hannah's fate.

He needed to let her know that somehow. "May I speak to her?" he asked. "I'd like to say goodbye."

Oblivious to the thoughts running through his son's mind, Abraham smiled magnanimously. "Of course, my boy, of course. I believe she has been scheduled to work in the bakery this week if you wish to seek her out. I'm sure she will be pleased to see you."

Daniel believed Hannah's reaction to seeing him would be anything but pleasure. If he hadn't abandoned her on their wedding night, she might never have mentioned the incident to anyone. She might have remained safely beneath the notice of the diviner. The girl couldn't possibly be happy to be married to a man old enough to be her great-grandfather. This was Daniel's fault. All his fault. He had already charged himself with the deaths of three people in obtaining his father's artifacts and now this. He didn't know how much more guilt his soul could bear. He stood up abruptly. "Do I have your permission to leave now, Father?"

Abraham had refocused his attention on the golden bee. He spoke absently. "Not right now, my son. I'd still like to have a full report of your journey. After that, I think we should spend some time in prayer and thanksgiving. Surely you can postpone your other duties until this afternoon."

The scion lowered himself back into his seat. It seemed his ordeal was to continue. Several more hours of uninterrupted attention from his father. Considering all the misery he had inadvertently caused, it hardly seemed penance enough.

Chapter 42—Marital Affairs

HANNAH PAUSED TO RUB a smudge of flour off her nose. She'd been kneading bread dough for what seemed like hours. Her fingers were beginning to cramp up. She stood at a long butcher block table flanked by a dozen other women engaged in the same occupation. Providing enough daily bread for two hundred people was a time-consuming chore. She happened to glance toward the door of the bakery and dropped the lump of dough she was holding. Daniel was standing there. He hadn't seen her yet. He was scanning the faces of the women to her right, obviously looking for someone. Looking for her it seemed because when he saw her, he gave a little start. Their eyes met. He offered a tremulous smile and motioned for her to join him at the door.

She hurriedly wiped her hands on her apron and scurried over to where he stood.

"H...hello," he began. "How are you?"

She blushed and looked at the floor. "I'm alright, I suppose."

"Will you please come for a walk with me?" he asked.

Could it be possible? Had something changed? Had he persuaded his father to give her back to him? She hadn't felt anything like hope for a long time. She nodded.

They walked down the corridor in silence, their footfalls echoing over the stone floor.

"Let's go in here where we can speak privately." Daniel motioned toward the chapel. It was deserted at this time of day.

Hannah realized it would be unseemly for her to invite him to her quarters now that she was married to another man.

They walked down the central aisle together. The irony was not lost on her. The last time they had met in public, it had been to walk down this same aisle on their wedding day. Daniel led her to the front row and indicated that she should sit down with him.

She complied wordlessly.

He seemed to have difficulty meeting her gaze. He looked at the floor and asked, "Are you happy with your new marriage?"

She didn't know what to say. He was the son of the diviner. If she told him how she really felt, he might report back to his father. If she didn't say anything, he might assume she actually wanted to be married to that old man. She hesitated for several more seconds.

When she didn't speak immediately, he finally looked at her. The expression on her face must have told him what he needed to know. "I am so sorry this happened to you, Hannah."

His apology meant that he wasn't in sympathy with what his father had done. That was good. Maybe there was a chance to fix things after all. "I'd rather be married to you," she offered shyly.

Unfortunately, his reaction wasn't what she'd hoped for. The blood drained out of his face. "I... uh..." He stammered and cleared his throat. "Um...I don't think that would be a good idea."

"Then why did you want to talk to me?" She was on the point of tears. It seemed she wasn't to be allowed to break free from her prison after all.

He steadied himself. "To tell you how sorry I am about all this. If there is anything I can do to make it up to—"

"But there is." She cut across his words. "You can tell your father that you want me back!"

"He would never agree to that," Daniel protested, squirming in his seat.

Tears of frustration and despair were running down her face now. "But you could try at least! Maybe it would make a difference!"

"It wouldn't," he countered in a small voice.

Deep down, she knew he was right. Abraham would never let her go. She wiped the tears away with her apron, leaving streaks of flour on her cheeks.

"Here now," he said gently, removing the smudges on her face with his handkerchief. "You mustn't grieve so."

She stared at him as a new thought occurred to her. "You really never wanted to marry me, did you?"

He dropped his eyes. "No, I'm sorry. That was my father's idea, not mine."

"Then why didn't you say something to him while there was still time?" she asked plaintively.

He gave a bitter laugh. "By now you're familiar with my father's temperament. He can't be dissuaded once he's made up his mind about something."

"No, I suppose not," she agreed in a weak voice, feeling all the hope drain out of her once again.

He took her hands in his. "Look at me, Hannah."

She forced herself to return his gaze.

"I truly am sorry for all of this. I wanted you to know that. If there is anything I can do to make your lot easier to bear, please tell me."

She noted the anguish in his expression and believed he was sincere. A frightening and audacious plan began to take shape in her mind, but she had to be sure first. She tilted her head, considering. "You've been to the Fallen Lands more than any of us, haven't you?"

He nodded uncertainly, releasing her hands. "Yes, that's true. I've seen many parts of the outer world. More than almost anybody in the compound except perhaps for father himself."

"Is it really as bad as they say? Do people murder each other in the streets? Are all the women painted harlots?"

Daniel laughed. "No, it's actually not like that at all. I was surprised when I first saw for myself how things are out there. It's not as clean as here, and certainly more disorganized with everyone going their own way but the people..." He furrowed his brow. "I don't know how to explain them. They're like us only they don't seem to worry as much."

"That doesn't sound so terrible," Hannah commented.

"No, it's not."

His description gave her courage to launch her plan. She tried to keep her next words casual. "You said you wanted to make things up to me. Maybe there is a way."

"Anything! Name it."

"I think I'd like to know more about the Fallen Lands. How people act and dress and how they travel about. Will you come visit me from time to time and tell me about them?"

He seemed taken aback. She knew that exhibiting curiosity about the outer world was considered an abomination. A sure sign of the devil's influence.

She watched him closely. Everything depended on the next few seconds. Would he realize why she wanted to know and, more importantly, would he help her?

He stared at her in silence, a look of shock and understanding dawning on his face. And then he seemed to reach a decision in his own mind. "Why yes. I see no harm in that. Of course, I'll tell you anything you'd like to know."

She needed to be sure he wouldn't betray her, so she nudged him one step further. "Can we keep this just between ourselves?"

He gulped and nodded. "Y...yes. Of course. Just as you say. Between ourselves."

She gave him a tremulous smile. "Thank you, Daniel. I'll feel much better about things if you just do that much for me. It will make all the difference."

He seemed both relieved that she'd forgiven him and troubled because he must suspect how she was going to use that information.

"Whenever you want to talk about the Fallen Lands, send for me. I'll be there. I promise." He leaned over and kissed her on the forehead just as he'd done on their wedding night, only this time she fancied there was some genuine emotion behind that kiss. "Goodbye, Hannah. Until next time."

"Goodbye Daniel and thank you."

He got up and left her sitting alone in the chapel.

She smiled to herself. All wasn't lost. She would have her freedom after all. Whether he knew it or not, Daniel was going to help her throw open the gates of hell.

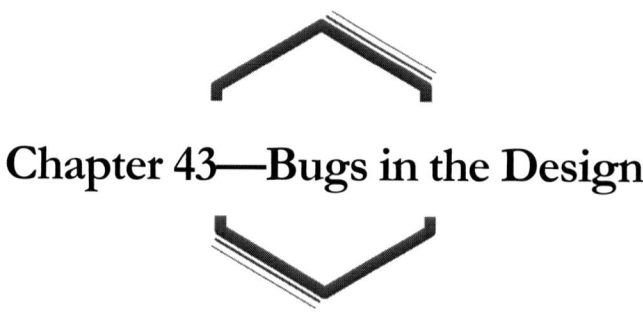

Chapter 43—Bugs in the Design

ABRAHAM ENTERED HIS secret treasury clutching the small wooden box to his chest. Words couldn't express the elation he felt. God was good. He was holding in his hands an object believed to be no more than a legend. Like so many of the other so-called mythical artifacts he had collected in this room, the golden bee was quite real. He walked to the table in the center of the treasury and took his most recent acquisition out of its container. He held it up to examine it more closely. Even under the fluorescent lights which seemed to drain the color out of most objects, this one still glowed with an inner fire. An indication of its hidden power.

He reminded himself sharply of the Lord's command against worshipping graven images. But he wasn't worshipping it. He worshiped the deity who had so graciously placed it in his possession. His gaze slid away from the bee to the storage compartments lining the walls. They were almost full now. Only six remained empty. After today, only five. They waited to house the Bones of the Mother and finally the Sage Stone. Once he possessed the latter, he would be ready to act. Then the world would see a change.

He had no doubt that Daniel would succeed in acquiring the rest of the artifacts. It was a mark of God's favor that they had prevailed thus far, even in the face of resistance from the Fallen. The young man who had tried not once, but twice, to steal the relics from the Nephilim had been justly vanquished. No doubt he was burning in hell at this very moment. God was good. He smote down the enemies of the righteous. Abraham uttered a silent prayer of thanksgiving.

He replaced the golden bee in its container and carried it reverently to a storage compartment in the corner of the treasury. It would remain sealed away here, waiting for its companion pieces. Its very presence, however, was a signal to Abraham to move forward with the next phase of his plan. He looked at his wrist watch. The hour was at hand.

DOCTOR RAFI ABOUD WAITED impatiently for his benefactor to arrive. He was used to secrecy in his line of work, but this compound out in the middle of nowhere and the people who lived here seemed otherworldly to him. Otherwordly in a way that made him uneasy. Uneasiness was a small price to pay, he reminded himself sternly. In order to be allowed to continue his work, he would have gladly struck a bargain with the devil himself. Aboud noted the time. His host should have been here by now.

At that moment the office door opened to reveal an old man with a white beard. He was dressed entirely in black.

"Doctor Aboud?" he held out his hand in greeting.

The visitor grasped it warily. "You are Abraham Metcalf?"

"Yes, I'm very glad to meet you. Was your trip difficult?"

Aboud shrugged. "Flying thousands of miles is never easy."

"And your accommodations," the old man pressed. "Are they sufficient for your needs?"

"Sufficient, yes," the visitor agreed. He didn't much like being surrounded by locked gates, but that was a minor inconvenience.

The old man appeared animated for some reason. He exuded a hectic energy which he only suppressed with difficulty. "May I offer you some refreshment?"

Aboud wished to keep the meeting short and impersonal. "No, thank you," he said curtly. "I would like to see the plans for my facility."

"Of course," Metcalf agreed readily. "Here they are." He picked up a long cardboard tube which had been standing next to his desk and removed the contents. He carried the rolled papers over to a conference table on the other side of the room and spread them out.

Aboud came to stand beside him, looking at the blueprints over his shoulder.

"As you can see, the entire laboratory will be underground," the old man explained. "That will allow you to work in maximum privacy."

"That is good," the visitor agreed. "How many of your people know of this plan?"

"Very few. Only a handful in fact. There's no reason why the rest should. I've acquired a tract of land a few miles away from the compound. The construction crew will be hired from the outside. They will have no occasion to deal with any of the Nephilim other than the men I've selected to supervise this operation. You may come and go as you please."

Aboud nodded his approval. So, he would be allowed to leave after all. He made a mental note to find alternative living arrangements as soon as possible. Transferring his attention back to the blueprint, he scrutinized every detail of the design. This Metcalf had been careful to follow his instructions. It looked very good. He traced his finger over the main laboratory. The dimensions were much larger than his old facility.

"I will need assistants," he said half to himself.

"My brethren are attempting to locate some of your countrymen whose work was also disrupted. I'm sure we can guarantee at least a handful of experienced laboratory technicians."

"I will need a dozen." Aboud's voice was expressionless. It wasn't a demand. It was a necessity if the work was to go forward as his benefactor wished.

Metcalf at first seemed taken aback by the comment. Apparently, he wasn't used to being contradicted. Then he smiled briefly. "Just as you say. A dozen."

The doctor returned his attention to the blueprint for a few moments, but then he paused as a new thought struck him. "Have you found a supplier for the animals I will need?"

Metcalf nodded. "Oh yes, that's all been arranged. Here is the card of the man who will be your contact."

He handed Aboud a business card with a name and phone number printed on it. The man's title indicated that he specialized in laboratory supplies.

The old man elaborated. "Once the facility is complete, you can contact him and let him know what you require. He assures me that he can get most anything. Cats, dogs, primates."

Aboud allowed himself to smile briefly. "That is good. We can institute a breeding program, of course, but that will take time. Initially, I will need a very large quantity to test my experiments."

"It's a shame your work was interrupted during the war."

The doctor shot Metcalf an incredulous look. The old man seemed to be trying to make conversation. This was hardly a pleasant topic to choose. Aboud thought back to his final days in his homeland. He had been forced to flee his country, one step ahead of the troops. His laboratory was destroyed and with it his hopes of completing his research. He gave a humorless laugh. "Not only my work was interrupted. My life as well."

"I realize it must be difficult adjusting to a new place," Metcalf offered consolingly.

Aboud shrugged philosophically. "Here, there. The science is the same. What you are planning to build for me here is much better than what I had in my own country. I can accomplish more in a facility like this one." He continued to trace the outline of the structure, but then his finger stopped. "There is one thing missing from this plan."

"Yes?" Abraham asked anxiously.

"I will need an incinerator. A very large one."

Chapter 44—Cliffhanger

FAYE CARRIED A TRAY over to the coffee table in her conference room at the vault. She sat down and added Darjeeling leaves to the pot of hot water.

"Good, you're here." Maddie breezed through the open door and dropped down across from Faye on one of the leather couches.

"Any word from our intrepid team?" Faye inquired as she stirred the liquid in the pot and replaced the lid.

Maddie shook her head. "Just my luck I was out of the office when they finally phoned. But I got a voice mail from Griffin saying they were planning to arrive back at the vault this morning with a full report. That's why I called you to come over." She gave her superior an arch look. "At least this time you answered your phone."

Faye smiled serenely. "My little world has been restored to order now that Zachary has been bundled off to his home. I am happy to announce that I am once more 'online' and fully functional as the saying goes."

"Let's hope the world of the Arkana is about to be restored to order too," Maddie commented worriedly. "I've been on pins and needles fretting over this business with Erik. I keep telling myself that it's no use bleeding before I'm cut."

"A wise practice," Faye concurred. "Any number of things might have happened, and there's no point speculating. Imagination has a way of amplifying any problem the real world can provide."

"Guess we'll know soon enough." Maddie reached for a cigarette but saw the look of mild reproach that Faye gave her. She threw the pack on the coffee table and smiled contritely. "Sorry. Force of habit. I really need a smoke to settle my nerves, but I'm afraid if I climb up to the chimney, they'll get here while I'm gone."

"What time did Griffin say they'd arrive?" Faye checked the color of the brewing tea.

Maddie consulted her wristwatch. "Right about now."

"Have some tea, dear. That might steady you a bit." She poured servings for both of them and handed one to Maddie.

"Might as well." Maddie accepted and drank the hot tea in a few gulps.

"My goodness," Faye said. "Would you like another?"

The operations director took a deep breath. "Nope, that'll do me for now." She set the cup down and began to drum her long fingernails on her knee. "I just wish they'd get here already."

"Your wish is our command," Griffin announced as he walked through the door trailed closely by Cassie. Bringing up the rear was Erik.

"Erik! Thank goddess!" Maddie cried. Springing off the couch, she engulfed the security coordinator in a smothering embrace.

He squirmed and tried to disentangle himself. "Maddie, let go. I can't breathe."

She stood back, holding him at arms length. Her joyous expression rapidly turned to a scowl. She shook him by the arms like a rag doll. "What the hell is wrong with you? You had us both worried to death! I swear I could kill you myself!"

Cassie and Griffin shrank back against the wall, but Erik took the tirade far more calmly than he'd taken the hug. He grinned and extricated himself from Maddie's grip. "Relax, chief. It's all good."

The operations director wasn't ready to calm down. "Why the hell didn't you call?"

Griffin cleared his throat. "If I may, that was my idea. We were afraid the Nephilim might attempt to retrace Erik's trail once they knew he'd been hunting the relic. They might have made inquiries and stumbled across us. We didn't want to lead them straight to HQ via telecom, so we thought it best to leave the country as quickly as possible and provide explanations later."

"Oh, you'll be doing that alright." Maddie glared at the Brit. "Right now, as a matter of fact. All of you, sit down and explain yourselves."

During this interchange, Faye had remained silent. She'd busied herself with pouring out cups of tea for the new arrivals and distributing them around the table.

The trio filed dutifully around the couches and sat.

"I don't know what you're fussing about," Erik objected.

"We thought you were dead!" Maddie shot back.

"But how did you—"

She cut him off. "We got a hold of Hunt's last call to Metcalf. He said he'd had some trouble on the mountain. From the description he gave, it sounded like he'd killed you."

Erik looked sheepish. "Jeez, I'm sorry, Maddie. It never occurred to us you'd hear about that."

"Especially not under those circumstances," Griffin added. "We're all terribly sorry."

"Yeah," Cassie concurred. "We would have called if we'd known."

Maddie seemed to have vented most of her frustration by this time. The looks of apology mollified her temper. "OK, so now you know," she grumped.

Faye took charge of the conversation. "I think what Maddie is trying to say is that we're very happy and relieved to see you all back safely." She smiled at each one of them in turn. "I take it you consider your mission a success?"

They all began chattering at once.

"I'll tell it. We have to start with the room key," Cassie said.

"I think we ought to begin with the bandit problem," Griffin objected.

"You'll start with why Erik isn't dead!" Maddie burst in. She focused her attention on the security coordinator. "You go first," she commanded.

"Yes, ma'am." He saluted playfully.

The operations director didn't appear amused.

Faye suppressed a chuckle.

Erik was on the point of speaking when he hesitated. "You know, my reappearance isn't going to make any sense at all if we don't start at the beginning."

Maddie tapped her fingers. "Fine."

"Let's see, the last time we talked was just before we went up the mountain to switch the fake relic."

"Has it been that long?" Cassie seemed surprised. "Then they don't know anything!"

"I think that's what I've been saying," Maddie commented pointedly.

"Well, I guess I should go first then," the pythia offered. "It all started right after we buried the fake. Everything was fine up till that point. We'd gotten back to the Jeep when I realized I'd dropped my hotel key back at the site."

Cassie recounted how they retraced their steps, only to find the relic had been unearthed by the three Turks. She then explained how the Arkana team trailed the men through the woods and how she was captured.

Both Faye and Maddie appeared horror-struck as the pythia zestfully recounted how the trio held her at gunpoint while they decided whether to kill her or hold her for ransom.

"You should have seen her," Erik butted in. "She was amazing."

Cassie blushed.

"I mean, she stood her ground. Didn't lose her head. Cool as a cucumber, she cut a ransom deal with those guys. It was incredible." He beamed at the pythia.

"Erik, stop," she murmured, obviously pleased by his approval.

Faye and Maddie exchanged raised eyebrows.

"You two seem to be fast friends these days," Faye observed.

"The new pythia is officially aces in my book," Erik enthused. "You can quote me on that."

"I'm glad you don't want to drum her out of the Arkana anymore," Maddie said sarcastically, "but can you get on with the story?"

"Oh, yeah, right." Cassie continued. "After that, the bad guys took me to this run-down cabin, and I wrote a ransom note to send back to the hotel." She described how her teammates stormed the shack and rescued her.

"You should have seen Erik," she added. "He came in with guns blazing."

"Me?" he protested. "What about you. The Turk had a knife to your throat. I was gonna put the gun down before he cut you, but then you stomped on his foot."

"She did what?" Maddie and Faye were both aghast.

"Swear to goddess!" Erik was beaming again. "Like I said, she was amazing. While the Turk was hopping around, I rushed him."

"Yeah, talk about amazing," Cassie smiled back at him. "The guy never knew what hit him."

Faye glanced at Griffin who had remained silent during this interchange. "Dear, you seem awfully quiet. Don't you have anything to add?" she prompted.

The scrivener shifted uncomfortably in his seat. "Nothing that would do me credit, I'm afraid. If I hadn't tripped over my own legs and stumbled into Cassie while we were following the bandits, she would never have been captured in the first place."

"Griffin!" Cassie protested. "You shouldn't think like that. It could have happened to any of us."

"Yeah, dude," Erik added. "Lighten up. If it hadn't been for you figuring out where to find that artifact, we would have come home empty-handed."

"At least you would have come home alive without needing to risk life and limb," the scrivener murmured.

Erik slapped him on the back consolingly. "It was a field mission, man. Stuff like that always happens on a field mission. I could tell you stories."

"Really?" Griffin brightened. "You're not just saying that to make me feel better?"

"Nope," Erik protested. "Swear to goddess."

"Like the time he trashed an entire hotel room in Venice," Maddie offered.

"Aren't you ever gonna forget about that?" Erik moaned.

Maddie folded her arms resolutely. "What do you think?"

Faye forestalled any further comment from Maddie by asking, "What happened next?"

"We tied up the bandits and left them for the sweepers," Griffin explained.

"By the way, I checked with Anatolian Security while we were at the airport," Erik interjected. "The creeps got bagged and tagged. Turns out they had a rap sheet as long as my arm." He paused to glance at Maddie who was several inches taller than he was. "Might have even been as long as your arm."

"So, they're in custody with the Turkish police?" the operations director asked.

"Yup," Cassie answered. "I hope they stay that way for a good long time. Nasty guys. Bad breath too."

"What about the Nephilim?" Maddie asked.

"Oh, they showed up at the worst possible second, and that's when everything got real interesting." Erik picked up the thread. "We were about to rebury the fake artifact when we heard their car coming up the trail. We were boxed in. Couldn't drive away and there was an empty hole in the ground where the relic should have been. If they found that, they would definitely know somebody else was looking for the same thing."

"And that's when Erik came up with the most incredible idea," Cassie burst in.

"Are you gonna let me tell it?" he scolded, but it was obvious he was enjoying her enthusiasm.

"I just had to say that. It was absolutely genius," she gushed. Then apparently realizing just how effusive she sounded, she waved him on. "You go."

"So anyway," he began, "we had to figure out how to get the fake into their hands without them knowing they were being set up. That's when I decided to act as a decoy."

"We hid ourselves while Erik staged a scene," Griffin chimed in. "He stood by the hole in the ground where we'd found the relic. That way when the Nephilim arrived, they would think he'd just dug it up."

"And they fell for it too," Erik continued. "Leroy Hunt saw me and ran down that hill waving a pistol. I hid behind one of the megaliths near the edge, so he couldn't corner me. I had the fake artifact in my hand. He was with that Daniel guy. Finally got a good look at the kid. Kind of nervous and jumpy for a Nephilim. There was a Turk with them too. He must have been their guide. Anyway, I gave them a line about how I escaped from the tomb at Karfi and my other two teammates were killed."

"Then they don't suspect that Cassie and Griffin are alive?" Faye asked.

"Nope. Swallowed the whole story," Erik replied. "I told them that I'd give them the relic if they let me leave. Daniel was all for it, but Hunt wanted to kill me. That's when I threw the relic into the air toward them. Then I fell off the side of the mountain."

"You did what?" both Faye and Maddie asked simultaneously.

Cassie giggled. "This is the genius part."

"They came rushing over to look and saw a body on a ledge about two hundred feet below. It was a sheer drop, so there was no way for them to climb down to get a good look. No way to shoot the body because Hunt was out of range. They just had to let it go. Daniel seemed kind of broken up about the whole thing, but Hunt said the vultures would get the body before anybody would know it was there. Then they left."

"But how did you manage to fall that far without being killed?" Faye asked in wonderment.

"It wasn't me. It was Fred," Erik explained proudly.

"You allowed Fred to die?" Faye sounded appalled.

"Who's Fred?" Maddie was mystified.

"Our guide, remember?" Cassie prompted. "You talked to him on the phone during our last group call."

"Oh, yeah" the operations director seemed to recall. "Now I remember him. Quiet sort." Then she scowled as a new thought hit her. "So Fred's dead?"

"No, he isn't." Griffin picked up the thread. Turning to his teammate, he added, "It really was a remarkable plan, Erik. To come up with something like that on such short notice. Absolutely brilliant."

"Aw shucks," Erik said mockingly. "You guys are gonna turn my head."

"I'm gonna turn your head backwards Exorcist-style if you don't wrap this story up soon," Maddie barked. "What happened to Fred?"

"Fred is alive and well." Griffin smiled.

"And living in Turkey," Cassie added.

"We got a couple of lucky breaks that day," Erik commented. "The first one was the fact that the mountain is honeycombed with hermit cells."

"Ah." Faye smiled knowingly. "I'm beginning to see the light." She was apparently several steps ahead of Maddie.

"So what if there are hermit cells?" the operations director asked.

"There are tunnels that lead through the mountainside out to the rock face. You can't see them if you're standing up above. It just so happens that one of those tunnels leads directly out to that ledge on the mountainside."

"Then that would mean Fred was able to position himself while you were above acting as a diversion." Faye summarized.

Cassie nudged Griffin in the ribs. "She's good."

Maddie turned to Erik. "But how could they mistake this Fred guy for you?"

"It was one of those lucky breaks I mentioned before. We were both wearing the same color clothes that day. Cassie pointed it out when we left that morning. Yellow shirt, blue jeans, white sneakers. He's blond too. From two hundred feet away, face down, he made a passable double."

"But I still don't understand, dear," Faye said. "You said you fell off the mountain. How did you keep from sliding all the way down? You couldn't have had more than a few moments lead time before your attackers would have reached you. Where did you go?"

"I got lucky again when we left the bandit shack. I decided to bring along the extra coil of rope that was left over after we tied them up. Because the Nephilim were standing in the middle of the stone circle and I was on the other side of a megalith, they couldn't see that I had a piece of rope lying right next to my foot. I grabbed it when I went over the side."

"Heavens!" Faye exclaimed.

"Cassie and Griffin were hiding in another hermit cell just a little below the top of the cliff. Griffin had the other end of the rope, and he pulled me up to where they were hiding." Erik glanced at his two companions. "We cut it close though. I'd just barely managed to tuck into the hole in the rock before I heard Hunt talking right above where we here hiding."

"Quite an extraordinary adventure," Faye observed.

"I need a smoke," Maddie announced abruptly. "Don't say anything important until I get back."

Her companions watched open-mouthed as the operations director grabbed her pack of cigarettes and headed for the chimney.

"She really has been worried about you," Faye apologized. "I think the stress this morning has been too much for her, poor dear. Let's give her a few moments to quiet her nerves. I'll just take this opportunity to phone downstairs for some food while we wait. I'm sure you're all hungry after your trip."

"That's why she's the memory guardian," Cassie confided to her teammates. "She remembers when it's time for a snack."

Chapter 45—Relic Redux

"OOOH, SPINACH DIP," Cassie enthused. "I haven't tasted that since we left."

"We haven't been gone that long, toots," Erik objected.

They were both diving into plates of cold cuts and crudités.

Cassie looked at Faye quizzically. "I didn't think there was a kitchen in the vault. Where did all this food come from?"

"We do have a cafeteria, actually," Griffin explained. "We're miles from nowhere out here, and people have to eat. I just didn't show you that part of the facility when I was giving you your tour. It didn't seem relevant."

"It's plenty relevant when you're hungry," Cassie said as she built herself a turkey sandwich.

At that moment, Maddie walked back into the conference room. Her clothes reeked of cigarette smoke, but she appeared to be in a much pleasanter mood than when she'd left. "That's better," she announced taking her seat on the couch and immediately helping herself to the deli platter.

Faye looked around at her team benevolently. "All's well that ends well," she observed.

"All isn't ended yet," Maddie said, crunching into a dill pickle. "What about the artifact?"

"Right you are!" Griffin wiped his hands on a napkin and reached into his duffle bag. He dug around until he located a small box. "Here it is." He held it out to Faye.

The old woman opened the lid and removed the tissue that surrounded the object. "Oh, my!" she exclaimed. "What exquisite craftsmanship."

She held the golden bee in the palm of her hand. It measured about three inches in length. The bee's wings were outstretched as if in flight. The entire surface of the wings was covered with the peculiar markings which had become all too familiar to the Arkana team.

"It was quite a feat to duplicate something this intricate on such short notice," Griffin commented. "We're indebted to the Anatolian goldsmiths who helped us out."

"I'll be sure to express your appreciation to Aydin," Faye remarked.

"Let me see." Maddie held out her hand, and Faye passed the object to her. She flipped the bee over and traced the hieroglyphs that covered the underside of the wings. She handed the piece back to Griffin. "Did you get a chance to translate what these symbols mean yet?"

The Brit sighed. "Translate, yes. Understand, no."

"He told us what the message says," Cassie offered.

"But it's all Minoan to us." Erik completed the thought.

"More tea?" Faye held out the pot, but everyone shook their heads now that a pitcher of cola had been brought up from the cafeteria. The old woman filled her own teacup and resettled herself. "Perhaps Maddie and I can help decipher the message. Just tell us what it says, dear."

Griffin set the bee on the table and reached back into his bag for a tablet. He flipped through several pages of field notes before he came to the right section. "Ah yes, here it is. I must say, this seems even more cryptic than our last riddle was."

The group waited in silence for him to begin.

"The first line reads: Let Eurus fill the sails twelve days, then follow Eberos where it climbs to the sky."

"I don't know about the Eurus or Eberos business, but the word 'sails' has to mean twelve days by boat to somewhere," the operations director speculated as she popped a handful of olives into her mouth.

"Twelve days' worth of sea travel to anywhere leads me to believe the relic won't be in Crete or Turkey," the scrivener said.

"I agree," Faye concurred. "You'll be traveling farther afield on your next expedition."

"Yeah, but they couldn't have gone that far," Cassie objected. "Everybody thought the world was flat so they all stayed close to home, didn't they?"

The old woman smiled knowingly. "The ancients were far more sophisticated in their navigation techniques and in their understanding of the world that our current history books would lead you to believe."

"Ooops." Cassie grinned sheepishly. "You can chalk that comment up to my overlord education."

Faye nodded and then directed her attention to Griffin. "What's next, dear?"

The scrivener consulted his notes. "Set your course three bees from the dragon's wing to the sea."

The memory guardian frowned in perplexity. "Are you sure you translated that correctly?"

"I'm afraid so. I checked it several times. I confess I'm as mystified as you are. It's some sort of nautical reference. That's all I can determine at this point."

Cassie reached across the table for the pitcher of soda and poured herself a refill. "We also figured the bee has something to do with it."

"She means that the bee is supposed to be used as some kind of yardstick for us to measure with," Erik expanded helpfully.

"How interesting," Faye murmured half to herself. "So even if one had the text of this clue, without the artifact itself, it would be impossible to determine the location of the next relic."

"Wish we'd realized that in time," Cassie said ruefully. "We might have made the fake relic half an inch shorter. Could have thrown the Nephilim off for a while."

"I don't think it's going to matter much," Maddie observed. "If you guys are having a tough time understanding it, I don't think they'll figure it out any quicker."

"I'll just keep reading, shall I?" Griffin flipped a page in his notebook. "When the bull turns the season, mark where the goat grazes the spinner's peak."

They all looked at one another blankly.

"Huh," Maddie grunted. "Sounds like complete gibberish to me."

"Is there any more?" Faye asked.

"One more line: There lies the second of five you seek."

"We figured that one out." Cassie laughed.

"Yeah, that was a freebie," Maddie murmured.

"Why don't you read the entire message back to us now," Faye suggested.

The scrivener obliged. "Let Eurus fill the sails twelve days, then follow Eberos where it climbs to the sky. Set your course three bees from the dragon's wing to the sea. When the bull turns the season, mark where the goat grazes the spinner's peak. There lies the second of five you seek."

"That sure is a mouthful." Cassie scowled as she considered the diminutive bee. "How the heck did they fit all those words on the wings?"

"My translation is somewhat liberal," Griffin admitted. "I attempted to turn the message into something coherent and, to whatever extent, poetical. In its original form, it reads more like Morse Code or semaphore."

Cassie regarded him skeptically. "You sure you didn't lose anything along the way?"

"Oh no, the gist of what I recited is faithful to the original symbols."

"Well if that's true," she remarked bleakly, "then we've got a ton of work ahead of us to figure this out. And I was hoping for a break!"

Griffin smiled. "Then I have good news for you."

"Really?"

"We will have quite a lot of time to figure this out."

Cassie picked up the bee, turned it over and shook it. "I don't see anything falling out that says, 'Take your time. No rush.'" She set it back down in dismay.

The scrivener was beaming smugly. "Ah, but that's exactly what it says. It's in the third line of the message."

By now, everyone around the table was staring at him.

"When the bull turns the season," he repeated, apparently expecting them to comprehend. When they didn't, he continued. "It's a clear reference to the vernal equinox."

"The what?" Cassie asked.

Faye took up the explanation. "The vernal equinox is the date when days and nights are of equal length." She turned to face Griffin. "But I don't understand why you would necessarily connect a bull to that date."

"I admit it's a bit of a stretch," the scrivener replied. "Due to precession, the constellation associated with the vernal equinox has shifted over time. Approximately every two thousand years, the sun rises on the equinox in a different constellation. It currently rises in Pisces and in a few hundred years will shift to Aquarius. At the time our Minoan friends buried their relic, the equinox would have occurred in the constellation of Aries the ram."

"So how come they're talking about a bull?" Erik asked.

"Because Minoan civilization first flowered when the equinox constellation would have been Taurus the bull. Their mythology continued the tradition of associating the vernal equinox with the bull long after it was no longer literally true."

"But what's this got to do with us?" Cassie urged impatiently.

"My dear girl, you really need to brush up on your astronomical phenomena. The vernal equinox is the first day of spring. It usually falls somewhere around March 21st."

Cassie began to count excitedly on her fingers. "But that's more than eight months from now!"

"Precisely," Griffin nodded. "Hence my assertion that we have plenty of time to solve this riddle."

"Which means you're convinced we can't find the relic till then?" Cassie asked dubiously.

"Well, it would certainly be consistent with what occurred on Ida," Griffin replied. "If we hadn't been in position at precisely that time of year, we wouldn't have found the bee."

"They've hidden these objects in space and time," Faye observed.

"Eight whole months," Cassie exhaled in wonder.

"We'll still need to apply ourselves before then," Griffin warned.

"Yeah, yeah," the pythia dismissed him. "But not tomorrow."

"And not next week either." Erik glanced around at his companions. "I don't know about you guys, but I vote for taking a week off."

Faye and Maddie exchanged a look.

The memory guardian replied, "It's fine with me if Maddie agrees."

The operations director smiled wryly. "Go on. Get outta here."

The trio didn't need any further encouragement.

Erik sprang out of his seat.

Cassie stood up too. "All the things I could do with a week off." She closed her eyes, imagining the possibilities.

Griffin collected his files and followed his teammates.

"There's a beach in Tahiti I haven't been to in a couple of years," Erik said half to himself. "Just hanging out. Sun, sand, surf, island chicks." He turned back to Maddie. "How about it, chief?"

"You expect me to foot the bill for that?" Maddie asked incredulously.

"Oh, come on. I risked life and limb on this last recovery. I deserve some R and R."

She eyed him appraisingly and then said, "I suppose we can work something out."

Taking that as a yes, Erik smiled happily and headed for the door.

Cassie followed him out. "I think I'll get a pedicure."

"A pedicure?" he echoed in disbelief.

"Hey, you relax your way, and I'll relax mine."

Griffin brought up the rear. "I confess I'm rather eager to get back to the vault. I miss my books."

His companions sighed in exasperation.

"Griffin, you really need a chia pet or something," Cassie muttered.

The trio happily continued to discuss their plans as they walked down the corridor. Maddie and Faye kept silent until their voices faded in the distance.

The operations director shook her head in disbelief. "They're the oddest mix of characters I've ever seen in the field. It's amazing they even found their way to the airport. Much less..." she trailed off.

Faye completed her thought. "Much less managed to accomplish the impossible." She picked up the golden bee and considered it, smiling. "I don't believe we've even scratched the surface of what they can do. Exciting times are in store for the Arkana, and they'll be at the forefront of it all."

"I can feel my ulcer acting up already," Maddie groaned.

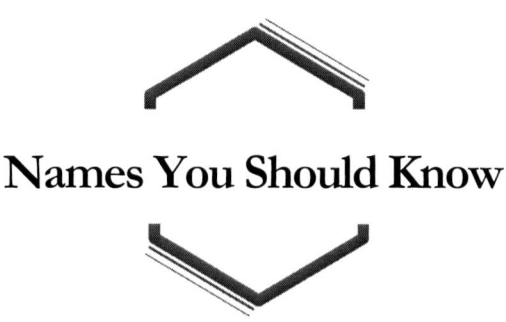

Names You Should Know

KEY TO BOOKS IN THE series through the end of Volume 1:
  GK – The Granite Key

❖ **Abraham Metcalf** – Prophet and autocratic leader of the Blessed Nephilim. In his seventies.

❖ **Annabeth** – Third wife of Daniel. Nervous and high-strung. Wants to improve her position in the Nephilim hierarchy by birthing more children.

❖ **Arkana** – Secret organization whose mission is to retrieve and protect the artifacts of lost pre-patriarchal civilizations around the globe.

❖ **Blessed Nephilim** – Fundamentalist religious cult which traces its lineage to the Nephilim of the Bible. They practice polygamy, live in isolated compounds, and maintain a strict separation from the rest of the world.

❖ **Bones of the Mother** – Collection of Minoan artifacts which have been hidden among the ruins of forgotten civilizations on every continent. Each artifact provides clues to the location of the next relic. Collectively, they will lead to the location of the Sage Stone.

❖ **Cassie Forsythe** – Psychic with the ability to touch an artifact and relive scenes from its past. She succeeds to the title of pythia within the Arkana after the murder of her sister. Nineteen-year-old college freshman at the beginning of the story.

❖ **Central Catalog** – Abandoned rural schoolhouse outside the Chicago metro area which contains the global records of Arkana troves throughout the world. Also known as the Vault.

❖ **Chief Scrivener** – Person responsible for managing the records of the Arkana Central Catalog. The title is currently held by Griffin.

❖ **Chris (David Christian)** – Librarian at the Chicago Public Library who assists Daniel with his research and becomes his friend.

❖ **Circle** – Governing body of the Arkana.

❖ **Concordance** – General Council of the Arkana.

❖ **Consecrated Bride** – Nephilim term for married women within the cult.

❖ **Daniel Metcalf** – Lesser son of Abraham whose skill with ancient languages has made him an unwilling participant in the quest to find the Bones of the Mother.

❖ **Diviner** – Title given to the prophet of the Nephilim. A role currently occupied by Abraham Metcalf.

❖ **Dr. Rafi Aboud** – Foreign doctor with a mysterious past who has been hired by Abraham to perform experiments at a secret laboratory. The purpose of his experiments is known only to the diviner.

❖ **Erik** – Martial arts and weapons expert, in his mid-twenties. His job is to protect the pythia on field assignments and arrange for the safe transportation of artifacts. His title is security coordinator.

❖ **Fallen** – Term used by the Nephilim to describe inhabitants of the outer world. Anyone who doesn't belong to the cult.

❖ **Faye** – Elderly leader of the Arkana. She holds the title of memory guardian. Her age is unknown, but it may exceed normal human limits.

❖ **Griffin** – Chief Scrivener. He is responsible for cataloguing all artifacts collected in troves around the world. British and in his early twenties, he has an eidetic memory.

❖ **Leroy Hunt** – Mercenary currently on the payroll of the Nephilim. His job is to protect Daniel as they attempt to retrieve the Bones of the Mother. He has no conscience and a taste for violence.

❖ **Maddie** – Short-tempered, chain-smoking operations director of the Arkana. She manages day-to-day global affairs.

❖ **Matristic Civilizations** – Arkana term for ancient goddess-worshipping societies which thrived without military fortifications, rigid social hierarchies, male dominance, or career warfare.

❖ **Memory Guardian** – Faye's title as head of the Arkana.

❖ **Operations Director** – Maddie's title as manager of global operations for the Arkana.

❖ **Operatives** – Members of Blessed Nephilim satellite communities assigned to help Daniel in the field. In order of appearance: Nikos (Crete-GK).

❖ **Overlord Cultures** – Arkana term for male-dominated warrior cultures fixated on territorial expansion through conquest and exploitation of indigenous inhabitants.

❖ **Pythia** – Title currently held by Cassie. The official seer of the Arkana.

❖ **Rhonda** – Antique store owner and Sybil's former business partner. Surrogate big sister to Cassie.

❖ **Sage Stone** – Mythical Minoan relic which is reputed to possess great power. Nephilim prophecy reveals that this relic must be acquired by Abraham if his secret plan to orchestrate a global apocalypse is to succeed.

❖ **Scouts** – Field agents of the Arkana deployed around the globe. Individuals tasked with assisting in the retrieval of Bones of the Mother.

❖ **Security Coordinator** – Title currently held by Erik. He reports to the operations director.

❖ **Sybil Forsythe** – Cassie's sister. Late pythia of the Arkana.

❖ **Trove** – Arkana collection point for artifacts related to a specific geographic region or culture.

❖ **Trove Keeper** – Person appointed to manage the collection of artifacts at a particular location or trove. In order of appearance: Xenia Katsouros (Minoan-GK).

❖ **Vault** – Another name for the Central Catalog.

About the Author

Nancy Wikarski is a fugitive from academia. After earning her Ph.D. from the University of Chicago, she worked in corporate America for two decades before becoming a historical mystery author. Her books highlight unknown aspects of women's history and contain elements of magical realism. In her Arkana series, she foregrounds the latest archaeological discoveries about prepatriarchal cultures around the planet and weaves these facts into fictional artifact hunts. Her Gilded Age Chicago books depict the real issues of first-wave feminism while following the fictional adventures of two amateur sleuths. Both series have been award-nominated and have ranked on Amazon's Top 100 bestseller lists.

The author is a member of Mystery Writers of America, the Society of Midland Authors, and has served as vice president of Sisters in Crime-Twin Cities and on the programming board of the Chicago chapter. Her short stories have appeared in *Futures Magazine* and *DIME Anthology*, while her book reviews and essays have been featured in *Murder: Past Tense*, *Deadly Pleasures*, and *Mystery Readers Journal*. She is currently writing an Arkana spinoff series called The Trove Chronicles that will continue to feature discoveries about global prepatriarchal cultures. More mysteries from the casebook of Gilded Age detectives Evangeline LeClair and Freddie Simpson are also in the works.

Read more at www.nswikarski.org.

33181017R00153